Eric Ambler was born into a f ... early years helped out as a puppeteer. However, he initially chose engineering as a full time career, although this quickly gave way to writing. In World War II he entered the army and looked likely to fight in the line, but was soon after commissioned and ended the war as assistant director of the army film unit and a Lieutenant-Colonel.

This experience translated into civilian life and Ambler had a very successful career as a screen writer, receiving an Academy Award for his work on *The Cruel Sea* by Nicolas Monsarrat in 1953. Many of his own works have been filmed, the most famous probably being *Light of Day*, filmed as *Topkapi* under which title it is now published.

He established a reputation as a thriller writer of extraordinary depth and originality and received many other accolades during his lifetime, including two *Edgar Awards* from *The Mystery Writers of America* (best novel for *Topkapi* and best biographical work for *Here Lies Eric Ambler*), and two *Gold Dagger Awards* from the *Crime Writer's Association* (*Passage of Arms* and *The Levanter*).

Often credited as being the inventor of the modern political thriller, *John Le Carre* once described Ambler as '*the source on which we all draw.*' A recurring theme in his works is the success of the well meaning yet somewhat bungling amateur who triumphs in the face of both adversity and hardened professionals.

Ambler wrote under his own name and also during the 1950's a series of novels as *Eliot Reed*, with *Charles Rhodda*. These are now published under the '*Ambler*' umbrella.

Works of **ERIC AMBLER** published by
HOUSE OF STRATUS

DOCTOR FRIGO
JUDGMENT ON DELTCHEV
THE LEVANTER
THE SCHIRMER INHERITANCE
THE SIEGE OF THE VILLA LIPP   (Also as 'Send No More Roses')
TOPKAPI   (Also as 'The Light Of Day')

Originally as Eliot Reed with Charles Rhodda:
CHARTER TO DANGER
THE MARAS AFFAIR
PASSPORT TO PANIC
TENDER TO DANGER   (Also as 'Tender To Moonlight')
SKYTIP

Autobiography:
HERE LIES ERIC AMBLER

The Levanter

eric Ambler

HOUSE OF
STRATUS

This edition published in 2009 by House of Stratus, an imprint of
Stratus Books Ltd., 21 Beeching Park, Kelly Bray,
Cornwall, PL17 8QS, UK.

www.houseofstratus.com

Typeset, printed and bound by House of Stratus.

A catalogue record for this book is available from the British Library and the Library
of Congress.

ISBN 0-7551-1763-8
EAN 978-0-7551-1763-5

LEVANTER [1] n *(Levant,* the countries of the eastern Mediterranean,
      +er)

    1.   A native or inhabitant of the Levant

    2.   A ship trading to the Levant, *rare.*

    3.   A strong and raw easterly wind in the Mediterranean.

    Also fig.

LEVANTER [2] n (f. Levant *v* + -er) One who absconds; esp. one who does
    so after losing bets.

From Webster's Third New International and
The Oxford English dictionaries

Contents

Chapter 1

Lewis Prescott

May 14

This is Michael Howell's story and he tells most of it himself. I think that he should have told all of it.

He may not be the most persuasive of advocates in his own cause, and as the central figure in what has come to be known as the Green Circle Incident, he is very much the defendant; but he alone can answer the charges and give the necessary explanations. It is upon his own words that he will be judged. In his sort of predicament declarations of sympathy and understanding from outsiders are apt to sound like pleas in mitigation. Instead of strengthening his case, my contributions could very well weaken it. I told him so.

He, however, did not agree.

"Supporting evidence, Mr. Prescott," he said earnestly; "that's what I need from you. Tell them what you know about Ghaled. Give it to them thick and strong. I can tell them what happened to me, but they have to understand what I was up against. They'll believe you."

"My opinion of a man like Ghaled, formed in the course of a single interview, isn't evidence."

"It will have the weight of evidence. I don't expect you openly to side with me, Mr. Prescott - that would be asking too much - but don't, I beg you, play into the hands of my enemies."

Fruity and false; this was the Levanter speaking. I gave him a bleak look.

"I am not playing into anybody's hands, Mr. Howell, least of all your enemies". I would have thought I had made that sufficiently clear."

"To me, yes." He held up a finger. "But what about the public and the news media? How cam I vindicate myself, *and* the *Agence* Howell, when important independent witnesses, those who know the truth, choose to remain silent?"

"I wrote a three-thousand-word feature on the subject, Mr. Howell," I reminded him. "I don't call that remaining silent."

"With respect, Mr. Prescott, your Green Circle article gave only a smattering of the truth." He began wagging the raised finger at me. "If I am to be believed, I must tell it all. In that telling I need your help. I ask you to stand up with me and be counted."

I paused before replying: "You may find yourself wishing that I had remained seated."

"I am prepared to take that risk. What we have to do between us, Mr. Prescott, is to tell the *whole* truth. That is all, the whole truth."

He made the telling of the whole truth sound very simple. He may even have believed that, in his case, it was.

For the record: at the time of which I am now writing I had neither met Mr. Howell nor even heard of his existence.

As a senior foreign correspondent working for the *Post-Tribune* syndicated news service, I am based in Paris. Two months prior to the Incident I had been assigned temporarily to the Middle East to cover the visit of a U.S. Secretary of State making yet another attempt to resolve the Arab-Israeli conflict. The tour had ended in Beirut and it had been there that I had encountered Melanie Hammad.

My wife and I had met her originally in Paris at the apartment of mutual friends. Knowing her to be a free-lance contributor to French and American fashion magazines, I had been surprised to find her sitting next to me at a Lebanese Ministry of Foreign Affairs press conference.

"A little off your usual beat, aren't you?" I asked after we had exchanged greetings.

She raised her eyebrows. This is my home. Didn't you know that I was an Arab?"

"I knew that you were from Lebanon."

In Paris she had been an attractive young woman with sultry eyes who dressed well, spoke several languages, and knew the high-fashion people. She had been helpful to my wife in the matter of getting special discounts on perfume, I remembered.

"Here," she said firmly, "I am Arab first and a Lebanese second."

"Muslim or Christian?"

"My parents are Maronite Christian, so I suppose I am, too." She lowered her voice to a whisper. "At present I am observing for the Palestinian Action Force."

"I see." I assumed that she was joking and added with a smile: "Unofficially, I take it."

"I could scarcely do so officially." She did not return the smile. "We could talk about it later if you wish." Her fine eyes became intense. "I think you might be interested, Mr. Prescott."

I hesitated. She seemed to be serious, but the only Palestinian Action Force I knew of was a splinter guerrilla group led by a man named Salah Ghaled with a gangster reputation. It was difficult to think of the elegant Miss Hammad as in any way connected with him. Still, I was intrigued.

"All right," I said. "I'm at the St. Georges. If you're free we might have lunch."

The syndicate's Middle East bureau has an office in Beirut. The man in charge is an Englishman named Frank Edwards who also acts as a stringer for one or two British newspapers. Before meeting

Miss Hammad for lunch I made some inquiries.

Edwards laughed. "So, our Melanie's picked on you, has she? I thought she was after the *New York Times* man."

"What are you talking about?"

"She's press agent for the Palestinian Action Force."

"But my wife and I know her. She's one of the Paris fashion girls."

"In Paris she may be a fashion girl, but in this part of the world she's a Palestinian activist. Ghaled recruited her when she was a student at the Sorbonne and he was still with Al Fatah. Her old man's rich, of course, or the police would be leaning on her. He owns that new office building you can see from the St. Georges and a few more like it as well She doesn't have to work for a living, and, anyway, where Ghaled is concerned it's love. We've got loads of stuff on them both. Do you want me to get it out?"

"I think I'll see what sort of a pitch she makes first."

"I can tell you that now. Extremism in the pursuit of liberty is no vice. Moderation is another name for weakness. I'm told that she can be very persuasive. You get handed an expurgated version of the PAF manifesto and, to warm the cockles of your heart, a mimeographed copy of the "Thoughts of Salah Ghaled.""

"She could have given me that in Paris."

There you weren't writing about the Middle East."

However, in one thing Edwards had been mistaken. Melanie Hammad had more to offer than pamphlets.

"You have," she informed me, "a reputation for being truly objective and independent, of not accepting uncritically a consensus of opinion, even when it would be prudent to do so."

That's very flattering, Miss Hammad, but I hope you're not suggesting that I am in any way unique."

"I am not so stupid. There are other Americans like you, of course. But they are not often here, and when they are they have no time to listen. I know what is said about the Palestinian Action Force. It is said that they are criminals using the Palestinian cause for their own ends, that Salah Ghaled deserted Al Fatah when they were under attack, that he is no fighter for freedom but a mere gangster. You may be inclined to believe these things. You will at least have taken note of them. But you may also question and wonder if this received view, this consensus, may be wrong. Given the chance, I think that you would prefer to form your own opinion."

"But since nobody has asked me to form an opinion about Mr. Ghaled and his Palestinian Action Force ..." I left the rest of the sentence in the air.

"I am asking you."

"Unfortunately you are not my New York editor."

"You have wide discretion. Your wife told me so. I am speaking of an important personal interview by you. Lewis Prescott. It would be exclusive, of course."

I thought for a moment.

"Where would this exclusive interview take place?"

"Here in Lebanon. In secret naturally. Great discretion would have to be observed."

"When would it take place?"

"If you agree today, I think I can arrange it within twenty-four hours."

"Does Mr. Ghaled speak English or French?"

"Not well. I would be the interpreter. You have only to say the word, Mr. Prescott."

"I see. Well, I'll let you know later today."

Edwards whistled when I told him of the proposal "So Ghaled wants to come out of the woodwork!"

"Has he been interviewed much before? Hammad mentioned that she had done pieces on him."

"That was when he was an Al Fatah man. Since he started the PAF caper he's been underground most of the time. The Jordanians put a price on his head and the PLO people in Cairo tried to persuade the Syrians to crack down on him. The Syrians wouldn't quite go along with them on that, but he's had to keep his nose clean there and be careful. Though he's based in Syria he never sends his goon squads into action on Syrian territory. He's poison here, of course. He could use an improved image, a little respectability."

"Frank, you're not suggesting, I hope, that, to please pretty Miss Melanie Hammad, I'd do a clean-up job on him."

Edwards held his hands up defensively. "No, Lew, but I am reminding you that a personal interview of the kind you do tends to become a profile of the institution with which the person interviewed is generally identified. If you were to do a job like that in this case you'd be giving Ghaled a lift, the sort of international identity that he doesn't at present have."

"If I were out to do a piece on the Palestinian guerrilla movement, which I am not, would I choose Ghaled as representative of it?"

"Representative?" He looked blank for a moment, then shrugged. There are ten separate Palestinian guerrilla movements, more if you include groups like the PAF. You might do worse than choose Ghaled. He's been in one or other of the movements since he was a boy."

"Isn't he a maverick, though, a far-out fanatic?"

"They're all far-out fanatics. By hatred out of illusion, the lot of them. They have to be. They couldn't have survived otherwise."

"No moderates at all? What about Yasir Arafat?"

"He isn't a guerrilla, he's a politician. He's against Palestinians killing Palestinians instead of Israelis. If he ever so much as hinted that a peaceful settlement with Israel might someday be possible, he'd have his throat cut within the hour. And it would be someone like Ghaled who'd order the cutting. Ghaled might even do the job himself."

"Well, I can see that *you* think he's interesting."

"Yes, Lew, I do." He screwed up his eyes. "You see, since the Second Betrayal..."

"Come again?"

That's what Ghaled calls the '71 Jordanian government

crackdown. The first crackdown, in '70, when Hussein's army turfed the guerrillas out of Amman, was the *Great* Betrayal The *Second* Betrayal was the mopping-up operation that followed a year later. A lot of the steam has gone out of the guerrilla movement since then, at least as far as the Al Fatah and the PFLP are concerned. You could say that events have proved Ghaled's original point for him. That alone makes him interesting. Personally I happen to think that he's got something more."

"A hunch, or reasons?"

"A hunch. But if Melanie had asked me, I'd have jumped at the chance of an interview."

"Okay them. I'll jump. We'd better wire New York. Can we put Ghaled's name in a cable from here?"

"Not unless you want to be tailed by the police."

"Is it that bad?"

"They'd probably tip off the local Al Fatah bureau, too. I told you. He's poison."

It took me some two hours with the bureau files to find out why.

Salah Ghaled had been born in Haifa, the eldest son of a respected Arab physician, in 1930, when Palestine was under the British Mandate. His mother had been from Nazareth. He had attended private schools and was said to have been an exceptionally gifted pupil. In 1948 he had been accepted as a student by the Al-Azhar University in Cairo. He was to have studied medicine there, as his father had. That program, however, had been interrupted by the first Arab-Israeli war.

The attacking forces were those of the Jordanian Arab Legion and an irregular Arab Liberation Army. On the defensive at first, but later counterattacking, was the Haganah, the Jewish army fighting to preserve the newly proclaimed State of Israel. Charges of atrocities committed against noncombatants were made freely by both sides. An Arab exodus began.

Over eight hundred thousand Arabs went; some in panic, some

because they thought that they were leaving the field clear for an advancing Army of Liberation. All expected soon to return to their land and their homes. Few ever succeeded in doing so. The Palestinian refugee problem had been born. Among those early refugees had been the Ghaled family from Haifa.

They suffered less than many of their fellow refugees; Ghaled senior was a doctor and had money. After a few weeks in a temporary camp the family moved to Jericho. At that point Salah could have gone to Cairo and the university as planned. Instead, and apparently with his father's blessing, he joined the Arab Liberation irregulars. This was the army which had boasted that it would "drive the Jews into the sea."

When, a year later, the war ended, with the Israelis more firmly established on dry land than ever and the Arab forces in hopeless disarray, Salah Ghaled had just turned eighteen. He had fought in an army which had been not only defeated but humiliated as well Both defeat and humiliation had to be avenged. In Cairo, where he at last went to pursue his medical studies, he was soon drawn into student politics. According to a statement he made some years later, he there became a Marxist. He never qualified as a doctor. In 1952 he went to work as a "medical aide" in an UNWRA Palestinian refugee camp in Jordan.

The guerrilla movement was in its infancy then, but he seems to have been a natural leader and was soon heading his own band of "infiltrators," as they were called by the Israelis, in raids across the Jordanian border into Israel. As he was still on the UNWRA payroll as a medical aide, it was necessary for him to use a cover name. The one he chose was El-Matwa - Jackknife - and before long it had achieved some notoriety. One of Jackknife's exploits, the shooting-up of an Israeli bus, was believed to have provoked a shattering Israeli reprisal raid. Among the Palestinian militants success was measured by the violence of the enemy's reaction. Jackknife's reputation as a local leader was now established. When Egyptian intelligence officers came looking for Palestinians who knew the border country and would be willing to serve with the *fedayeen*, Ghaled was among the select few who were approached.

The Egyptian *fedayeen* were heavily armed commando forces. Operating from Egyptian and Jordanian bases, they penetrated deep into Israeli territory, murdering civilians, mining roads, and blowing up installations. The Sinai campaign of 1958 put an end to their activities, but among the Palestinians the *fedayeen* idea persisted. The guerrilla groups which now began to be formed were trained and organized by men like Ghaled who had soldiered with the Egyptian *fedayeen*. One of the larger groups became known as Al Fatah, and Ghaled was one of its early leaders.

In 1963 he was wounded in the left leg during an Israeli reprisal raid. The wound was serious and the early treatment of it inadequate. Toward the end of the year his father advised him to go to Cairo for corrective surgery.

His presence in Cairo at that time had decisive effects on his future. The Palestine Liberation Organization was in the process of being formed there, and Ghaled, convalescing after the operation on his leg, was drawn into the discussions. As an Al Fatah leader of note he was consulted about the PLO's new official field force, the Palestine Liberation Army, which was to be armed with Soviet weapons. Though he refused the battalion command which was offered to him, he was appointed a member of the PLO's new "Awakening Committee."

Under the PLO charter this committee was to devote itself to "the upbringing of the new generations both ideologically and spiritually so that they may serve their country and work for the liberation of their homeland." During his convalescence Ghaled was given the job of lecturing to groups of Arab students attending, or about to attend, Western universities, and of leading discussions. It was at one of these student meetings that he met Melanie Hammad.

There were two articles by her in the Ghaled file. The first had been published by a French left-wing quarterly and was a dull restatement of the Palestinian case enlivened by direct quotes from Ghaled. One of them, a comment on the Balfour Declaration, gave me a foretaste of the sort of thing I might have to listen to.

"The British are unbelievable," Ghaled had said. "They promised to provide the Zionists with a national home in Palestine and in the same breath promised that they would do so without infringing on the rights of the existing inhabitants. How could they? Did they think that, because they were dealing with the Holy Land, they could count on another of those Christian miracles of loaves and fishes?"

The other Hammad piece, also in French, had been written in 1933 for a big-circulation newspaper noted for its sensationalism. In this Melanie Hammad had let herself go. Ghaled, then commanding an Al Fatah training camp in the Gaza Strip, was eulogized as the white knight *sans peur et sans reproche* of the Palestinian cause, a resolute yet honourable fighter for freedom, a Nasser-like politico-military leader of the kind needed if there were ever to be true unity of purpose in Palestine.

Edwards had written a note in red ink across this clippings *PLO Cairo spokesman went out of his way to dismiss this estimate of G. as "grossly distorted" and said that it "impugned his loyalty to the Palestinian cause." Hammad dubbed "irresponsibly inaccurate and naive." Picture declared phony.*

The picture referred to, which appeared with the article, showed a tall man in desert uniform studying a map spread out on the tailgate of a truck. He was wearing a head cloth which shaded most of his features. All you could see was a prominent, somewhat aquiline nose and a thin moustache. Since there was no authenticated photograph of Ghaled in the file with which to compare it, I had no way of judging its possible phoniness. What interested me more was the suggestion, implicit in the spokesman's strictures, that in 1988 Ghaled's loyalty to the PLO was already suspect I looked for evidence of disciplinary action of some sort.

All I found was an announcement put out by the PLO radio

some weeks later (November '66) that Ghaled had been relieved of his duties as a member of the Awakening Committee in order to "concentrate upon his operational duties with Al Fatah in the field." In other words he had been told to stay clear of politics, stop playing personality games, and get back to killing Israelis.

Presumably they believed that this public admonishment had brought Ghaled to heel; and, presumably, his general demeanour encouraged them in that belief. Subsequent references to him in PLO communiqués were laudatory in tone. His sudden turnaround, when the crunch came in Jordan, had obviously taken them by surprise.

Following the Six-Day War with Israel and the fresh influx of West Bank refugees which it produced, tension in Jordan between the government of the Hashemite King Hussein and the Palestinians had grown steadily. Half the population of that small country were now Palestinian refugees. The Al Fatah and other refugee guerrilla organizations began to present the king and his government with a serious challenge to their authority. In 1970 the Palestinians were warned by Ghaled that the Jordanian government was planning to make a unilateral peace settlement with Israel. It was time, he declared, to take over the government in Amman and make it their own. Quite suddenly he became the most militant and vociferous of the anti-Hashemite Palestinians. In a speech to his *fedayeen,* reported by the Damascus guerrilla radio, he had thrown down the gauntlet. "By Allah," he had shouted, "we will wade through a sea of blood if need be. I tell you, comrades, we must risk everything now for our honour."

From the self-styled Marxist, Salah Ghaled, this sort of hysteria was new. Frank Edwards thought that the fact that Ghaled's parents had once again become refugees when the West Bank was occupied, and that Ghaled senior had subsequently died in an UNWRA camp, had precipitated the change. I wasn't so sure. It seemed to me more likely that Ghaled had decided that the moment had come for him to snake his bid for power, and that the hysteria had been calculated.

Anyway, he got the sea of blood he had called for. When he and the other Al Fatah guerrilla leaders attempted to take control of the capital, Amman, King Hussein ordered the Jordanian army to stop them, and the army obeyed.

At this point, the series of events which Ghaled was later to denounce collectively as "the Great Betrayal" took place. Alarmed by the spectacle of what was, in effect, an Arab civil war, the PLO Central Committee hastened to intervene. Negotiating with the king and his government, they secured a cease-fire, then an extension of it, and finally signed am agreement under which all Palestinian guerrilla forces would be withdrawn; to begin with from Amman, and later from all other urban areas in Jordan. This tragic conflict, it was said, had been the result of Israeli provocations designed to incite brother to fight brother instead of the common Zionist enemy.

Ghaled was not the only guerrilla leader to defy the Central Committee by refusing to honour either the cease-fire or the withdrawal agreement, and sporadic fighting continued in and around Amman for many weeks; but, with the acceptance of the agreement by most of the Al Fatah forces, the Jordanian army was free to concentrate on and to isolate those that remained. One by one, as they saw their positions becoming untenable, Ghaled and the rest had slipped away, taking their men, their arms, and their equipment with them.

Ghaled and his *fedayeen* went north, first to a base at Ramtha near the Syrian border, and then, when the Jordanian army moved to clear that area too, into Syria itself. Most of the dissident leaders, having taken to the Jordanian hills to await developments, now set about composing their differences with the Central Committee. Not Ghaled, however; he remained loudly defiant.

From a subsidiary camp in Lebanon he proclaimed his independence of the POL "running dogs" in the Al Fatah and his support for the Maoist-Marxist Popular Front for the Liberation of

Palestine. At the same time he announced the formation of the super-militant Palestinian Action Force.

I found a copy of the original PAF manifesto in the file. It was subtitled, *Who Are Our Enemies?* Stripped of all the dialectical circumlocutions, his answer to that question could be summed up as, "Those who now falsely profess to be our friends."

How were we to distinguish between false professions of faith and true ones? Simple. *All* would be regarded as suspect until tested in secret. How tested? The PAF had its own security service and its own sources of information. It would conduct its own secret courts-martial. Lists of convicted traitors would be published; PAF purification squads would carry out the court's sentences. Only thus could the Palestinian movement be purged of the poison of the Great Betrayal and become purified.

What Ghaled meant by "purification" and "purified" had soon become clear. Only five or six well publicized "courts-martial" death sentences and "purification" squad executions had been necessary. After those demonstrations there were few men of sense And substance in the Fertile Crescent who did not see that it was better to contribute to the PAF's fighting fund than to run the risk of being named on one of Ghaled's purification lists.

The PLO denounced him as a criminal extortionist. The Popular Front for the Liberation of Palestine dissociated itself from the PAF and its "revisionist" leader Ghaled's "adventurism." The Jordanian government outlawed him. In Lebanon he was wanted on various felony charges. As Frank Edwards had said, he was poison.

"As far as I can see," I said, "this character is completely unrepresentative of the Palestine guerrilla movement. I'm not talking about what he used to be when he was with Al Fatah, Frank. I'm talking about what he has become lately".

He nodded. "I Suppose it's the extortion bit that you don't like. Would you feel that he was more representative if he planted bombs on foreign airliners or in Israeli supermarkets?"

"Yes I would.".

"I can tell you one thing. This extortion thing wasn't started to line his own pockets. The PLO cut off his supplies and subsidies. He had to turn somewhere. Maybe the Russkis are helping him, maybe the Chinese, but he still has to have some cash to operate."

"But to operate what? Does he really believed that he is serving the Palestinian cause with this purification racket of his?"

"No, that's a means to an end."

"What end?"

"Why not ask him? You talk as it you already know what he's become lately-a mere extortionist. That's the PLO line and I don't buy it I don't know what he's become. That's why I'm interested in him, and curious. I'd like to know what he's up to."

"Okay," I said. "I'll try and find out."

I called Melanie Hammad then and told her to go ahead with the arrangements for the interview.

"At once," she said. "I am pleased to be of service, Mr. Prescott. There will, of course, be certain conditions."

I would have been surprised if there had not been. "What conditions, Miss Hammad?"

"The interview must not be published until two days after it has taken place. Security, you understand. And there can be no photographs taken."

"Okay. Accepted. What else?"

"The interview must be tape-recorded."

"I don't use a tape recorder for interviews. I take notes."

"Salah will wish it. He will not ask you to submit your copy to him before you file your story. Obviously that would be difficult But he will wish exact records of what is said."

"Very well."

"I will supply the two recorders."

"Two?"

"You also must have an identical record."

"I don't need one."

"That will be Salah's wish."

"Okay. Anything else?"

"I will telephone you tomorrow with arrangements for the following day."

We met in the early afternoon at the museum in Beirut - "I am known to too many people at the St. Georges Hotel, Mr. Prescott" - and two tape recorders on the front seat of the car were committed to my care.

Miss Hammad drove as iff we were being pursued. The mountain road we were soon climbing was narrow and poorly surfaced, the Buick softly sprung. Clutching the armrest as she flung the car through the hairpin bends, I began to wonder if, for the first time in my life, I was going to be carsick. I was about to protest that we had made good time from Beirut and that there was really no need to go so fast when she braked hard. I had to grab for the two tape recorders on the seat beside me to stop them slithering to the floor.

We had just come through a very sharp bend onto a short, level stretch. I saw now that there was a roadblock ahead of us. It consisted of a striped barrier which could be raised and lowered, and, to prevent anyone crashing the barrier, a staggered arrangement of concrete posts on either side of it A concrete guardhouse with weapon slits crouched beside the barrier, and three Lebanese army men with sub-machine guns stood outside. As the car rolled to a halt one of the soldiers lounged forward.

By the time he reached the car Miss Hammad had her window down and was talking fast. The soldier talked back while looking at me. I wasn't unduly concerned. I didn't speak or understand Arabic myself, but I had heard enough of it spoken to know that, although Miss Hammad's conversation with the soldier might sound like an exchange of threats or insults, it could very well be an exchange of pleasantries. This judgment was proved correct when she gaily laughed at something he had said, wound up the window, and was waved on past the barrier.

"What was all that about?" I asked.

"We have entered the military zone," she said. "Because this is near the Syrian and Israeli borders the army polices the area. You see how it is? Those cowards in Beirut use the army to oppress the *fedayeen.*"

"Those fellows didn't seem very oppressive. They didn't even ask for our papers."

"Oh, they know me and they know the car. It is my father's. He has a chalet in the hills here. I said that you were an American friend of his."

"Is that where we're going, your father's chalet?"

"Only until it is time to go to the rendezvous. That is at another place."

We had passed through an Arab village and were climbing steeply again. Although it was May, up there in the mountains the snow was still unmelted in the gullies. Soon after we left the roadblock behind us she switched on the car heater.

"You didn't tell me I might be needing a topcoat," I said.

"Someone at the hotel might have thought it curious if you had left with an overcoat to go to the museum in Beirut. But it is all right. There are coats at the chalet that we can use."

The chalet proved to be a sizable house with servants to welcome us and a wood fire blazing in a big stone fireplace. Sandwiches had been prepared and there was a well-stocked bar.

"I know it is early for dinner," she said, "but we shall get nothing to eat where we are going."

"Which is where?"

"There is a village two kilometres from here, and above it an old fort. That is the rendezvous. What will you drink?"

"Can I say that the interview took place in an old fort near the Syrian frontier?"

"Of course. There are dozens of them in the mountains here." She smiled. "You could call it a ruined Crusader castle if you like."

"Why?"

"It would sound more romantic."

"Is it a ruined Crusader castle?"

"No, it was built by Muslims."

Then it's an old fort. Thanks, I'll have Scotch."

Over the drinks she tried to pump me about the sort of questions I was going to ask. I replied vaguely and as if I had not given the matter much thought She became irritated, though she tried not to show it. Conversation flagged. I ate most of the sandwiches.

When the sun began to set she said that it was time to go. She donned a voluminous, poncho like garment, which looked as if it had been made out of an old horse blanket, and black felt ankle boots. I was handed a fur-lined anorak belonging to her father that was uncomfortably tight across the shoulders. The Buick had been put away and we travelled now in a Volkswagen fitted with snow tires. She had a haversack with her. I carried the tape recorders on my knees. The two kilometre journey over weather-scoured tracks took twenty minutes.

We stopped just short of the village by a ramshackle stone barn that smelled strongly of animals.

"From here we must walk," she said and produced a flashlight from her haversack.

It was still light enough to see the outline of the fort, a squat, ugly ruin perched on a ledge of rock jutting out from the hillside above. It wasn't far, but the way up to it was rough and we needed the flashlight. In some places there were stone steps and these were dangerous because most of them were broken or loose. Unimpeded by having to carry tape recorders, Miss Hammed bounded ahead nimbly, however, and was obviously impatient when I failed to keep up with her. Finally, as the track straightened out and we approached the scrub-covered glacis of the fort, she told me to wait and went on alone. At the foot of the glacis she made some sort of signal with the flashlight When it was answered from above she called to me that all was well. I plodded on up. By then I didn't much care whether all was well or not. My chief concern was to avoid spraining an ankle.

The stone archway which had been the entrance to the fort had long ago collapsed, and stunted bushes grew in the rubble. There was, however, a path of sorts through it, to which she guided me with the light. There was an Arab in a black wool cape waiting. He motioned me forward with the lantern he carried.

Inside there was more rubble and then a clearing. One of the old walls was still intact, and against it had been built, probably by some local goatherd using stone from the ruins, a lean-to. It had a roof made of bits of rusty iron sheeting patched with tar paper, and a door with cracks in it through which light filtered. In the clearing beside the hut were tethered three donkeys.

"I will go first," said Miss Hammad. "Give me the recorders, please, and wait here."

She said something in Arabic to the man in the cape, who granted an assent and moved up beside me as she went to the hut When the light spilled out from the opening door he peered at me curiously and licked his lips. He had a gray stubble on his jaw and very bad teeth. He smelled bad, too. He asked me in halting, guttural French if I spoke Arabic. I said I didn't and that was that. Two minutes went by, then Miss Hammad reappeared and beckoned to me.

The light in the hut came from a kerosene pressure lamp standing on a battered oil drum. The only other furniture consisted of a crude bench like table and two stools; bat rags had been spread to cover the earth floor for the occasion and a smell of cigar smoke almost masked those of kerosene and goat.

As I entered, the cigar-smoker, who wore a sheepskin coat and a knitted wool cap, rose from one of the stools and inclined his head.

"Mr. Prescott," Miss Hammad announced with awe. "I am permitted to present to you the commander of the Palestinian Action Force, Comrade-leader Salah Ghaled."

He was not handsome; he had a beak of a nose that was too big for his head and a thin moustache that emphasized the disproportion, but in his hawklike way he was impressive. The eyes, heavily lidded, were both keen and wary. Although I knew that he had only just turned forty, he seemed to me to be a much older man. A very fit one, however; every movement he made was precise and economical, and those of his hands had a curious grace about them.

He inclined his head fractionally and then straightened up.

"Good evening, Mr. Prescott," he said in strongly accented, hesitant English. "It is good of you to make this journey. Please sit down." His cigar hand motioned me to the second stool.

Thank you, Mr. Ghaled," I replied. "I am glad of this opportunity of meeting you."

We sat down on the stools.

"I regret," he said, "that I am unable to offer you coffee here, but perhaps you will accept a glass of arrack and a cigarette."

He stumbled over the words and they were the last he said in English. Miss Hammad now took over as interpreter.

A bottle of arrack and two glasses stood on the bench beside the tape recorders along with a pack of the cigarettes I usually smoke. Obviously the arrack, the glasses, and the cigarettes had been brought by her in the haversack.

"Mr. Ghaled does not, of course, normally drink alcohol," she said as she opened the bottle, "but he is not bigoted in these matters and as this is a private occasion he will join you in a glass of arrack made in Syria."

I happen to loathe arrack, wherever made, but this did not seem the moment to say so.

"I am told that Syrian arrack is the best kind."

She translated this as she poured.

Ghaled nodded and motioned to the glasses. We each picked one up and took ceremonial sips.

"I will now prepare the tape recorders," said Miss Hammad. She was sitting cross-legged on the floor now and went on talking alternately in English and Arabic as she set up the microphones and inserted the cassettes.

"Each tape will record for thirty minutes at the slow speed, and I will warn you when I am about to change them. Perhaps it will be as well if I repeat the conditions under which the interview is conducted."

She did so. Ghaled said something.

"Mr. Ghaled has no objections if Mr. Prescott wishes to take written notes to supplement the tape recording."

"Thank you." I put my glass down and took out the scratch pad on which I had already made notes of the preliminary questions I would ask - the easy ones. I could feel Ghaled watching me as I thumbed through the pages; he was trying to weigh me. I took my time looking over the notes and lit a cigarette to extend the silence. If he became impatient, so much the better.

It was Miss Hammad who became impatient.

"If you will say something into the microphones to test them, Mr. Prescott, we can begin."

"It is an honour to be received by Mr. Ghaled."

She translated his reply. "It is gracious of Mr. Prescott to say so."

She played it back on the recorders. They were both working. She pressed the "Record" buttons again and said in English and Arabic: "Interview of the commander and leader of the Palestinian Action Force, Salah Ghaled, by Lewis Prescott, correspondent of the American *Post-Tribune* news service syndicate, meeting in the Republic of Lebanon on . . ." She looked at her watch to check the date before adding it.

It was the fourteenth of May.

Chapter 2

Michael Howell

May 15 to 16

On the fourteenth of May I was in Italy, and I wish to God I had stayed there.

Even an airport strike - if it had delayed me for twenty-four hours or so - would have helped. At least my ignorance would have been preserved a little longer. With luck I might even have escaped direct involvement But no. I went back on the fifteenth and walked straight into trouble.

The fact that the poison had already been in the system then for over five months - ever since the man calling himself Yassin had come to work for me - was something I did *not* know. I have been accused of having turned a blind eye until circumstances forced me to do otherwise. Nothing could be further from the truth.

Unfortunately, those who know me best, business friends, for example, have found the fact that I was both ignorant and innocent hard to accept. My admission that never once during those months had I had the slightest inkling of what was going on seems to them no more than a highly unconvincing, but in the circumstances necessary, claim to incompetence. Well, I can scarcely blame them, but I am sorry. That admission, which I certainly did not enjoy making and of which I am anything but proud, happens to be true.

One thing I would like to be clearly understood. I am not trying to justify myself or my conduct; I am only attempting to repair some of the damage that has been done. It is not my personal reputation that matters now, but that of our company.

The week prior to the fifteenth of May I had spent in Milan on company business. Having completed that business, I flew to Rome, where I picked up two new suits which had been waiting for me at my tailor's. The following day, the fifteenth, I took a Middle East Airlines flight to Damascus.

As usual I had cabled the flight number and expected time of arrival and so, as usual, I received the VIP treatment. At Damascus this meant that I was met at tike foot of the stairway from the plane by a Syrian army corporal in a paratroop jump suit, with a Czech automatic rifle, loaded and at the ready, slung across his stomach. Escorted by him, I then went through passport control and customs to the waiting air-conditioned Ministry car.

My feelings about being met am this way were, as always, mixed. It was convenient, of course, to be spared the interrogations and searching to which most of my fellow passengers would be subjected. It was also reassuring to know on landing that one was still considered of value to the state, and that no long knives had been out during one's absence: modern Syria must still be considered one of the 'off-with-his-head' countries.

On the other hand, while there was no denying that Damascus airport was at times a dangerous place, I could never quite rid myself of the conviction that should any of the potential dangers - a bomb outrage, say, or a guerrilla shoot-out - suddenly become immediate, I as a foreigner, a civilian, and an infidel, would be among the first to perish in the crossfire. The corporal, whom I had encountered before, was a friendly oaf who smelled of sweat and gun oil and was very proud of the fact that his firstborn was now attending a village primary school; but to me, his uniform and his loaded rifle seemed as much a threat as a protection. I was always relieved when we reached the car, and the porter arrived with the luggage.

My appointment with the Minister was not until four thirty so I drove first to the villa our company owned in the city - and to Teresa.

The villa was in the old style with a walled courtyard and was part office, part pied-à-terre. Teresa was in charge of both parts of the establishment. With the help of a Syrian clerk she ran the office for me; with that of two servants she took care of our private household.

Teresa's father had been the Italian consul in Aleppo. He had also been an enthusiastic amateur archaeologist. With Teresa's mother and members of the Aleppo Museum staff he was away on am archaeological expedition in the north when the party was attacked by a gang of bandits, believed to be Kurds. Supposedly the Kurds mistook the party for a Syrian border patrol. Teresa's parents had been among those killed.

She had been nineteen then, convent-educated in Lebanon, and a good linguist. For a time she worked as secretary-translator in the local office of an American oil company. Then she came to me. Having spent most of her life in the Middle East, she knows the form. She has been and is, in every way, invaluable to me.

I have always had to do a lot of travelling around for our company, and whenever I returned to Damascus from a trip there was a set office routine. Teresa would have ready for me a brief summary report on the state of our local enterprises. This report usually consisted chiefly of figures. She would supplement the report verbally with comment and any interesting items of information that she thought I should have.

On this occasion she told me about the manoeuvring of a competitor who was bidding against us on a job in Teheran, That story amused me.

What came next did not amuse me at all.

"I've noticed that the laboratory costs seem to be getting higher and higher," she said, "so while you were away I looked into them. The accounts come here for payment, but the invoices showing the details of items purchased go to the factory with the goods. There most of them seem to get lost. So I wrote to the suppliers in Beirut for a duplicate set of last month's invoices."

"And?"

"I found one recent item that was really very expensive. We also had to pay a lot of duty on it It was an order for ten rottols of absolute alcohol."

A rottol, I should explain, is one of those antediluvian weights and measures which are still used in some parts of the Middle East One rottol equals two okes, one oke weighs just over a kilo and a quarter. So ten rottols would be about twenty-five kilos.

"Issa ordered that?"

"Apparently. I didn't know we used that much alcohol in the laboratory."

"We shouldn't use any. Did you ask him about it?"

She smiled. "I thought you might prefer to do that, Michael"

"Quite right I'll look forward to it. The little bastard!" I glanced at my watch; the Minister was a stickler for punctuality. "We'll talk about it later," I said.

"Did you get what you wanted in Milan?"

"I think so." I picked up my briefcase. "Let's hope His Nibs likes the look of it, too."

"Good luck," she said.

I went down and got back into the Ministry car. The sound of the first warning note was already becoming faint in my mind. I imagined, with reason, that I had more important business to attend to that afternoon.

In view of the libelous and highly damaging statements which have been made about our company and its operations, particularly in certain French and West German 'news' magazines, I feel it necessary at this point to give the essential facts. Slander, the verbalized bile of jealous competitors and other commercial opponents, may be contemptuously ignored, but printed vilification cannot be allowed to go unchallenged. True, these published libels are actionable at law and, of course, the necessary steps have been taken to bring those responsible before courts of justice. Unfortunately, since different countries have different laws on the subject of libel, and what is clearly actionable in one place may be only marginally so in another, the paths to justice are long and tortuous. Time passes, the lies prosper like weeds, and the truth is stifled. That I will not permit. The weed-killer must be applied now.

One of the news magazine reporters to whom I granted an interview described my defence of our company's position as "a garrulous smokescreen of misinformation." Mixed metaphors seem to be a characteristic of heavily slanted reporting, but as this sort of charge was fairly typical, I will answer it.

Garrulous? Maybe. In trying to break down his very obvious preconceptions and prejudices I probably did talk too much. Smokescreen? Misinformation? He came with a closed mind and that was its condition when he left. The truth wasn't newsy enough for him. His quality - and that of his editor - was well displayed elsewhere in the piece where it was stated that I wore "expensive gold cuff links." What was that supposed to prove, for God's sake? Would my credibility have been enhanced if I had secured my shirt cuffs with inexpensive gold links, should such things exist, or plastic buttons?

No. I am not saying that all newspaper men are corrupt - Mr. Lewis Prescott and Mr. Frank Edwards, for instance, have at least tried to tell the truth - but simply that the only way you can win with those who *are* corrupt is to fight them on their own ground, and discredit them publicly in print.

That is what I am doing now, and if any of those spry paladins of the gutter press feels that anything that I have said about him is libelous and actionable, his legal advisers will tell him where to apply. Our company retains excellent lawyers in all the capitals from which we operate.

Agence Commerciale et Maritime Howell, along with its associated trading companies, has always been very much a family concern. The original *société à responsabilité limité* was registered by my grandfather, Robert Howell, in the early 1920's. Before that, since the turn of the century in fact, he had grown licorice and tobacco on big stretches of land held under a *firman* of the Turkish Sultan, Abdul, in what used to be called the Levant.

The land, in the *vilayet* of Latakia, was granted to him as a reward for political services rendered to the Ottoman court. The exact nature of the services rendered I have never been able to determine. My father once told me, vaguely, that "they had something to do with a government bond issue," but he was unable, or unwilling, to amplify that statement. The original land grant described Grandfather's occupation as that of "entrepreneur-negotiator," which in Imperial Turkey could have meant many different things. I do know that he was always very well in, in Constantinople, and that even during World War I, when as an Englishman he was interned by the Turks, his internment amounted to little more than house arrest. Moreover, the land remained in his name, as, too, did the businesses there - a tannery and a flour mill - which he had acquired before the war. "Johnny Turk is a gentleman," he used to say.

With the collapse of the Ottoman Empire and the establishment of the French Mandate over the areas mow known as Syria and Lebanon, some changes had to be made. Although his tenure of the lands he had previously held was eventually confirmed by the new regime, his experience under the French colonial administrators - less gentlemanly than Johnny Turk by all accounts - had taught him a sharp lesson. Personal ownership of a business made one vulnerable. He made arrangements to acquire a corporate identity in Syria and to transfer gradually most of his subsidiary businesses, chiefly those which did not depend directly on landholding, to

Cyprus.

Grandfather died in 1933, and my father, John Howell took control. He had been in charge of the Cyprus office in Famagusta, which had been established originally to find cargoes for the fleet of coasters which the parent company owned and operated out of Latakia.

As his Cyprus office had grown in importance my father's interest in the mainland of Asia Minor had waned. He had married in Cyprus. My sisters and I were born in Famagusta and baptized in the Greek Orthodox faith. My name, Michael Howell, may look and sound Anglo-Saxon but, with a Lebanese-Armenian grandmother and a Cypriot mother, I am no more than fractionally English. There are lots of families like ours, rich and poor, in the Middle East. Ethnically, I suppose, my sisters and I could reasonably be described as "Eastern Mediterranean." Personally I prefer the simpler though usually pejorative term, "Levantine mongrel." Mongrels are sometimes more intelligent than their respectable cousins; they also tend to adapt more readily to strange environments; and in conditions of extreme adversity, they are among those most likely to survive.

The World War II years were difficult ones for our Syrian interests. Those in Cyprus gave little trouble. The coasters, prudently reregistered in Famagusta before the war, were all on charter to the British. They lost three of them off Crete, but their government war-risk insurance covered us nicely; I think we even made money on the deal In Syria, though, it was a different story. The fighting between the Allies and the Vichy French brought business virtually to a standstill. The demand for licorice root and Latakia tobacco at that time was, to put it mildly, minimal. In 1942, when the Allies started driving the enemy out of North Africa, Father moved our head office to Alexandria and registered a new holding company, Howell General Trading Ltd. The Syrian and Cypriot businesses became subsidiaries. In that year, too, I was sent around the Cape to purgatory in England. Had I been consulted I would have chosen to stay at the English school in Alex, or, failing that, go to the one in Istanbul where there were family friends; but my mother wouldn't have Istanbul - unlike Grandfather Howell she is very anti-Turk - and anyway my father's mind was made up. War or no war, I had to go through the same prep and public school mills as he and his father had.

Not all my father's ideas were so fixed, however. After the move to Alexandria the whole character and direction of our business began to change. This was Father's doing and he was quite deliberate about it. He had sensed the future. Some things remained - the coasters and the bigger ships that later replaced them had nearly always been profitable-but from 1945 on, when the war in Europe ended, the whole emphasis on the trading side of our business shifted from bulk commodities to manufactured goods. During those postwar years we became selling agents throughout the Middle East (after 1948, Israel always excepted) for a number of European and, later, some American manufacturers.

This change had a direct effect on my life. The first of these agencies of ours was that of a firm in Glasgow which made a range of rotary pumps. It was my father's realization that it is difficult to sell engineering products effectively when the buyer knows more than you do about them that made him decide on a technical education for me. So, instead of going from school in England to Cairo University, a transition to which I had been looking forward, I found myself committed to a red-brick polytechnic in one of the grimier parts of London.

At the time, I am afraid, my acceptance of this change of plan was more sullen than dutiful. Born in Cyprus when it was a British colonial possession, I held a British colonial passport. By the simple process of threatening me - quite baselessly, I later discovered - with the prospect of National Service conscription into the British army unless I enrolled as a student in London, my father had his way. It wasn't, I know, a nice trick for a loving father to play on a son; but I can admit now that, as a businessman, I have had no reason to regret that he played it.

One way and another, then, I learned a lot from my father. He died in 1962, of a heart ailment, eighteen months after we moved our head office to Beirut in Lebanon and registered our second holding company in Vaduz.

The testing time for me, as the new head of our business, came the following year, when I had to make my first major policy decision.

It was that decision, made almost nine years ago, that started me on the road which has proved in the end to be so very dangerous.

Our Syrian troubles had started in the early fifties when Soviet penetration of the Middle East began. In Syria it was particularly successful. Friendship with the Soviet Union grew with the rise to power of the Syrian Arab Socialist Renaissance movement, later to be known as the Ba'ath Party. They were not communists - as Sunnite Muslims they could not be; they were, however, Arab nationalists committed to socialism and strongly anti-West. The Ba'ath program called for union with Egypt and other Arab states, and rapid socialization of the Syrian economy.

In 1958 they got both union with Egypt and, at the same time, the first of their socialization measures, "agrarian reform." In that year an expropriation law was passed which stripped the Agence Howell of all but eighty hectares of its irrigated land. We had held over a thousand hectares. As a foreign-owned company we received "compensation," but since the compensation was paid into a blocked account in the state-owned Central Bank, it didn't do us much good. We were not permitted to transfer the money out of the country, we could not buy foreign currency or valuta, and we were not even allowed to reinvest or spend the money inside the country without permission from the Central Bank. It was in limbo.

They let us keep the tannery and the flour mill for the time being. Nationalization of industry was to come later.

In 1959 my father formally applied for the release of the blocked funds for reinvestment purposes. He planned to buy a 2,000-ton cargo vessel that was up for sale in Latakia and me it in the Aegean. It was a way of exporting some of the capital that he thought he might just get away with. But that was a bad year in Syria. There was a prolonged drought and the harvests were so poor that Syria had to import cereals instead of exporting as usual. The Central Bank, which clearly saw through the ship-purchase idea, regretted that, owing to the current shortage of foreign exchange resulting from the adverse trade situation, the application for release must be refused.

In 1960, when he applied again, the bank did not even reply to his letters.

In 1961 there was a military coup d'état aimed at dissolving the union with Egypt, restoring Syria's position as a sovereign state, and setting up a new constitutional regime. It succeeded, and for a while things looked better for us. Property rights were to be guaranteed. Free enterprise was to be encouraged. The Central Bank was giving our latest request its sympathetic consideration. If the squabbling politicians could have agreed to compose their differences, even temporarily, and allowed the situation to become stable, all might have been well; but they couldn't Within six months, the army, tired of the "self-seeking" civilians, had moved in again with yet another coup.

Then, in 1963, there was a revolution.

I have used the word "revolution" because the Ba'athist coup of that year, though once again mainly the work of army officers, was more than a mere transfer of power from one nationalist faction to another; it brought about basic political changes. Syria became a one-party state and, while rejoining the UAR, managed to do so without re-surrendering its sovereign independence. The program of socialization was resumed. In May of '63 all the banks were nationalized.

It was at that time that I came to my decision.

I knew a good deal about the Ba'ath people. Many of them were naive reformers, doomed to eventual disillusionment, and they had their windbags who could do no more than parrot ritual calls for social justice; but among the party leaders there were able and determined men. When they said that they meant to nationalize all industry, I believed them. Later, no doubt, there would be some pragmatic compromises, and gray areas of collaboration between public and private sectors would appear; tout in the main, I thought, they meant what they said. What was more, I believed that they were there to stay.

How best, then, to safeguard the interests of the Agence Howell?

I had, I considered, three options open to me. I could side with the resisters. I could temporize. Or I could explore the gray areas of future compromise and see what sort of a deal I could make.

Siding with the resisters meant, in effect, taking to the political woods and conspiring with those who would attempt to overthrow the new government. For a foreigner contemplating suicide this course might have had its attractions. For this foreigner it had none.

The temporizers, of whom there were many among my business acquaintances, seemed to me to have misjudged the new situation. Having observed with mounting weariness the political antics of the past decade, they tended to dismiss the nationalization of industry threat, with smiles and shrugs, as mere post-coup rhetoric. The banks? Well, the British and French banks had been sequestrated for years, hadn't they? Nationalizing what was left had been an easy gesture to make. No, Michael, the thing to do now is sit tight and wait for the next counter-coup. Meanwhile, of course, we'll have to keep our eyes open. When all this dust begins to settle a bit some of your new men will be coming out of it with their palms beginning to itch. They'll be the ones to talk to about nationalization of industry. How can we pay them if they nationalize us, eh? Watch and wait, my boy, watch and wait. It's the only way.

The temporizers, I thought, might be in for some surprises. I went my own way, exploring.

Obviously, yet another application to the Central Bank for the release of our blocked funds would fail unless I could apply some sort of leverage. Just as obviously, the only kind of lever that would work with the Central Bank would be one operated by its masters in the government. What I needed, then, was an endorsement of my application by a government department It would have to be a high-level endorsement, too, preferably ministerial. What did I have to offer in exchange for such a thing?

At that point, the catch phrase, "If you can't lick 'em, join em," came to mind. After that, once I had accepted the fact that I might do better working *with* the government people than by attempting artfully to outwit them, I made progress. The problem was then simplified. How could I join them in a way which would ultimately benefit us both?

I did a lot of thinking, some intensive market research, and formulated the plan.

In '63 I was not as used to negotiating with government officials as I am now. If I had been, I would not have given the proposition I was out to sell them even a fifty-fifty chance of success. Perhaps the fact that I was only thirty-two at the time, and consumed by the need to prove myself, helped. I was very aggressive in those days, too, and, I am afraid, given to finger-wagging exhortation when opposed.

My first encounter with the decision-making machinery in Damascus was a meeting with two bureaucrats, one from the Ministry of Finance, where the meeting took place, and one from the Ministry of Social Affairs and Commerce. They listened to me in silence, accepted copies of an *aide-mémoire* which summarized my proposals in veiled, but what I believed to be intriguing, terms, and indicated politely that they had other appointments.

A month went by before I was summoned by letter to a meeting at the Ministry of Social Affairs and Commerce. This meeting was in the office of a senior official to whom I had once been introduced at a Greek Embassy picnic. Also present were the two bureaucrats who had interviewed me before and a younger man who was introduced as representing the recently created Department of Industrial Development After the usual preliminary politenesses had been exchanged the senior officials invited this younger man to question me on the subject of my proposals.

His name was Hawa - Dr. Hawa.

My subsequent dealings with Dr. Hawa have been the subject of much misrepresentation. He himself has lately seen fit to assume the role of innocent betrayed, and to accuse me publicly of every crime from malfeasance to murder on the high seas. Under the circumstances it may be thought that no account I give of our relationship can be wholly objective.

I disagree. I have every intention of remaining objective. As far as I am concerned the only effect of his diatribes has been to relieve me of any lingering disposition to pull my punches.

Dr. Hawa is a thin, hard-faced man with tight lips and dark, angry eyes; obviously a tough customer, and particularly formidable when met for the first time. I remember that it was something of a relief to find that he was a chain-smoker; I knew then that he wasn't as formidable as he appeared. Though we later became better acquainted I never discovered the academic discipline to which his doctorate belonged. I do know that he had a degree in law from the University of Damascus and that he later spent a year or two in the United States under a post-graduate student-exchange arrangement. There, I gather, he managed to pick up a Ph.D. from some easygoing academic institution in the Middle West. His English is fluent, with North American intonations. However, that first conversation was conducted mainly in Arabic with only occasional lapses into French and English.

"Mr. Howell, tell me about your company," he began.

The tone was patronizing. I had noticed that he had a copy of my *aide-mémoire* on the table in front of him, so I nodded toward it

"It is all there, Dr. Hawa."

"No, Mr. Howell, it is not all there." He flicked the papers disdainfully. "What is described there is a gambit, an opening move in which a small piece is sacrificed to secure a later advantage. We would like to know what game it is that we are being invited to play."

I knew then that I would have to be careful with him. Chain-smoker he might be, but he was certainly no fool. If he had been English he would probably have described my *aide-mémoire* as a sprat to catch a mackerel, but gambit was also a pretty accurate description - too accurate for my liking. I looked at the senior official.

"What I had hoped for here, sir," I said sternly, "was a serious discussion of serious proposals. I have no intention of playing any sort of game."

"Dr. Hawa was speaking figuratively, of course."

Hawa had a thin smile. "As Mr. Howell appears to be so sensitive I will put the matter another way." He looked at me again. "You ask, Mr. Howell, for ministerial endorsement of an application for the release of blocked funds in order that they may be reinvested here. In return you undertake to confer on the state a number of economic blessings, the nature of which you hint at, but the value of which you leave to the imagination. More specifically, however, you offer to relinquish control of your remaining enterprises here, including a tannery and a flour mill, so that they may become cooperatives working under government auspices. Naturally we are curious about the spirit and temper of this strange gift horse, and about the business philosophy of the giver, the man who is seeking funds for reinvestment. So, I ask you to satisfy our curiosity."

I shrugged. "As you probably know our company here has hitherto been a family affair. My grandfather and my father before me have done business in this country for many years. I think it fair to say that it has been useful business."

"Useful? Don't you mean profitable?"

"For me that is a distinction without a difference, Dr. Hawa.

Useful *and* profitable, of course. Is there any other kind of business worth doing?" I thought I had his measure mow. In a moment he was going to start talking about ownership of the means of production. I was wrong.

"But useful to whom, profitable to whom?"

Useful to all those of your people to whom our company pays good wages and salaries - here, I may remind you, we employ only Syrian nationals. Profitable certainly to our company's shareholders, but profitable also to the successive governments, Turkish, French, and Syrian, which have taxed us. Dividends have not always been certain, but wages and taxes have always been promptly paid." And, I might have added, so had the bribes, petty and not so petty, which were part of any Levantine overhead; but I was still trying to handle him tactfully.

"Then why, Mr. Howell, are you so eager to relinquish control of these useful and profitable businesses?"

"Eager?" I gave him a blank stare. "I assure you, Dr. Hawa, that I am not in the least eager. My impression is that ultimately I will have no choice in the matter."

"Ultimately, perhaps, but why this premature generosity? Understandably, I think, we find it puzzling, and a little suspect."

"Only because you are not looking at my proposals as a whole. I think I am being realistic."

"Realistic? How?"

I might have replied that had I not puzzled them by offering to hand over the Syrian assets of the Agence Howell, we would not have been sitting there discussing what was to become of its blocked funds. Instead I gave my prepared answer.

"At present the government lacks the administrative machinery to implement its socialist program for industry. But only at present. I am looking to the future. I might retain control for a year or so, but sooner or later I will certainly lose it. I prefer to lose it sooner and devote my time and energies to retrieving the situation. Does that seem foolish, or even generous, Dr. Hawa?"

"If we knew better what you meant by 'retrieving the situation' we might be able to judge."

"Very well. Then let us begin with two assumptions. First, that the government takes over the operation of our remaining business in Syria for its own account and profit. Second, that the government compensates us in the usual way, with paper."

He was lighting yet another cigarette. "There is no harm in our speaking hypothetically. Let us, for the purposes of your explanation, accept both acquisition and compensation. What then?"

"The Agence Howell is left without businesses here but with substantial assets. Some of these assets are intangible - management skills, knowledge of world markets and access to them, trading experience - but they are real enough nonetheless. However, without the capital to exploit them they are useless. The capital is there, but it is blocked. So, since the capital is not allowed to work, nothing else can. The loss is only partly ours. Your economy loses, too. The remedy I propose would work to our mutual advantage and would be in line with announced government policies for industry."

"If you could be more specific."

"Certainly. I propose a series of cooperative ventures, under government auspices and control, in the light industry field. Their primary object would be the manufacture of goods suitable for the export markets."

"What sort of goods, Mr. Howell?" He had now the intent look of a cat who has suddenly seen a plump and rather somnolent field mouse.

"Ceramics to begin with," I said. "Then I would go over to furniture and metalwork."

The cat's tail twitched. "In case you are unaware of the fact, Mr. Howell, I must tell you that we already have a considerable ceramics industry."

"I am well aware of it, Dr. Hawa, but as far as I am concerned it is making the wrong things."

"And as far as I am concerned, Mr. Howell, I begin to suspect that you are barking up the wrong tree."

He was beginning to annoy me. "Of course, Dr. Hawa, if you find it too painful to listen to new ideas on old subjects, there is nothing more to be said."

He decided that it was time to pounce. "New ideas, Mr. Howell? Decorated junk in quantity - pots, plates, and vases - for export to the trashy tourist shops of the Western world? Is that the way you would like to get your money out?" He laughed shortly at the others and they smiled back dutifully.

I nearly lost my temper, but not quite.

"I realize, Doctor, that you must be a very busy man," I said, "and that before this meeting you were unable to make the usual departmental inquiries about my qualifications and reputation."

He shrugged indifferently. "You were trained as an engineer. That could mean anything."

"Then you cannot have heard that it is not a business habit of mine to talk nonsense. At the mention of ceramics your mind goes to pots and plates and vases. And why not? That is all you know about in the context. When I say ceramics I have something different in mind, because I have done some market research. I am talking, for one thing, about mass produced tiling."

He frowned. "Tiles? You mean the tiles we use on our floors?"

"Not of the kind you mean. I mean ceramic tile sold by the square meter and made up of two centimetre mosaics glazed on one surface in plain colours, and not sold in any tourist shops, trashy or otherwise. I will give you an example. There is at the moment a modern two-hundred bedroom hotel going up in Benghazi. Each bedroom has a bathroom tiled in this material - floors and walls, plain colours - pink, blue, green, black, white. Approximately fifty square meters of tiling go into each bathroom. There is the same kind of tiling in the kitchens and on the verandas. About twelve thousand square meters were involved in the contract which went to an Italian manufacturer. It was worth forty-five thousand American."

"Dollars?"

"Dollars. There is a big demand for this material. All over the Mediterranean hotels and big apartment blocks are being built, all over Europe for that matter. Marble is expensive. Tiling is comparatively cheap. Tiling is now the preferred material. Could Syria have had this order for Benghazi? If it had been equipped to produce the right article in the quantities needed and on time, the answer must be yes. True, Libya still has commercial ties with Italy, but what of her religious, ethnic, and political ties with the UAR? Besides, Syria's price could well have been lower."

"Where else is this special tiling made?"

"You mean is it an Italian monopoly? By no means. The French and the Swiss are already in the business. There is a tile factory near Zurich employing over two hundred persons."

He made a face. "So a tiling factory, and when the building business slumps . . ."

"We shall be much older men. In any case the tiling is only one example of the kind of thing I mean, Egypt is now building an electric power grid. It will take years to complete, and overhead high voltage power lines need glazed ceramic insulators, massive things, six or eight to a pylon. Tens of thousands will be needed. Of course, they could all come from the Soviet Union or Poland, but would the Russians care if these insulators were made in Syria? They might even be glad to subcontract the work to a friendly neighbour. It would be interesting to find out. I am sure that a request passed through their commercial attaché for drawings and specifications would be sympathetically received."

"Yes, yes, of course." He had risen nicely to that bait, as I had hoped he would.

The senior official leaned forward. "I take it that your proposals for furniture manufacture are equally unconventional, Mr. Howell?"

"I believe so, sir. No camel-saddle chairs, no ornamental coffee tables, but modern office and hotel furniture of Western design and, again, mass-produced. Some relatively inexpensive machine tools would have to be imported, as would the plastics we would meed for surfacing, but the metal fittings could be made here."

Dr. Hawa returned to the attack. "But in the metal-working field you would surely be thinking in terms of such things as Western-style cutlery."

"No, Dr. Hawa."

A sly smile. "Because your Lebanese and Egyptian companies already sell expensive cutlery imported from the United Kingdom?"

So he had done some homework after all.

"No," I answered, "because the Japanese already dominate the market for mass-produced cutlery. We could never compete. I am thinking in terms of door fastenings, catches, bolts, hinges - building hardware that can be made in quantity using jigs and dies and some inexpensive machine tools such as drill and stamping presses. There must also be modern finishing processes. Handicraft standards would not be adequate."

The senior official intervened once more. "You again emphasize the use of inexpensive machines, Mr. Howell, but isn't it the expensive machines which make the inexpensive and competitively priced goods?"

I replied carefully. "Where labour costs are-high that is certainly true. We should endeavour to strike a balance. Labour intensive projects, I agree, are of no value to Syria. But in the refugee camps we have a source, still largely untapped, of unskilled and semi-skilled labour. Under Syrian foremen it could be trained and made useful. I have no doubt that as we progressed we would need, and could use, machine tools that were less simple and more expensive. Our ability to buy them would certainly be one measure of our success. Our inability to do so in the beginning, however, should not foredoom us to failure. In properly guided hands even simple machines can do a lot."

"It is a relief," said Dr. Hawa nastily, "to know that Mr. Howell has at least considered the possibility of failure."

"I have tried to consider all the possibilities, Doctor. I have proposed that the government uses our company and its assets to advance the public interest. Whether you use us or not, or how you use us, are questions which will not, I imagine, be answered today. But if we are to be used, and used successfully, I submit that we can serve you best in the ways I have suggested, employing our limited resources to reach limited but realistic objectives in the foreseeable future."

The senior official was nodding encouragingly, so I went on quickly before Hawa could interrupt "The projects I most favour, the ones we have been discussing in general terms, are those which can be most easily tried and tested by means of pilot operations. I believe such operations to be essential. When we make mistakes, as we will, they should be on a small scale and rectifiable. On the other hand, all pilot operations, to be of real value, must be big enough for us to snake accurate forecasts, projections of our full-scale needs-for raw materials, for example. Simple arithmetic can sometimes be misleading."

"It can indeed!" Dr. Hawa blew smoke across the table; he had taken charge again. "Having been treated to some entertaining flights of fancy, perhaps we may now return to more prosaic matters. Mr. Howell, are you in fact proposing that the Agence Howell's blocked funds should be employed entirely to finance these splendid schemes of yours?"

"No," I said bluntly, "I most certainly am *not* proposing that."

Then I fail to see..."

"Allow me to finish, please. Firstly, the amount of company capital available, if it can be made available, would be quite inadequate for the projects we have been discussing. What I am proposing is that company funds are employed to finance and manage the *pilot* operation in each case. When, and only when, a pilot project has proved itself does it go forward into full-scale production. At that point the government takes over the financing and the company becomes a minority shareholder in a government owned cooperative."

Dr. Hawa rolled his eyes in theatrical amazement.

"You would expect me to believe, Mr. Howell, that you and your company would be prepared to work for nothing?"

"No, I don't. We would expect something in the way of management fees for our work in organizing and developing the projects. They could be nominal, enough to cover normal overhead expenses, let us say. Naturally, all such arrangements would be covered in the formal agreements made between the department of the government concerned and the company." I paused slightly before I added: "It would, of course, be one of the conditions of our entering into such agreements that our company is granted exclusive agencies for the sale abroad of the products of these joint ventures. I think that sole and exclusive agencies for a period of, say, twenty-five years would be fair and reasonable."

There was a silence, and then the senior official began making a throat-clearing sound which developed after a moment or two into words of protest.

"But . . . but. . ." He did not seem quite able to go on. Finally, he threw up his hands. "You could make a fortune!" he cried.

I shook my head. "With respect, sir, I think we are more likely to lose one. However, since our fortune here is now at risk anyway, I would like to reduce the odds against it if I can."

"The government would never agree."

"Again with respect, sir, why not? They will be running no risks. By the time they are asked to fund a project, all the risks will have been run for them. It can only be for the good of the economy then, and for the people. Why should they not agree?"

Dr. Hawa said nothing; he was lighting yet another cigarette; but he seemed to be amused.

A month later the first of the draft agreements was initialled; by me on behalf of the company and by Dr. Hawa on behalf of the newly formed People's Industrial Progress Cooperative.

41

The news had a mixed reception in Beirut, and I had to preside over an unusually prolonged board meeting. My sisters, Euridice and Amalia, both had husbands who, with one qualifying share apiece, attended these meetings as voting directors.

This lamentable arrangement had been initiated by my father in the last months of his life; mainly, I think, because it made him uneasy to see more women than men seated around a board-room table-even when the women in question were his own wife and daughters. Having dealt so much with Muslims over the years, he had become inclined in some ways to think like them. By the time he had learned to regret the arrangement, however, he was too ill and tired to do anything about rescinding it. That task he had bequeathed to me, and, since I was unwilling to precipitate a major family quarrel during my first year in command, I had postponed taking the necessary action.

I don't dislike my brothers-in-law; they are both worthy men, but one is a dentist and the other an associate professor of physics. Neither of them knows anything about business. Yet, while both would be understandably affronted if I offered to advise them in their professional capacities, neither has ever hesitated for a moment to tender detailed criticisms of, and advice about, the management of our company. They regard business, somewhat indulgently, as a sort of game which anyone with a little common sense can always join in and play perfectly. With the dreadful persistence of those who argue off the tops of their heads from positions of total ignorance, they would make their irrelevant points and formulate their senseless proposals while my sisters took it in turn to nod their idiotic heads in approval. Having to listen to these blithe fatuities was almost as exhausting as having later to dispose of them without being unforgivably offensive. No, I don't dislike my brothers-in-law; but there have been times when I have wished them dead.

Their immediate and enthusiastic approval of my Syrian agreement was, therefore, both disconcerting and disquieting.

Giulio the dentist, who is Italian, became quite eloquent on the subject. "It is my considered opinion," he said, "that Michael has been both statesmanlike and farsighted. Dealing with idealists, ideologues perhaps in this case, is no easy matter. In their minds all compromise is weakness, and negotiation a mere path to treason. The radical extremist of whatever stripe is consistently paranoid. Yet there are chinks even in their black armour of suspicion, and Michael has found the most vulnerable-self-interest and greed. We have no need of gunboats to help us do our business. This agreement is the modern way of doing things."

"Nonsense!" said my mother loudly. "It is the weak and shortsighted way." She stared Giulio into silence before she turned again to me. "Why," she continued sombrely, "was this confrontation necessary? Why, in God's name, did we ourselves invite it? And why, having merely discussed am agreement, did we fall into the trap of signing it? Oh, if your father had been alive!"

"The agreement is not signed, Mama. I have only initialled a draft."

"Draft? Hah!" She struck her forehead sharply with the heel of her hand, a method of demonstrating extreme emotion that did not disturb the careful setting of her hair. "And could you now disavow that initialling?" she demanded. "Could you now let our name become a byword in the marketplace for vacillation and bad faith?"

"Yes, Mama, and no."

"What do you say?"

"Yes to the first question, no to the second. A draft agreement initialled is a declaration of intent. It is not absolutely binding. There are ways of puling out if we wish to. I don't think we should, but not for the reasons you give. There would be no question of bad faith, but it might well be thought that we had been bluffing. In that case we could not expect them to deal generously with us in the future."

"But it was you, Michael, who took the initiative. Why? Why did you not wait passively until the time was ripe to employ those tactics which your father knew so well?" She had leaned forward across the table and was rubbing the thumb and third finger of her right hand together. Her second diamond ring glittered accusingly.

"I have explained, Mama. We are dealing with a new situation and a different type of man."

"Different? They are Syrians, aren't they? What can be new there?"

"A distrust of the past, a real wish for reform and determination to bring about change. I agree that a lot of their ideas are half-baked, but they will learn, and the will is there. I may add that if I had attempted to bribe Dr. Hawa, or even hinted at the possibility, I would certainly have been in jail within the hour. That much at least is new."

They are still Syrians, and new men quickly become old. Besides, how do you know that the parties to your agreement will still be there in six months' time? You see a changed situation, yes. But remember, such situations can change more than once, and in more than one direction."

I removed my glasses and polished them with my handkerchief. My wife, Anastasia, has told me that this habit of mine of polishing my glasses when I want to think carefully is bad. According to her it produces an effect of weakness and confusion on my part. She may be right; I can always count on Anastasia to observe my shortcomings and to keep the list of them well up to date.

"Let me be clear about this, Mama." I replaced the glasses and put the handkerchief away. "There are many in Damascus, persons of experience, who think as you do. I believe that if Father were alive he would be among them. I also believe that he would be wrong. I don't deny the value of patience. But just waiting to see which way the cat is going to jump and wondering which palms will have to be greased may simply be a way of doing nothing when you don't think it safe to trust your own judgment. By going to these people rather than waiting for them to decide our fate in committee, we have secured solid advantages. With luck, our capital there can be made to go on working for us."

She shook her head sadly. "You have so much English blood in you, Michael More, I sometimes think, than your father had, though how such a thing could be I do not know." Coming from my mother these were very harsh words indeed. I awaited the rest of the indictment. "I well remember," she went on steadily, "something that your father said in 1929. That was before you were born, when I was" - she patted her stomach- "when I was carrying you here. A British army officer had been staying in our house. An amateur yachtsman he was, and the yard had been doing some repairs to his boat When he left he forgot to take with him a little red book he had been reading. It was a manual of infantry training, or some such thing, issued by the War Office. Your father read this book and one thing in it amused him so much that he read it aloud to me. To do nothing,' the War Office said, 'is to do something definitely wrong." How your father laughed! 'No wonder," he said, 'that the British army has such difficulty in winning its wars!'"

Only my brothers-in-law, who had not heard the story so many times before, laughed; but my mother had not finished yet.

"You, Michael," she said, "have done things for which you claim what you call solid advantages. First advantage, compensation for loss of our Syrian businesses which we will not receive and which is therefore stolen from us. Second advantage, a license to subsidize with the stolen money, and much too much of your valuable time, some nonexistent industry producing nonexistent goods. Yes, we have the sole agency for these goods, if those peasants and refugees there can ever be made to produce them. But when will that be? If I know those people, not in my lifetime."

She had, of course, put her finger unerringly on the basic weakness of the whole arrangement. I was to be reminded of that phrase about "nonexistent industry producing nonexistent goods" all too often during the months that followed. At the time all I could do was sit there and pretend to an unshaken calm that I certainly did not feel.

"Are there any questions?"

"Yes." It was my sister Euridice. "What is the alternative to this agreement?"

"The alternative that Mama proposes. We do nothing. In my opinion this means that eventually we will have to cut our losses in Syria, write them off. The best we could hope for, I imagine, would be a counter-revolution there which would restore the status quo. I don't see it happening myself, but ..." I shrugged.

"But you could be wrong!" Giulio the dentist was back in action, with bulging eyes and one forefinger tapping the side of his forehead - presumably to inform me that the question came from his brain and not his stomach.

"Yes, I could be wrong, Giulio. What I meant was that the sort of counterrevolution in which the radical right overthrows the radical left doesn't usually restore a former status quo."

"But surely action and reaction are always equal and opposite." This was René the physicist. He had a maddening habit of quoting scientific laws in non-scientific contexts. Entanglement in one of his false analogies was a thing to be avoided at all costs.

"In the laboratory, yes."

"And in life, Michael, and in life."

"I am sure you're right, René. However, the political future of Syria is not something that we can divine in this board room. I think that there has been enough discussion and that we should put the motion to a vote. You first, Giulio."

At that point, I think, I had pretty well made up my mind to go against the agreement myself. The instant enthusiasm expressed by Giulio and René had engendered misgivings which my mother's shrewd disparagement had deepened considerably. By abstaining from voting on the ground that, as the author of the agreement I was *parti pris,* I could have backed away from the issue without too much loss of face. If Giulio had chosen to repeat his idiotic dithyramb in praise of my sagacity, that, I think, is what I would have done.

Unfortunately, he decided to change his mind. "My considered opinion is," he said weightily, "that time is on our side. No agreement, however ably negotiated, can in the end serve our interests if the regime with which the agreement is made is essentially unstable. If time is on our side, and we may hope it is, then I say let time work for us."

"You are against the motion, Giulio?"

"With deep regret, Michael, yes."

René had a few words to say about game theory mathematics and the possibility of applying them to the solution of meta-political problems. Then he, too, voted against.

I looked at my mother. She would now decide the matter, whatever I wanted; my sisters would follow her lead.

I said: "I think, Mama, that even the silliest generalization, even one made in a little red book by the British War Office, may once in a while have its moment of truth. I believe that this is just such a moment and that to do now what you and Giulio and René want to do - that is, nothing - would be to do something definitely wrong."

For a moment her lips twitched and she almost smiled, but not quite. Instead, she threw up her hands. "Very well," she said. "Have your agreement. But I warn you. You are making a lot of trouble for yourself - trouble of all kinds."

In that, of course, she was absolutely right.

The trouble was of all kinds, and I had no one to blame for it but myself.

For almost two years the only party to the Syrian agreement who profited from it in any substantial way was Dr. Hawa. Our company lost, and not only in terms of its unblocked assets. As my mother had predicted, the Syrian cooperatives took up far too much of my time. Inevitably, some managerial responsibility in the profitable areas of the company's operations had to be delegated to senior employees. They, naturally, took advantage of the situation and had to be given salary increases.

In the early days, I must admit, the work itself was fairly

rewarding. Pulling rabbits out of a hat can be fun when the magic works. The ceramics *pilot*, for instance, which I started up in a disused soap factory, went well from the beginning. That was partly luck. I found a man to put in as foreman, and later manager, who had worked for three years in a French pottery and knew something about coloured glazes. He also knew where to recruit the semiskilled labour we needed and how to handle it. Within four months we had a range of samples, realistic cost accountings, and a complete plan for volume production which I could submit to Dr. Hawa under the terms of the agreement. Within weeks, and after am incredibly brief period of haggling, the government funding had been authorized and the project went ahead. By the end of the year we had received our first export orders.

With the furniture and metalworking projects it was a different story. In the case of the furniture some of the difficulties arose from the fact that, under pilot plant conditions, a lot of work which should have been done by machines had to be done by hand. That made much of our costing little better than guesswork. However, the biggest headache with that pilot was its dependence on the metalworking shop. The trouble there was shortage of skilled labour.

It was understandable. Why should a metalworker who had been his own master for years, and earned enough to support himself in the style that his father and grandfather before him had found acceptable, go to work in a government factory? Why should this craftsman be compelled to use unfamiliar tools; tools that didn't even belong to him, to produce unfamiliar objects of, for him, questionable virtue? You could argue, and I did until I was purple in the face, that in the government factory he would work only a fifty hour week instead of the sixty-hour one he had been working on his own, and make more money in the bargain. You could talk about job security. You could promise him overtime and bonus rates for bringing in apprentices. You could plead, you could cajole. The answer in most cases was still a slow, ruminative, maddening shake of the head.

In the end I had to take the problem to Dr. Hawa. He solved it by putting through a regulation controlling the sale of nonferrous metals such as copper and brass. Each buyer was given a quota based on his previous year's purchases. However, if he had kept no written records, no receipts, for instance, to prove his case, he was in difficulty. He was entitled to appeal, of course; but, even if he was literate, he would find that part of the regulation hard to understand. He would need a lawyer. As the hazards, uncertainties, and frustrations of self-employment thus became more evident, many of those who had previously shaken their heads eventually decided to reconsider.

That Dr. Hawa should have been in a position to legalize this Byzantine method of recruiting labour by coercion is not as remarkable as it may appear. I have said that he found our agreement profitable from the first Perhaps "advantageous" would have been a better word. From the day we signed the final papers scarcely a week went by without some manifestation of what he called "our public relations and information program." In practice this meant personal publicity for Dr. Hawa. I don't know how he learned to perform his image-building tricks. Clearly, most of them had been collected during those postgraduate years in the United States, but he performed them all with impressive ease. Teresa believes that he has a natural talent for self-advertisement of which he is only dimly aware, and that he works almost entirely by instinct. She may be right.

It was quite fascinating to watch him in action. On the day we took possession of the disused soap factory, a decrepit and rat-infested structure then, Dr. Hawa suddenly appeared flourishing a large rolled-up blueprint - of what I never discovered - and, attended by photographers and journalists, proceeded to tour the premises. The photographs, which later appeared in the newspapers, of Dr. Hawa pointing dramatically at the blueprint, and the accompanying stories extolling the dynamic yet modest personality of the Director of Industrial Development were most effective. He could make an occasion out of the most trivial happening. The arrival of a new piece of machinery, the rigging of a power line, the pouring of concrete for a workshop floor - if there was anything at all going on that could be photographed, Dr. Hawa was there; and, when the photographs appeared, not only was he always in the foreground, but also quite obviously in direct charge of the operations. He had a way of pointing at something whenever he asked a question, and of keeping his head well back as he did so, that made it look all the time as if he were issuing orders. And, of course, before long ours were not the only such fish he had to fry. All the extravagant publicity given to our pilot projects had led several of the former temporizers to conclude, mistakenly, that I had been coining money while they had slept, and to leap hastily onto the cooperative bandwagon. Some of these ventures, notably a glass works, a galvanized-wire mill, and a bottling plant producing an odd-tasting local imitation of Pepsi-Cola, were successful, and, of course, Dr. Hawa got the credit.

In 1988, when all industry in Syria was nationalized, occasions for self-advertisement became even easier for him to contrive. His official position as development expert enabled him to poke his nose into practically anything, and be photographed doing so. The only opposition to his methods came from the Russians, who had their own ideas about the way the publicity for Soviet aid projects should be handled. Deference, not direction, was what they expected from Dr. Hawa; they flourished their own blueprints. He conceded these defeats gracefully; he was as adaptable as he was ingenious. On the radio, and, later, on television he was astonishingly effective; very simple and very direct, an apolitical public servant, dedicated to the new, but respectful of the old, whose only thought was for the betterment of the people.

Nobody, then, was surprised when, with the announcement that the Department of Industrial Development was to be upgraded and to become a Ministry, came the news that the newly created ministerial portfolio had been offered to and accepted by Dr. Hawa. That he succeeded in retaining it for so long, even through the turmoils and upheavals of the late sixties, was due to a combination of circumstances.

As an appendage of the more potent ministries of Finance and Commerce and with little political or financial muscle of its own, Dr. Hawa's Ministry could never provide the kind of operational base camp sought after by senior dissidents and would be coup-makers. It controlled no deployable forces, armed or unarmed, and was outside the inner power sector of government. Its function had been defined by Hawa himself as essentially catalytic - a phrase of which he became increasingly fond as time went by - and the image which he projected of himself was that of the super-efficient specialist quietly doing his own job as only he knew how, and with eyes for nobody else's.

Never once did he attempt to display himself as a potential leader. He must have been tempted at times. Men with his vanity, ambition, and peculiar abilities are rarely able to set limits to their aspirations, but he was one of the exceptions. A threat to no one with the power to destroy him, he had accordingly survived.

Although I would have preferred someone lazier and less alert to deal with, I could have had worse taskmasters than Dr. Hawa. It was clear, from the moment of his promotion, that ministerial office agreed with him. He seemed to smoke fewer cigarettes and was often quite relaxed and amiable. On occasion, over a game of backgammon and with a glass or two of my best brandy inside him, he would even make jokes that were not also gibes. Of course, he could still be unpleasant. When, for the first time, it became evident that the Howell companies abroad were beginning to make worthwhile profits out of the exclusive agencies granted to us under the agreement, I had to listen to bitter sarcasms and veiled threats. Naturally, I had figures to prove that on balance we were still well in the red, but he was invariably difficult about figures. His were always unassailably accurate and complete; everyone else's were either irrelevant or cooked.

He had other quirks that made him hard to handle. For instance, you had to be careful with ideas for new projects. It was most dangerous to discuss a possible development with him unless you had already made up your mind that it was something you really wanted. If he liked a new idea he would seize upon it, and after that there was no escape. Almost before you were back in your office there would be a Ministry press release going out announcing the new wonder. From then on, whether you liked it or not, you were committed.

That, in fact, was how this whole miserable business over the dry batteries started. Dr. Hawa forced me into it.

It was the same with the electronics project. Under an arrangement made by Dr. Hawa's Ministry with a trade mission from the GDR, we had to set up a plant to assemble electronic components manufactured in East Germany. We produced telecommunications equipment of various kinds, including highly specialized stuff for the army, as well as small radio and television sets. They gave me an Iraqi manager who had received special training in East Germany to run the plant, but the whole setup was wrong from our point of view. Being labour intensive it was economically unsound anyway, and the military contracts, on which I had thought we might possibly have made money, were dished out to us on a cost-plus basis which was ruinous. With the electronics it was all we could do to break even.

But the dry-battery project was much worse. That cost me more than money; that became a nightmare.

Don't misunderstand, please. I am *not* blaming Dr. Hawa for everything that happened; I should have been quicker on my feet. What I *am* saying is that, far from having cunningly planned the battery operation, as some of those scavengers who call themselves reporters have hinted, I tried hard to stop it going forward, not only before it began but afterwards, too.

The thing started purely by accident. It was the year after the Six-Day War with Israel.

All government ministries everywhere have to send out lots of pieces of paper; it is in the nature of the beasts. One of the pieces regularly sent out by the Ministry of Industrial Development was a list of bulk commodities held in government warehouses and available for purchase. Normally, the list was of no immediate business interest to me, but I used to glance at it sometimes, for old times' sake, to see what they were asking for tobacco. That was how I came to see this rather unusual item. In one of the Latakia warehouses there were sixty metric tons of manganese dioxide.

It gave me an idea. Although the ceramics factory was doing extremely well, with production and sales both going up nicely, our stocks, particularly of tile, were building up a trifle faster than we could move them. I had been looking for other lines to manufacture so as to diversify a bit. This stuff in the warehouse suggested a possibility. I inquired about it.

Originally, I learned, it had been part of the mixed cargo of a Panamanian freighter out of Iskenderun in Turkey. South of Baniyas she had engine trouble and a southwest gale had blown her aground on a bank near the Arab-el-Meulk light-buoy. Tugs from Latakia had pulled her off eventually, but only after some of the cargo, including the manganese dioxide, had been transshipped to lighten her. Later there had been a dispute over the tug-masters' salvage claims, and she had sailed, leaving the transshipped cargo impounded. The manganese dioxide wasn't all that valuable anyway, except possibly to me. I requested samples.

Hawa's spies were everywhere. Within hours of my making that request, his Chef de Bureau was on to me, wanting to know what my interest in the material was. I said that it was hard to explain on the telephone and that, in any case, there was no point in trying to explain until I had received the samples and run tests. He said that he would await the results of the tests. A week later I was summoned to see the Minister. That didn't surprise me. I had long ago learned that, once his curiosity was aroused, Dr. Hawa was quite incapable of delegating its satisfaction to an underling. However, the summons came while I was away in Alexandria straightening out some of our Egyptian problems. Teresa told the Chef de Bureau where I was, of course, and they made an appointment for me to see Hawa on the day of my return; but I was quite unprepared for the VIP treatment at the airport that Hawa had laid on.

That was the first time I had had it, and it scared me stiff. Nobody could tell me what was going on, so naturally I assumed that I was under arrest. It wasn't until I was in the air-conditioned car and on the way to the Ministry that I began to get angry. I thought that this was Hawa's way of getting back at me for not being on instant call when he wanted to see me, and also of reminding me, in case I had forgotten, that he could control my comings and goings if he wished.

He was very affable when I was shown into his office.

"Ah, Michael, there you are. All quite safe and sound." He waved me to a chair.

"Thank you, Minister." I sat down. "I am most grateful to you for the airport reception. It was unexpected but welcome."

"We try to protect our friends." He lit a cigarette. "Doubtless you heard in Alexandria of our latest troubles. No? Ah well, it only happened last night. A civil airliner, European, destroyed by bombs at the airport. Israeli saboteurs, of course."

"Of course."

This was the ritual way of accounting for the bombings and other terrorist acts then being carried out by local Palestinian guerrillas. These were splinter groups mostly, with Marxist and Maoist leanings, who, when they weren't plaguing the insufficiently cooperative Jordanian and Lebanese authorities across the frontier, busied themselves with provocations which could be blamed on the Israelis. Such activities also served notice on any of their Syrian "brothers" who might be hankering after peace that they had better think again.

"Were they caught?" I asked.

"Unfortunately, no. Time bombs were used. Our security forces don't yet seem to have learned the right lessons."

And they never would learn, of course. According to Mao, guerrillas should move like fish in a friendly sea of people. If, in Syria, the sea was not all friendly, hostile currents were few. Those of the security services who did not actively assist the guerrillas adopted an averted-eyes policy. The magic labels "Palestine" and "Palestinian" could transform the most brutish killer into a gallant young fighter for freedom, and, providing that he did not go too far too openly, he would be safe. Dr. Hawa knew this as well as I did. Besides, no guerrilla was going to blow up a Middle East Airlines plane, even as a provocation. I still thought that he was using the bomb scares to get at me.

The coffee came in. "However," Dr. Hawa went on, "it is easy to be critical when one has not the responsibility. We must be patient. Meanwhile, as I say, we take precautions to protect our friends - especially those friends who are helping us to build for the future." He gave me a whimsical smile. "Would you like to take over the management of a tire re-treading plant, Michael?"

"Thank you, Minister, no." I smiled, too. He *had* been getting at me.

This tire thing was a rather bad standing joke. The retreading cooperative had been the brainchild of an Armenian who had made his money out of crystallized fruit, and it had been a disaster. At least fifty percent of the retreads produced had proved defective, in some cases dangerously so. An accident involving a long-distance bus, in which three people had been killed, was known to have been caused by a blowout of one of these tires. Hawa had had difficulty in hushing the story up, and was still looking for a face-saving way out of the mess. Although he well knew by now that I had no intention of providing it, he continued to ask the question. It was a way of letting me know that, while my refusal to do him that particular favour would not necessarily be held against me, it had by no means been forgotten.

"Then let us talk about this manganese dioxide." He chuckled. "I must say that when I heard of your interest I was puzzled. I know that you order strange chemicals to make your coloured glazes, but this was obviously exceptional. Sixty *tons?*"

This is not for a glaze, Minister. The idea was to use it to make Leclanché cells."

"I don't think I understand."

The Leclanché is a primary cell, a rather primitive source of electrical energy. It has been largely superseded by the dry battery, though they both work on the same principle. The Leclanché is a wet battery and a bit cumbersome, but it has its uses."

"Such as what?"

"Many things that a dry battery can do - ring door bells or buzzers, work concierge locks, power internal telephone' circuits, and so on. They have the advantages of long life and low initial cost."

He was nodding thoughtfully, a faraway look in his eyes. "A primary source of electrical energy," he said slowly.

He made it sound like the Aswan High Dam. His ability instantly to scramble a sober statement of fact into a misleading PR fiction was extraordinary.

"The point is," I said, "that it is a very simple thing. The cathode consists of a porous ceramic pot, which we could easily make, packed with manganese dioxide and carbon around a carbon plate. The anode is a zinc rod. The two of them stand in a jar, usually glass, but we could make it of glazed earthenware. The electrolyte is a solution of ammonium chloride, a very cheap material, in ordinary tap water. The zinc we would have to buy abroad, but the rest of it we could manage ourselves - that is, if this manganese dioxide is all right."

"What could be wrong with it?"

"For one thing it could have been contaminated with seawater. That is why I asked for samples to test."

He opened a drawer in his desk and took out a small jar. "In your absence," he said, "I also asked for samples and had tests made. I am told that it is the standard pulverized ore, probably from the Caucasus, with only the usual minor impurities. With sixty tons how many of these batteries could you make?"

"More than I could sell probably, tens of thousands."

"But here we could create the demand?"

"By cutting down on the imports of certain sizes of dry battery, yes."

"You said that the principle of this battery is the same as that of the dry battery. Why could we not make dry batteries ourselves?"

"I would have to have notice of that question, Minister. Dry batteries are mass-produced by the billions nowadays in Japan, America, and Europe. I can investigate, of course. But the battery I am talking about can be made in the ceramics factory. We would need an extra shed or two and a few men under a charge hand to do the work, but that is all No big capital expenditure, and something useful produced with our own resources."

"Dry batteries are labelled. Could we label these batteries?"

"Yes, we could." I did not add that labels stuck on glazed jars very quickly come unstuck, because I knew what was bothering him. Few of the products we made carried any sort of advertisement. For a man with his taste for publicity it must have been very frustrating.

"The labels should be highly coloured," he said. "And we should have a brand name. I will think about it."

The brand name he eventually decided upon was "Green Circle."

During the next two years we made over twenty thousand Leclanché cells bearing the Green Circle label, and managed to dispose of most of them at a decent profit. In Yemen and Somalia we did particularly well with them. As a sideline for the ceramics factory they had been useful.

If I had been able to leave it at that all would have been well. Unfortunately, Dr. Hawa was by then no longer interested in sidelines, however useful. Now he wanted the more ambitious kind of project which could be used to dress up the monthly reports which his Ministry issued; reports designed to show that the pace of development was continually accelerating and to confound his critics, who were becoming vocal, with evidence of fresh miracles to come. The truth was that too much had been promised too publicly, and now he was having to pay the penalty. Dr. Hawa was beginning to slip.

He never even consulted me about the feasibility of the dry battery project. He had one of his minions do some hasty research on the manufacturing processes involved. The minion, who cannot have done much more than browse through an out-of-date textbook, reported back that the processes were simple, the necessary materials in good supply, and that, with good management and some unskilled female labour, the thing could be done.

That was enough for Hawa. He announced the new project the following morning and handed it over to me in the afternoon. He didn't ask me if I would accept it; those days were over. I was assigned the project, and if I didn't like it - well, a private company under contract to a government agency was always vulnerable unless protected by its friends. For example, the Ministry of Finance had often pressed for the cancellation of those exclusive selling agencies granted to the company so long ago. So far these pressures had been resisted and the company's interests protected, but such protection must be earned.

I could not even argue that the information on which he had based his decision was false. Manufacturing dry batteries *can* be a simple business, but only if you are prepared to use the manufacturing methods employed fifty years ago, and to accept along with them the kind of battery they produced and the cost of its production. I tried to explain this to him, but he would not listen.

"The difficulties," he said idiotically, "are for you to overcome.

Knowing you, Michael, I am sure they will be overcome."

It is easy to say now that I would have done better to have refused him there and then and taken the financial consequences. As my mother pointed out, our net profits from the Syrian export operation at that stage amounted to over seventy percent of the original blocked funds. That, in her opinion, was better than anyone had thought possible. None of the shareholders would have thought ill of me if I had chosen to cut our losses at that point and get out; they were only too grateful for what had been accomplished to date.

She had some less pleasant things to say, too, of course. She even went as far as to suggest that the real reason for my going ahead with the dry battery project was not my reluctance to abandon some profitable lines of business, but my unwillingness to give up what she called "that *cinq-á-sept* affair of yours" with Teresa.

That was utterly absurd, and only the acid-tongued mother of my children could have put such an idea into my own mother's head. The truth is, and Teresa herself can vouch for this because I discussed the whole problem with her that same night - not between *cinq* and *sept,* by the way, as those are office hours with me - the truth is that I did seriously consider pulling out at the time. I didn't do so, firstly because it was the obvious and easy thing to do, and secondly because I thought there might be a way around the situation. That way, the only one that I could see, was to go through the motions of setting up a dry battery pilot and give Hawa a practical demonstration of the total *im*practicability of what he had proposed. Then, when the time came for him to accept defeat, I would have already planned for him a face-saving alternative project. I still say I did the right thing. How was I to know about Issa and his friends?

When I said that we would go through the motions of setting up the pilot project, I didn't mean that we weren't going to try to do our best. After all, on the pilot projects it was always Howell money that was being spent. I expected failure, yes; but the kind of failure

I expected was the commercial kind you normally associate with attempts to sell a technologically obsolete product at an uncompetitive price in a highly competitive market. What I had not bargained for, and was not prepared to submit to, was the humiliation of being responsible for the manufacture of a product which was not only antiquated but also hopelessly inferior in quality by *any* standards, old or new. Even the tire-retreading bunglers at their worst had managed to get their product right fifty percent of the time. With the first lot of batteries we turned out, our percentage of success hovered around the twenty mark. While we didn't actually kill anybody with our product, as the retread people had, we certainly did a lot of damage.

The trouble with a dry battery is that, except on the outside, it isn't really dry. Inside it is moist, and this moisture, the electrolyte, is highly corrosive. For a variety of reasons, foremost among which were my carelessness and inexperience, our batteries tended to leak as soon as you started to use them and very soon went dead. The leaking was the worst defect. Just one leaking battery, even a little penlight cell, can ruin a transistor radio. With the local radio dealers the Green Circle label and the product it enclosed soon became anathema. It was the subject of much angry laughter and the cause of many shrill disputes.

Something had to be done quickly. The Howell reputation was at stake, and my own self-confidence had taken a beating. After an exceedingly unpleasant session with Hawa, I secured his agreement to my withdrawing all unsold stocks from the dealers. I also stopped production and did the quality-control research that I had neglected to do before we started. Most of this work concerned the zinc containers. These were formed on jigs and had soldered seams. Obviously, faulty soldering would cause leaks, but the chief problem was with chemical impurities. For example, zinc sheeting of a quality that could be used for covering a roof would not necessarily do for bakery production. Certain impurities, even in very small amounts, would, in contact with the electrolyte, start up a chemical reaction. The result was that the zinc became porous. The same was true of the solder used on the seams. In the future, all materials used would have to be checked out chemically before we accepted them from the suppliers.

I worked out a series of standard tests for each material. Then I had to find someone to carry out the tests. As usual, trained and even semi-trained manpower was in short supply. I knew I wasn't going to be able to hire a qualified chemist; in fact, I didn't need one. I had already done the necessary elementary chemistry, and the actual testing would be routine work; but I did need someone with sufficient laboratory experience to carry out the routine procedures faithfully and without botching them.

That was how I came to employ Issa.

He was a Jordanian, a refugee from the West Bank territory who had come north with his family after the war, first to the UNWRA camp at Der'a, then to live with relatives in Quatana.. He was in his mid-twenties, a dropout from the Muslim Educational College in Amman where he had received some schooling in inorganic chemistry. More important for me, he had worked part-time as a lab assistant during his second year at the college.

I found him through a department in the Ministry which had started, or was trying to start, a technical training program. Representing himself as a science graduate, Issa had applied to them for a job as an instructor. In the absence of any papers to support his claim to graduate qualifications - he told them that they had been lost when the family fled from the Israelis - the Ministry took the precaution of writing to Amman for confirmation. When the truth had been established they referred him to me.

On first acquaintance he seemed a rather intense young man who took himself very seriously and had a lot of personal dignity. Later, I found him quick to learn, intelligent, and hard-working. The fact that he had previously lied about his qualifications should, I suppose, have prejudiced me against him, or at least made me wary.

It did neither. He was, after all, a refugee; one had to make allowances. If, in his eagerness to better himself and make the most of his intelligence, he had gone too far, well, he could be excused. The lie had done no one any harm.

When we started production again I gave him a small wage increase and made him responsible for ordering the battery-project raw material supplies as well as checking them. It seemed a reasonable thing to do at that time.

Until that afternoon in May the idea that the punctilious, hard-working Issa might have other, less desirable qualities of mind and character had never once crossed my mind. And, as I have said, even that first warning signal - Teresa's news about the alcohol orders - didn't really register.

Naturally, the conclusion I immediately jumped to - that Issa had been carrying on a private bootlegging business at my expense - wasn't exactly welcome; but until I had questioned him on the subject there was nothing to be done. He might have a perfectly innocent explanation to offer. I couldn't imagine what that might be, but the matter could, and would have to, wait.

As I drove to the Ministry that afternoon I had pleasanter things to think about, for this was a moment I had been looking forward to for months. This was showdown time for Dr. Hawa. If I played my hand properly the dry battery project would soon be no more than a disagreeable memory.

Before leaving for Italy I had prepared the ground carefully by sending him a statement of the financial position of the dry battery project Along with this profoundly depressing document, however, I had sent a cheerful little covering letter saying that I hoped, on my return, to be able to submit proposals for saving the entire situation.

As the situation was patently catastrophic, this promise of good news to come would, I thought, soften him up a little. The drowning man offered a line does not much care, when it arrives, whether the hempen rope he had been expecting turns out to be made of nylon.

Although it would have been a gross exaggeration to describe Dr. Hawa's political difficulties at the time as those of a drowning man, he was certainly floundering a little and in need of additional buoyancy.

His first words to me after the coffee had been brought in suggested that I had overdone the softening-up process.

"Michael, you have failed me," he said mournfully.

This would not do. In his pity-me mood, which I had encountered once or twice before, he wouldn't have bought IBM at par. I wanted him braced in his embattled PM-warrior stance, beady-eyed and looking for openings. I took the necessary steps.

"Minister, we have made some rectifiable errors, that is all"

"But these figures you sent me!" He had them there on his desk, sprinkled with cigarette ash.

"The obituary notice of an unsuccessful experiment which may mow be forgotten."

"Forgotten!" That stung him all right. "Forgotten by whom, may I ask? The public? The press?"

"Only by you and me, Minister. For the public and the press there will be nothing to forget. The battery project will go forward."

"On the basis of these figures? You expect the Ministry of Finance to fund the project when all we have to show them is this miserable record?"

"Of course not. But if you will recall our original conversation on the subject of dry batteries, the feasibility of the project was always in question. What I have in mind now is the rectification of an original error."

"Which error? There have been so many."

"The error of making primary batteries. We should have made secondary batteries."

"What are you talking about? Batteries are batteries. Please come to the point, Michael."

"With respect, Minister, that is the point. Secondary batteries are rechargeable storage batteries, the kind you have in cars and buses."

"But...'"

"Please, Minister, allow me to explain. I propose that the battery project should go ahead, but that we phase out the dry battery operation and change over to the manufacture of storage batteries."

"But the two things are totally different!"

"They are indeed, but they are both *called* batteries. That is the essential point We should not be abandoning the announced battery project, only redirecting it along a more profitable path. As for the changeover, I have had exploratory talks in Milan with a firm of car accessory manufacturers. They are willing to send us experienced technicians to train our own people and help us to set up an efficient plant for making storage batteries here."

"But that means another pilot project."

"No, Minister, not this time. You cannot make these things on a pilot scale. That is one reason for our present failure. This would have to be a full-scale operation from the start. That means a joint-venture arrangement between the Italian company and your agency."

"But why should they be willing to do this? Why should they help us? What do they get out of it?"

I knew then that I had him.

They have no outlet for their products in the Middle East at present. The West Germans and the British have most of the market. They were looking for a way in and came to me." That was not quite true; I had approached them; but it sounded better the other way. "I advised them to manufacture here and take advantage of low labour costs and the favourable UAR tariffs."

"But it would be *their* product they would be making and selling."

They are willing to put it out here under our Green Circle trademark."

That clinched it; but, of course, he did not give way immediately. There were doubts to be assuaged about the plant's value to the economy. The standard complaint was made that all the raw materials would have to be imported and that, as usual, money and cheap labour were all that was being asked of poor Syria. I countered with a question.

"Minister, when will the new plastics factory which has been promised be going into production?"

This factory was to be a present from Russia via East Germany and I wasn't supposed to know about it. My indiscretion threw him for a moment.

"Why do you ask?"

The battery cases could be made there."

"Have you a plan on paper yet for this project? Figures, estimates?"

I opened my briefcase and handed over the bound presentation that I had worked up with the people in Milan. It was quite a tome, and I could see that the size and weight of it impressed him. He leafed through it for a moment or two before looking up at me.

"In the matter of phasing out the present operation," he said thoughtfully, "if that is finally decided upon, there would have to be continuity, Michael. If we were to go ahead with this revised Green Circle plan there could be no sudden changes, no loss of employment. The two would have to overlap."

"I understand, Minister." What he meant was that he didn't want the press or radio picking up the story until we had papered over the cracks.

"Then I will study these proposals and we will have a further meeting. Meanwhile, this will be treated as confidential. There must be no premature disclosure."

"No, of course not." It was all right to browbeat the Agence Howell into squandering its money on a half-baked experiment after sounding off about it to the press; but to release the news of a sizable joint-venture deal involving an Italian company and his agency before clearing it with the ministries of Finance and Commerce would be asking for trouble. I was fairly sure that he would get the clearance, however. All I could do now was hope that he would get it quickly. The sooner I could start "phasing out" the dry battery fiasco the better.

Still, I was pleased with the way things had gone. Back at the house I told Teresa all about the meeting and we had some champagne to celebrate.

It wasn't until after dinner when we were in bed that I thought again about Issa. We had taken a bottle of brandy with us, and as I poured some into her glass the fact that it was alcohol reminded me.

"I was trying to work it out earlier," I said. "Ten rottols of alcohol would be how many litres?"

She shrugged. "I don't know how much alcohol weighs. Over fifty litres I suppose. Can you drink that stuff?"

"Absolute alcohol? Heavens no, it would kill you. What you could do, though, if you had fifty litres of it, would be to dilute it with a hundred and twenty-five litres of water and add a little burnt sugar flavouring. You would then have over two hundred bottles of eighty-proof whiskey. Whiskey of a sort anyway."

I did not have to tell her what that would be worth on the black market; we bought our own drink supplies there.

She was thoughtful for a moment "You know, Michael," she said then, "alcohol isn't the only expensive stuff that Issa has been ordering. I told you about that because of the duty we had to pay on it"

"What else? Gold dust?"

"Mercury. There have been orders for mercury."

"Mercury?"

"Four orders, each for one oke. I did ask him about those because two were marked urgent and we had to pay extra delivery charges."

"What did he say?"

"That he was experimenting with mercury cells. He said that the Americans make a lot of them. They have am extra-long life." She gave me a sidelong look

"I gathered that you knew all about it."

"Did he say that I knew?"

"Not in so many words, but he conveyed that impression."

"Well, I *didn't* know." The idiocy of it hit me. "Mercury cells, for God's sake! It's almost more than we can do to make the ordinary kind. What sort of mercury did he order, mercuric oxide or the chloride?"

"Just mercury, I think, the kind you have in thermometers. He said that it was a very heavy metal and that one oke wasn't much."

I swallowed my brandy and put on my glasses. "Teresa, have you still got those invoices here?"

"They're in the office, yes."

I got out of bed. She followed me through to the office and found the invoices for me in the files.

It took me about twenty minutes to go through them all and mark the items which should not have been there. By the end of that twenty minutes I wasn't concerned any more about bootlegging. I was, though, both angry and alarmed.

I glanced across at Teresa. Even with no clothes on she managed, sitting at her desk in front of the ship models in their glass cases, to look businesslike.

"Have we a spare set of keys to the battery works stores?" I asked.

"Yes, Michael."

"Would you get it for me, please?"

"Now?"

"Yes."

"Is it something very bad?"

"Yes. I think it may be very bad indeed," I said, "but I'm not spending a sleepless night waiting to find out. I'm going to the battery works to do a little stock taking."

"I'll come with you."

"There's no need."

"I'll drive if you like." She knows that I dislike driving at night

"All right."

We got dressed in silence. It was after ten, so the servants were off duty and in their own quarters. I opened the gates in the courtyard and closed them again after Teresa had driven out. Then I got in beside her and we set off.

Teresa is in the habit of crossing herself in the Catholic manner before she starts to drive a car. The gesture is made briskly, almost casually - she is fastening a spiritual seat belt - and it seems to work very well. She has never had a traffic accident or even scratched a fender. On Syrian roads and with Syrian drivers all about you, that is a considerable achievement.

However, on that occasion - perhaps because I was opening and shutting the gates instead of the houseman - I think that she must have neglected to take her routine precaution. I don't know which saint she counts upon for this security arrangement, but I am quite sure that he, or she, was not alerted. We made the journey not only safely but also in record time.

A divine agency with any concern at all for our welfare that night would have guided us gently but firmly to a soft landing in the nearest ditch.

The battery works was on the Der'a road ten kilometres south of the city. During the French Mandate it had been a district gendarmerie. When I took the place over it had been empty for several years and stripped of everything removable, including the roof and the plumbing fixtures. All that remained had been the reinforced concrete structures - a latrine, the shell of the old HQ building, and the high wall which enclosed the compound.

In a country where pilfering is a way of life, walls which cannot easily be scaled are extremely useful. I chose the site partly because the government would lease it to me cheaply, but partly because of the walls. Inside the compound I had built three work sheds. When refurbished, the old HQ building housed the offices and the laboratory. Two rooms in it had been set aside for safe storage, under lock and key, of the more marketable of our raw materials, such as the zinc sheet.

At the entrance to the compound there was an iron-bar main gate with a chain-link postern on one side. Both were secured by padlock. Just inside the postern was a hut which, during working hours, was occupied by the timekeeper, and at night by the watchman. Beyond the hut was the loading platform of number-three work shed, where the finished batteries emerged.

There was some moon that night and I could see the shapes of all this from outside. What I could not see was any sign of the watchman, and there was no light in the hut. I assumed that he was on his rounds. As he was supposed to carry a heavy club and I had no wish to be mistaken for an intruder, I kept my flashlight switched on after I had unlocked the postern.

"What about the car?" Teresa asked.

"Leave it. We won't be long."

Further evidence of divine indifference! The sound of the car would have made our presence inside the compound known sooner and given those already inside time to avoid a decisive confrontation. It was my fault. The main gate was very heavy and hinged so as to stay closed. I would have had to drag it open and hold it there while Teresa drove in. That meant getting my hands dirty and probably scuffing my shoes as well. I couldn't be bothered.

We went in. I re-locked the postern and we walked toward the loading platform and the path leading to the office building.

The battery works was not the tidiest of places, and in that particular area empty containers and loops of discarded baling wire were hazards to be watched for. So I had the flashlight pointing down and my eyes on the ground in front of me. It was Teresa who first saw that there was something wrong.

"Michael"

I glanced back. She had stopped and was looking toward the office building. I looked that way, too.

There was light on in the laboratory.

For a moment I thought that it might be the watchman's lantern, though he wasn't supposed to enter the office building except in a case of an emergency such as fire. Then, as I moved along the path and my view became unobstructed, I saw that all the lights in the laboratory were on. And I could hear voices.

I had stopped, staring; as I started to go on, Teresa put a hand on my arm.

"Michael," she said softly, "I think it might be better to leave now and come back in the morning, don't you?"

"And lose a chance of catching him at it red-handed?"

I was too incensed to realize that, as I had not told her what I now suspected, she could not know what I was talking about. Her mind was still on bootleggers, eighty-proof whiskey, and black-marketeering. She thought that what we had stumbled on was either a drinking party or an illicit bottling session, neither of which it would be useful or wise to interrupt.

"Michael, there is no point..." she began, but I was already going on and she followed without completing her protest.

The place had been built on high concrete footings with an open space between the ground floor and the bare earth. Concrete steps led up to a roofed terrace which ran the length of the building. The offices were to the right of the entrance, the laboratory to the left.

The window openings were barred with no shutters or glass in them, only wire mesh screens of the old meat-safe type to keep out the larger insects. You could see through them fairly well and hear through them easily. Issa's voice was distinctly audible as we went quietly up the steps.

"For the process of nitrosis," he was saying, "the nitric acid must be pure and have a specific gravity of one-point-four-two. I have shown you how we use the hydrometer. Always use it conscientiously. There must be no slovenly work. Everything must be exactly right.

For the reactive process, which you see going on, the alcohol must be not less than ninety-five percent pure. Again we use the hydrometer. What is the specific gravity of ninety-five percent ethyl alcohol?"

A young man's voice answered him. By then I had moved along the terrace and could see into the room.

Issa was standing behind one of the lab tables wearing his denim lab coat and looking every inch the young professor. His "class," squatting or sitting cross-legged on the floor in front of him, consisted of five youths, Arabs, with dog-eared notebooks and ballpoint pens. Lounging in Issa's desk chair, looking very neat and clean in a khaki bush shirt and well-pressed trousers, was the watchman. He had an open book in his lap, but his eyes were on the class.

"Very good," said Issa. He was speaking mostly Jordanian Arabic but using English technical terms. "Now observe." He pointed to an earthenware jar on the table in front of him from which fumes were rising. "The reaction is almost complete and precipitation has begun."

From where I stood I could smell the fumes. It was not hard to guess what was about to be precipitated.

"What will be the next procedure?" asked Issa.

One of the young men said, "Filtration, sir?"

"Filiation, exactly." Issa was obviously a natural pedagogue who enjoyed the teaching role. As he droned on I found myself remembering his application to the Ministry people for a post as an instructor, and wishing that they had been less punctilious about checking up on his qualifications. Why did it have to be me who had to deal with this little menace?

I was wondering how to handle the immediate situation, whether to clear my throat before entering or just fling the door open and make them jump, when the two men moved in.

I smelled them before I heard them, and so did Teresa. We both turned at once and she clutched at my arm. Then we saw the carbines in their hands and froze.

The carbines were very clean; but, in their filthy work clothes and faded blue *kaffiyehs,* the men who held them looked like labourers from a road gang. They were middle-aged, leathery, and tough; they were also tense and, quite clearly, trigger-happy.

They stopped well clear of us, the carbines pointing at our stomachs. The older man motioned with his carbine to the flashlight in my hand.

"Drop it. Quick!" He had a loud, harsh voice and broken teeth.

I obeyed. The glass of the flashlight shattered as it hit the concrete.

"Back! Back!"

We backed against the wall.

By this time Issa, followed by his class, was coming out to see what was going on.

Issa's face when he saw me was a study in confusion, but before he could say anything the man with the broken teeth started to make his report.

"We saw them come stealthily. We have been watching them for minutes. They were listening, spying. The man had a light Look, there it is."

He made the flashlight sound highly incriminating.

I said: "Good evening, Issa."

He tried to smile. "Good evening, sir. Good evening, Miss Malandra."

"They were listening, spying," said Broken Teeth doggedly.

"That's right, we were," I said. "And now we'll go inside."

I had started to move toward the entrance when the man hit me hard in the kidneys with the butt of his carbine. It was agonizing for a moment and I fell to my knees.

When I got up, Teresa was protesting angrily and Issa was muttering under his breath to the two men. I leaned against the wall waiting for the pain to subside. Finally, Issa told the class to wait there on the terrace and the rest of us went into the laboratory. Issa led the way, Teresa and I followed, the armed men brought up the rear.

The watchman had not moved from Issa's desk chair. As we came in he gave me a vague nod, as if he had been expecting me but could not quite think why. It struck me that he was behaving very oddly; I wondered if he were drank. Then I decided to ignore the watchman; I would deal with him later.

"All right, Issa," I said briskly, "let's have your explanation. I take it you have one?"

But he had had time to recover and was ready now to try to bluff his way out "An explanation for what, sir?" He was all injured innocence. "If, as you say, you have been listening, you will know that I was instructing a class of students in the techniques of chemistry. Having had the advantages of higher education, I consider that I also have a duty to pass some of those advantages on, when I can do so, to those less fortunate. I would only do so in my own time, of course. If you think that I should have asked your permission before using the laboratory out of working hours as a classroom, I apologize. It did not occur to me that a man of your character could conceivably refuse."

He was really quite convincing. If I had not been through those invoices and if my back had not been hurting as it was, I might almost have believed him.

"And these two men behind me?" I asked. "Have you been instructing them also in the techniques of chemistry?"

He tried a deprecating smile. "They are uneducated men, sir, older men from the village where my students live. They come to see that the young men behave themselves."

"They need guns to do that? No, Issa, don't bother to answer. You have given your explanation. It is not acceptable."

There was a flash of anger. "Simply because I wish to teach-----"

I cut him off sharply. "No. Simply because you are lying. You aren't instructing anyone in the techniques of chemistry, as you so elegantly put it. What you are giving is a do-it-yourself kitchen course in the manufacture of explosives. What is more, you are giving it at my expense."

"I assure you, sir-----" He died hard.

"You can't assure me of anything, Issa. I know what I'm talking about." I pointed to the jar on the table. That precipitate you were so lovingly anticipating is fulminate of mercury. How many detonators would that have filled? A hundred? A hundred and fifty? You're not passing on any advantages, Issa, you're passing on recipes for amateur bomb-making."

"My work is not amateur," he protested hotly.

I had a sudden feeling that I wasn't handling the situation very well. Now that the truth was out he should have been on the defensive and trying to make excuses, not arguing. I concluded that it was the armed men who were giving him confidence.

"I'm not interested in the quality of your work," I snapped. "The point is that you're not doing any more of it here - any work of any kind. As of this moment you are dismissed. You can consider yourself lucky, and so can your bomb-making friends, if I don't inform the police as well."

For the first time the watchman spoke. "But why will you not inform the police, Mr. Howell? If this man has stolen from you and is also making explosives illegally, is it not your duty to inform them?"

He had a high, rather thin voice, but it was the voice of an educated man. I suddenly realized that I knew very little about the watchman, and that, except when I had given him his original instructions, I had never spoken with him. There had been no occasion to do so. I looked at him coldly.

I said *if* I don't inform the police. If I do decide to inform them, your name will certainly be in the complaint as an accomplice, so don't tempt me by telling me my duty."

He rose very slowly to his feet. He was a tall man of about my own age with a long nose, a moustache, and deeply lined cheeks. "Perhaps then," he said, "I should introduce myself."

His self-assurance irritated me. "Your name is Salah Yassin," I told him, "and I engaged you six months ago as a night watchman. I was told that you were an ex-army man with a wound disability and of good character. Obviously, I was misinformed. You, too, are now dismissed. I want the lot of you off these premises within five minutes. After that you will be trespassing on government property and I shall certainly call the police. Now, leave your keys on the table there and get out."

The watchman looked pained. "It is ill-mannered, Mr. Howell, to refuse to hear a man when he offers politely to introduce himself. Ill-mannered and foolish." His eyes hardened as he stared into mine. "My name is Salah, yes. But it is Ghaled, not Yassin. Salah Ghaled. I am sure you have heard of it"

Teresa drew in her breath sharply.

With me shock and disbelief fought a brief battle. Shock won. I daresay I gaped at him stupidly. Anyway our consternation was obvious enough to please him.

He gave us a satisfied nod.

Chapter 3

Lewis Prescott

May 14

Michael Howell has left us in no doubt about his attitude toward reporters. I cannot altogether blame him. Some of my European colleagues have given him a rough time. However, as he has seen fit to exempt Frank Edwards and me from his blanket indictment, I hope he won't mind too much if I now suggest that much of the hostile press and TV criticism of his part in the Ghaled affair he brought on himself.

In his anxiety to protect his company's reputation - to say nothing of the reputations of his father, his mother, his grandfather, his sisters, Miss Malandra, and his brothers-in-law - he damaged his owe. Under questioning he did himself less than justice. He said either too little or, more often, far too much; and invariably he sounded evasive. When a reporter asked a direct question - "Mr. Howell, did you know what these arms were going to be used for?" - and received in reply, say, a lecture on the difficulties of dry-battery manufacture, the reasons why the Agence Howell had hired a Palestinian-refugee chemist, and the problems of the Agence Howell's blocked Syrian assets, he was apt to conclude that Mr. Howell was dissembling. Mr. Howell's too frequent protestations that what he was trying to do was to give the whole picture, background as well as foreground, didn't help either. Reporters are inclined to believe that, given the essential facts of a story, plain and unadorned, they are quite capable of drawing the picture for themselves. "Garrulous smokescreen" may be a mixed metaphor, but I can understand the feelings of the man who mixed it.

That said, however, I am prepared to go on record as believing most of Michael Howell's account of his part in the Ghaled affair. The situation in which he found himself was an appalling one. It is easy to say, as have his critics, that in reacting to it he should have thought less of his own safety and business interests and more of his higher responsibilities, but to do so is to miss the point With even less knowledge of Ghaled's plans and intentions than I had at that time, he did what he believed he had to do. To accuse him of irresponsibility is unfair; he did not then know what his responsibilities were. When he eventually did know he assumed them. At no time did he behave stupidly, and in the end he showed courage.

Those who condemn Mr. Howell and question his good faith were never in his shoes and don't understand what he was up against. They have never met Salah Ghaled.

I did meet him, and it wasn't an enjoyable experience.

I don't usually take strong likes or dislikes to the persons I interview. I am not there to defend or prosecute, but to gather information and, hopefully, insights, which I can pass on to others. But Ghaled I actively disliked.

I am not going to quote the whole of my interview with him - a lot that he said was standard guerrilla radio hate stuff - but this edited version contains the essentials. I am also giving, from notes made at the time, accounts of my subsequent conversations with Miss Hammad and Frank Edwards. They have a bearing both on Ghaled's thought processes and on my estimate at that time of his intentions.

The interview began easily enough with some questions about Ghaled's early life and career as a guerrilla leader. They were not important, and I already knew the answers, but I don't like microphones and tape recorders when interviewing; they tend to have an inhibiting effect. When I am obliged to use them, I find that a series of simple, easily answered questions at the beginning helps the subject to forget the microphone and tape. After this preparatory work I went on: "Mr. Ghaled, you seem to have devoted all your adult life to fighting on the Palestinian side in the Arab-Israeli conflict"

The Arab-Zionist conflict, yes."

"Most of the fighting, on your part, having been with guerrilla forces."

"Not all, but most, yes."

"Even when the armies of the Arab states, Egypt, Jordan, and Syria, have not been engaged, you have continued to fight?"

"Yes."

"Even when there has been peace?"

"There has never been a peace between the Arab states and the Zionists."

There have been peaceful periods, surely, prolonged cease-fires when things were peaceable enough for, say, Jordanian farmers to cross the border and sell their produce in Israel?"

He smiled faintly at my innocence. "Certainly there have been such periods. You speak of Jordanian farmers selling produce in so-called Israel. Let me tell you that there was a time when I used to cross the border that way myself. But one in five of the grapefruit that my donkeys carried to market had grenades in them. Peace at any price, Mr. Prescott, was never acceptable to us Palestinians. With or without our allies in the Arab states, we the *fedayeen* have always fought on."

"But what do you think you have accomplished by doing so, Mr. Ghaled? To put the question another way, what do you consider has been the main achievement of the guerrilla, the *fedayeen* movement?"

"It has ensured feat fee Palestinian cause has been neither lost nor conveniently forgotten."

"You say fee Palestinian cause. I want there to be no misunderstanding. What, in your particular view, *is* the Palestinian cause?"

"I have no particular view, Mr. Prescott. My view, in that respect, is the same as Yasir Arafat's or Dr. George Habash's or Kemal Adwan's - and Kemal, an Al Fatah man, is on the Central Committee of the PLO. We may disagree about means, but the end, our ultimate *aim,* is common ground."

He went on to mention the names of other former colleagues in Al Fatah and the Popular Democratic Front for the Liberation of Palestine with whom he shared this common ground. Had I not seen the bureau files so recently I would never have guessed that these were the men he had been denouncing as "running dogs." "We ask only for justice," he concluded proudly.

"Could you be more specific, Mr. Ghaled? What justice?"

"First, the destruction of the Zionist state. Note, please, that I do not ask for destruction of the Jews, only the destruction or dismemberment of the artificially created Zionist state. Second, the return of all Palestinian refugees to their lost lands and possessions. Third, the establishment of a Palestinian Arab state. Nothing less."

"All or nothing, Mr. Ghaled?"

"Less than all would amount to nothing."

"But hasn't the history of the past twenty-three years shown this uncompromising, all-or-nothing demand to be self-defeating?"

There was some trouble over translating the phrase "self-defeating." I was asked to put the question differently.

"As far as the Palestinian cause is concerned," I said, "hasn't the all-or-nothing policy failed? The all that it has achieved has been Israeli unity. The Israeli state that might once have been contained has instead been enlarged. The Palestinian cause may not be forgotten, Mr. Ghaled, but, as you present and define it, do you not think that it may reasonably be considered lost?"

"Considered lost by whom, Mr. Prescott? The United States

government?" Jocular.

"I don't speak for the United States government, Mr. Ghaled. I am merely trying to get your thoughts on the realities of the situation. Do you really believe that the destruction or dismemberment of the State of Israel, even if it were desirable, is any longer possible without a third and final world war?"

"Why should it not be possible, Mr. Prescott?" I could tell by his expression as he went on that there were more jokes on the way. "The West, and particularly the United States, is always expressing its wish to be helpful in resolving what it calls the Middle East conflict. Excellent. We accept. Let the United States send all the ships of its mighty Sixth Fleet to the ports of Haifa, Acre, Tel Aviv-Yafo and Ashdod. Then let them embark their Zionist dependents, all three million of them, and sail away forever. Where to, you ask? I hear that there are plenty of wide-open spaces in Texas and New Mexico that could accommodate these people. Of course, it is possible that the present owners of those spaces may object to three million Zionists taking possession of their lands. Such unreasonable persons will naturally have to be driven out and accommodated elsewhere. But this difficulty can be overcome. I am sure that UNWRA will be glad to build refugee camps for the dispossessed in the Arizona desert."

Miss Hammad's translation of this speech was accompanied by snickers.

"I am sure," I replied, "that Mr. Ghaled's suggestions would impress and entertain a junior college debating society. However, I am seeking information. I was asking if, as one of those Arabs who fought the Israelis in the '48 war and lost, and who has remained on the losing side ever since, Mr. Ghaled may not sometimes have begun to suspect that Israel is here to stay."

I knew that she didn't translate the whole of that because of his answer.

"In '48 there was no proper unity among the Arab States. If there had been, the Jews would have been driven into the sea."

I thought of asking him about '56 and '67 but decided to skip it. He had given me the lead I wanted.

"Then if we may return to the matter of the Palestinian guerrilla movement and its success in keeping the Palestinian cause from becoming lost or forgotten. Has unity between different sections of the movement been a factor in that success?"

He saw at once what I was getting at, of course, and sidestepped.

"The operations of conventional forces and those of commandos are differently conceived, of a different quantity, and hence qualitatively different. Unity of strategic command among allied states fighting a full-scale war is essential. In a commando struggle there must be unity of purpose, of course, but individual leaders may, and should, decide how best to contribute to the advancement of that purpose."

"There have been as many Arab casualties as a result of the guerrilla fighting in Jordan and Lebanon as there were Israeli casualties in the full-scale Six-Day War. More perhaps. You have attributed these Arab losses to betrayals of the Palestinian cause. The Great Betrayal and the Second Betrayal you call them. But isn't betrayal in this case just another word for disunity?"

"Why play with words, Mr. Prescott? A moment ago you were asking me to speak of reality. That I am ready to do."

"Very well. Has the Palestinian Action Force so far played a unifying or a disunifying role in the Struggle?"

"As I have already said, we Palestinian militants share a common purpose. Our methods of achieving it may differ. That is all."

"You agree about the ends but differ about the means. I see. Then may we discuss the merits of some of these means?"

"We may discuss anything."

"There have been bombs planted in European civilian airliners which have killed many persons who have never been near Israel. There have been attacks on airliners and hijacking which have also led to civilian loss of life."

"The work of the Popular Front for the Liberation of Palestine."

"So I understand. But do you approve of these means?"

"They would not be my means, but I do not disapprove."

"You approve of these murders of airline passengers, of innocent bystanders?"

"While we in Palestine fight for justice, no bystander is innocent."

I could tell by the gusto with which Miss Hammad translated this that she thoroughly approved and thought the statement important.

"How would you describe your favourite means, Mr. Ghaled?"

"My policy is to defeat the enemy closer to home."

"Are you referring now to the PAF purification campaign?"

"That has been a transitional campaign, a necessary housecleaning carried out in the interests of all in the movement."

"You have been called an extortionist, Mr. Ghaled. How do you respond to such charges?"

"With contempt and silence. Those persons who make such charges know nothing of my plans."

"Plans for defeating the enemy closer to home?"

"I have said so."

"But *which* enemy, Mr. Ghaled? The Jordanian government, the PLO Central Committee?"

The PAF has only one enemy, the Zionist state. I have said so repeatedly."

"And you intend to destroy it?"

"Defeat it."

"You were once quoted, Mr. Ghaled, as saying that when the British set out to implement the Balfour Declaration in Palestine, they were counting on a miracle. Do you not think that a similar charge might now be made against you?"

"I count on men and high explosives, not miracles."

"But it is against Israel that the PAF intends to move?"

"It is. I remind you that we are the Palestinian *Action* Force. Action, Mr. Prescott, is what we intend."

"When are we likely to see it, Mr. Ghaled?"

"Surely you do not expect me to tell you our plans so that they may be published."

"Naturally not. But while you said that the methods used by the Popular Front would not be yours, you would not deny that their exploits have a spectacular quality. From your point of view they would be valuable in that they reminded the world of the Palestinian cause. I was wondering if your plans for action are likely to provide similar reminders."

"I said that we intend to defeat the Zionists, Mr. Prescott. Did that not answer your question?"

At that moment Miss Hammad said that she had to change the tape. I almost told her not to trouble, that I had had enough. I didn't, because I was fairly sure that we had not been talking for anything like half an hour, and that she was changing the tape simply in order to interrupt a line of questioning and distract me from it.

When the tape had been changed I went on:

"Mr. Ghaled, when you said that the PAF intended to defeat the Zionist state, Israel, I assumed, I think with reason, that you were speaking figuratively. Was I wrong in that assumption?"

"Quite wrong."

"You would not object to my quoting you on that?"

"Not in the least."

"I do not ask for precise figures, naturally, but may I know the approximate strength of the PAF?"

"Not at this time."

"Not even an approximate figure, Mr. Ghaled? Over one thousand men? Under one thousand?" According to Frank Edwards it was probably less than three hundred.

"Not at this time."

"What about allies?"

"They will come with success."

"When the defeat of Israel is seen to be imminent?"

"When the manner in which it may be destroyed is seen and understood."

"I see."

"Give me a fulcrum and I will move the world. Have you not heard that expression, Mr. Prescott?" He was staring at me earnestly.

"I believe that a lever is necessary as well as a fulcrum."

"Be in no doubt. We have our lever." He paused. "Have you ever seen a man's house and his possessions in it dynamited before his eyes, Mr. Prescott?"

"I have seen lots of bad things happen to people's possessions in war areas, and worse things to the people themselves."

"I am not talking of war areas, Mr. Prescott, but areas of so-called peace. One night two months ago, in an Arab village near Haifa, a man was sleeping when there was a knock on his door. He went and opened the door. Outside stood his brother whom he had not seen for three years. The brother was one of my men who had crossed the border secretly. He asked for shelter for the night. That is all he asked, a place to sleep, no more. He was refused. The brother, whose house it was, stood in fear of the Zionist police. Trembling, he told his brother to go away, and the brother, understanding his fear, left without crossing the threshold. Sad, was it not?"

"Very."

"But now what happens? The brother in the house has a duty under the Zionist law to go to the police and report the incident, report that his brother who is with the *fedayeen* has been there, and is in the area, in order that he may be searched for and captured. This he cannot bring himself to do to one of his own blood, so he commits the offense of remaining silent, But a neighbour has seen and heard what has happened and the neighbour goes to the police. The brother who remained silent is arrested and condemned for harbouring and assisting one of those who fight for freedom. The sentence is that his house shall be destroyed, and he is led out with his wife and children to watch the sentence being carried out. The Zionist soldiers come then and place the dynamite charges. Then, before his eyes and those of his family, everything he possesses is destroyed. What do you think of that proceeding, Mr. Prescott?"

"In some countries I know, Mr. Ghaled, the man would have been shot"

"Better to shoot him than to destroy what makes his life."

"His wife and children might not agree. Besides, as you pointed out earlier, a state of war exists between Israel and her neighbours. I take it that your man had not crossed the border just to pay a social call."

"He was a courier, that is all."

"When was this sentence carried out?"

"Three weeks ago."

"What was the name of the village?"

"Majd el-Krum. But I mention this incident, Mr. Prescott, not because it is rare or special, but to remind you how Arabs live under the Zionist police dictatorship." He fumbled inside his sheepskin coat. "I will show you something." He dragged out a fat tooled-leather wallet and pulled a sheaf of photographs from it.

From the size and the way the edges of the prints were trimmed I could see that they had been made with an old-style black-and-white Polaroid. There were ten or twelve of them in plastic covers. He sorted them through, them thrust the lot into my hands.

"Take them, Mr. Prescott Look at them."

For a moment his eagerness reminded me, incongruously, of the lonely man on the long plane flight who wants to share his homesickness with you. "Look, *there's a shot of us all together up at the lake last summer.*"

Only these were not family snaps. The top one was a picture of a young woman. Her throat had been cut and she was dead.

She was lying on a patch of bloodstained earth at the base of a concrete wall. The cut in the throat was deep and gaping; you could see the severed ends of the veins and arteries. Her clothing was up over her waist and there were stab wounds in her thighs and belly.

Ghaled said something else and again Miss Hammad interpreted.

"Look well, Mr. Prescott, look well."

I slid the top print aside and looked at the next. It was of a dead man. He was naked except for a torn shirt, and his genitals had been cut off. The next was of a child of ten or so. I went through the rest of them.

The attitudes of violent death do not vary much. When the cause has been sudden, the rag-doll effect is usual, though muscular spasm can sometimes freeze the limbs in strange ways; when death comes less suddenly the knees and arms are often drawn up together in the fetal position; a human being incinerated by napalm becomes a gray-black clinker effigy of a dwarf boxer with fists up ready to do battle. There were no burn cases among these pictures, however; all the subjects had been cut, stabbed, or hacked to death; you could believe that they had been human beings. One or two of the bodies, those of children, had obviously been rearranged, by or for the photographer, and posed so as to dramatize the death agonies.

In war it is possible, as well as necessary and advisable, to get used to horrors. What I have never been able quite to get used to is the man who chooses to collect and keep pictures of them. Ghaled's private gallery would have an ostensible propaganda purpose, of course, but the prints had been well thumbed before they had been protected by plastic. The last collection I had seen like it had been carried by a Special Forces lieutenant in Vietnam. He had claimed a propaganda purpose. He had said piously that he kept it to remind him of what he was fighting against. I didn't believe him. He kept it for kicks. The British policeman in Malaya who treasured a jungle photograph of himself, shotgun in hand with one raised foot resting sportively on the disembowelled body of a Liberation Army Chinese, had been less inhibited. He was grinning proudly in the picture and he had grinned proudly when he had shown it to me.

I handed his photographs back to Ghaled.

"Well, Mr. Prescott?"

"Well what, Mr. Ghaled? I've seen pictures like that before. What are those dead bodies supposed to prove?"

"Those were Arab villagers murdered and mutilated by Zionist forces."

"You say so, Mr. Ghaled. I say that they could equally well be Arab villagers killed by other Arabs, or Israeli villagers killed by the *fedayeen*. Where were the pictures taken? When were they taken? On one occasion or several? Who was the photographer or was there more than one? Of what value are these photographs as evidence?"

"These photographs were taken on my orders and under my supervision after a raid, a typical raid, by Druse commando traitors of the Zionist army, on a refugee village in Jordan."

"In this typical raid were no bullets used?"

"What do you mean?"

"None of the wounds shown in those photographs was made by a bullet. For a commando raid that seems odd."

"They do not waste bullets on helpless women and children and crippled men."

"I must accept what you say, of course." In fact, all I would have accepted from him after that was his claim to have supervised the taking of the pictures; but there was no point in pursuing the argument. I wanted no more of him, and it seemed a good moment to bring the interview to an end.

"One or two final questions, Mr. Ghaled. Does the fact that so many of your Palestinian colleagues, your fellow leaders in the guerrilla movement, profoundly disagree with your views and policies ever cause you to question them yourself?"

"Naturally. Self-examination and self-criticism are always necessary. As for disagreement, I would remind you that many of Lenin's closest colleagues profoundly disagreed with him. But who in the end was proved right?"

"You see yourself as the Lenin of the Palestinian revolutionary guerrilla movement?"

"I see myself as the Ghaled of the Palestinian Action Force."

"And time in the end will no doubt prove you right.

I see. Thank you, Mr. Ghaled. You have been most patient and helpful."

When Miss Hammad had translated that she looked at me questioningly.

"That's all," I said.

"Interview between Salah Ghaled and Lewis Prescott concluded," she said and switched off the recorders. While she packed them up again Ghaled took the bottle of arrack and refilled the glasses.

He seemed pleased with the way the interview had gone and lit up a fresh cigar with the air of a man who has just concluded a successful deal. If he had spoken enough English he would probably have fished for some expression of satisfaction on my part.

He took the two tape cassettes which Miss Hammad handed him and one of the recorders. While she showed him how to operate it, I sipped the arrack and wondered how I was going to get back to Beirut The prospect of being driven down that mountain road in the darkness by Miss Hammad was not attractive.

I need not have worried. After the ceremonial leave-taking and the scramble back down to the Volkswagen, she explained the position. There was no question of our driving back to Beirut right away. During the hours of darkness nobody was allowed through the military roadblocks. We would have to wait at the chalet until it was light.

There I had a Scotch to take away the taste of the arrack, and Miss Hammad began to question me about my "impressions" of Ghaled.

I had expected that and was ready for her.

"Frankly," I said, "I was disappointed."

"Disappointed!"

"You're a Journalist, Melanie. You should know that there's no story in what he gave me."

"No story!" She was amazed.

"Melanie, forget your own interest in the man and your sympathy with the cause. Look at it professionally. Ghaled moved out of the mainstream of the Palestinian movement when he formed the PAF and denounced the PLO and Al Fatah. The Popular Front people have brushed him off. He's little more than a gangster now and he has sense enough left to realize it. So he's trying to talk his way back in with this crackpot stuff about destroying Israel single-handedly."

"That is not what he said." She was indignant now. "He said 'defeat,' not 'destroy,' and he did not say 'single-handed.' You are seriously underestimating him."

I shook my head. "A punchy has-been still kidding himself that he's in line for a championship bout. That's all I see."

"That is a ridiculous comparison!"

"I don't think so. Destroy, defeat the Zionist state? Don't tell me you can take that seriously."

"Indeed I can, and I do."

"All that nonsense about fulcrums and levers?"

"It is not nonsense!"

"Sorry, Melanie, I think it is."

"That is because you do not know what is planned."

"And you do?"

"I know a little, yes."

That was the first thing I had wanted to find out. I went on needling her.

"Plans for defeating Israel are easy to make. The Arabs have made quite a few. Carrying them out, though, doesn't seem to be so easy. The combined forces of Egypt, Syria, and Jordan couldn't do it. I can't see your Mr. Ghaled improving on their efforts."

"He will"

"What with? Bombs in grapefruit?"

"You were not so contemptuous of bombs when they were planted in airliners by the Popular Front."

"No. But what did that little campaign achieve against Israel? Did it stop the tourists going to Israel by air with their travellers' checks? It did not. More tourists than ever went. When your Mr. Ghaled's friends shot up the Israeli buses taking tourists into the occupied territories, did they stop the buses running? At no time."

"It will be a different story when Salah has finished."

That was the second piece of information she gave me.

I shrugged "So what? A few unfortunate tourists are killed. Okay, the tourist trade is important to the Israeli economy, but it's not *that* important. A slight letup in the dollar flow isn't going to destroy Israel."

"Who can tell what it might lead to?" She was becoming angry now. I didn't think I would get any more out of her, but after a moment she went on. "You said 'destroy' again. The word Salah used was "defeat' You see now why he insisted on tape recordings."

"Destroy, defeat? What's the difference? He used both words."

"But in different contexts. Where Israel is concerned the distinction is important. If it cannot be destroyed from without it must be defeated from within,"

"Sorry, I don't get it."

"You said yourself that Israeli unity has been an Arab achievement."

"That was part of a loaded question I was asking. Israeli unity is a product of many things - religion, faith, history, the drama of the Ingathering, the toughness of the sabras, the dedication of the aliyah immigrants, common purpose, self-respect - all the ingredients of high national morale are there. The presence of Goliath and the continued success of David against him are only parts of the story."

"They are the parts that count most. Without the pressure on it from the outside the Israeli state would have fallen to pieces. Even now, with Goliath, as you call it, still at the gate, they are torn by hate and dissension."

"Dissension is part of democratic government."

"But not hatreds such as theirs. The Ashkenazim hate the Sephardim, and both are hated by the Oriental Jews, the underprivileged proletariat. The Aduk hate the Ostjuden and the Taymanim hate those of Mea Shearim and their like who are Jewish anti-Zionists. The sabras hate everyone, even themselves."

"You mean Ghaled is counting on Israel becoming politically unstable and falling apart? Because if so…"

Who can say," she challenged, "what will happen when, for the first time, David's boasts are proved empty, when it is Goliath who has the sling and the simple bag of stones, when the Israelis have to taste defeat?"

"I'd say they'd close ranks and make damn sure it didn't happen again."

"Perhaps, perhaps not Defeat does strange things to those without experience of it."

"Israel isn't going to be defeated by pinpricks."

"One pinprick will collapse a balloon, especially if the pressure inside is high."

"And if Ghaled had the right fulcrum he could move the earth, I know. Let's skip it, Melanie." I yawned. I didn't want her to realize how much of the cat she had let out of the bag, so I didn't leave it there. "One thing I forgot," I went on, stifling the yawn. "How do you spell the name of that village Ghaled mentioned, the one near Haifa? Majd el something, wasn't it?"

"Majd el-Kram." She spelled it out. "But I thought you said that there was no story."

"I don't think there is, not for me anyway, but the tapes will be transcribed. We may as well have it right"

I had another drink and slept for a couple of hours in a spare room. She got me back to Beirut in time for a late breakfast. When I had showered and changed I went to the bureau office.

Frank Edwards was there and expectant,

"How did it go, Lew?"

I told him about the setup of the meeting and gave him my two tape cassettes.

"Most of it's there," I said. "There's one thing I'd like to check if it's possible here. There was an incident in Israel about three weeks ago in a village called Majd el-Krum near Haifa. An Arab was sentenced for not informing the police about a visit from his brother who was a member of the PAF. Is that sort of thing reported in the Israeli press?"

"Sometimes. We get the Israeli papers by mail via Cyprus. Three weeks ago you say?"

"About then."

He found the item to the English language *Jerusalem Post*.

"Here we are. The case was heard in the Haifa District Court. The man Ali gave the brother a drink of water and them turned him away."

"The Israelis blew up his house for that?"

"What do you mean, blew up his house? He was sentenced to three months in jail and then the judge suspended the sentence. Ali left the court amid the cheers of friends from his village."

"What about the PAF man?"

"He was caught. In fact, it was he who told the police that he had been to see his brother Ali. Charmimg fellow. He'll be up for trial soon. The judge won't suspend *his* sentence."

"What'll he get?"

"Eight to ten years. He was caught armed, you see." He picked up the tapes. I'll have these transcribed for you right away."

"No hurry, Frank," I said. "I'm not filing any story yet on Ghaled."

"No story?"

"Yet. You wanted to know what he's up to. You'll read some of it to the transcript, but I can sum up. He's out to defeat the State of Israel. No less."

"They all are, to a manner of speaking."

"He means it literally. I quote: 'Give me a fulcrum and I will move the world." Well, he cla<u>im</u>s to have found a fulcrum. Incidentally, he told me that the Israelis blew up that man Ali's house. He probably thought that I couldn't or wouldn't trouble to check. Stupid of him, and a bit odd, because he didn't strike me as a stupid man, at least not stupid in that way. Very close-mouthed. Lots of cute double-talk about M's plans. I got more out of La Hammad afterwards."

"What sort of thing?"

I told him.

"What did you make of it?"

"I don't think she knows as much as she thinks she knows," I said. "All that stuff about internal pressures in Israel, pricked balloons, and disintegration through factional hatreds are her personal fantasies. I'm inclined to believe that Ghaled has a definite plan of action involving a terrorist attack on some tourist centre inside Israel. By "defeat' all I think *he* means is that the location and nature of the place or installation attacked would make prompt Israeli armed countermeasures difficult or impossible. My guess is that this fulcrum he babbles about is simply the vulnerability of innocent bystanders - visitors, tourists - about whom he is openly callous. 'While we in Palestine fight for justice, no bystander is innocent.' He enjoyed saying that. What he's after, I think, is political mileage. If - a very big if - he could show that the PAF was capable of striking with impunity inside Israel, Cairo would have to take him seriously again, wouldn't they?"

He nodded. "Something showy, well inside Israel, yes. That would certainly give him a leg up. If he could get away with it - and that, as you say, is a big if - without being squashed like a bedbug." He grinned. "It's just occurred to me why he told you that phony story about the Majd el-Krum case."

"Why?"

"Because he wanted to impress upon you the fact that there are PAF men operating in the Haifa area."

"But why lie about it?"

"If he'd told you the true story about the Israeli judge suspending sentence, would you have bothered to check the story? Wouldn't you have forgotten about it?"

"Probably. But why does he want to draw my attention to the Haifa area?"

"I'd say because that's where the operation he's planned will *not* take place. He wanted to put you off the scent."

"Sounds farfetched to me."

"Maybe, but that's the way these birds' minds work. Lew, I think you're wrong about this. I think you ought to file some sort of story now. In personal interview PAF leader Salah Ghaled threatens new guerrilla strikes in Israel. Something like that. Portrait of a terrorist. What makes such men tick?"

"Do what Hammad wants, in fact? Give her hero the needed boost?"

"I don't imagine that she'd consider what you'd write about him a boost."

"To her I compared him with a punchy fighter who's still kidding himself that he can make the big time. I think I was right If - big if again - he delivers what he promises, or even attempts to do so, there'll be a story. Until then, as far as I am concerned, he's a waste of time - just a lot of talk."

I was wrong, of course; inexcusably wrong, moreover, because I had allowed my personal dislike of Ghaled to influence my judgment.

Chapter 4

Michael Howell

May 16 to 17

I don't see why Lewis Prescott should have taken such an instant dislike to Ghaled. To me it seems that at that interview the man was on his best behaviour. According to Prescott, he even smiled.

With Teresa and me twenty-four hours later it was a very different story. No soothing arrack for us; no seats, no politeness. Instead he sat in my office chair with my office bottle of brandy in front of him and glowered up at us. He knew we were afraid of him.

The office door was open and the two gunmen were there on guard. From the laboratory came Issa's voice as he continued his interrupted lecture. He was on filtration now and telling the class how to dry out the fulminate of mercury on plates of glass. Youth training programs, Ghaled had said, must not be interrupted.

He took a swig of my brandy, slammed the bottle down on my desk, and pointed a finger at me.

"You will now answer questions. First, why are you here tonight? Who or what sent you?"

"I came here to confirm a suspicion."

"What suspicion?"

"That Issa was doing what in fact he is doing, making explosives."

"Who told you?"

"Nobody told me. I guessed."

He leaned forward across my desk. "I realize, of course, that you are at present experiencing feelings of confusion. The stupid night watchman turns out to be somewhat less stupid, and a person who gives orders instead of taking them. I am prepared to make allowances, but don't try my patience too far. You will give truthful answers and you will give them promptly. No wriggling, no evasions, Mr. Howell. I ask you again. Who told you?"

"I have already answered you. I guessed."

"You expect me to believe that?"

"I know my own business, Mr. Ghaled. I know which chemicals are needed in the laboratory and I know which are *not* needed. I can also read an invoice."

"The invoices for the special chemicals have always been destroyed."

Teresa spoke. "I asked Beirut for duplicates."

"Why?" he snapped. "What made you ask?"

She was calm now, much calmer than I was. "Invoices may be destroyed, but bills have to be paid. These bills were too high. I wanted to know why. Then I showed the duplicate invoices to Mr. Howell."

Ghaled was wearing a cotton *kaffiyeh* with a pink key pattern. He brushed it away from his face and sat back. His eyes shifted from her to me.

"Is that the truth?"

That's the truth," I said.

"When did you make this discovery about the chemicals?"

This evening."

"Bid you tell anyone else?"

There was no one else to tell."

"And now?" He lit a cigar with an engraved silver lighter.

"Now what?"

"Who is there to tell now?"

I shrugged. "Still no one, I suppose."

He nodded. "I am glad that you do not again insult my intelligence with foolish talk about informing the police. I don't have to tell you why it was foolish, of course."

"You know, I take it, that the police would do nothing."

"Against me, little or nothing, that is true. But that was not what you were thinking, my friend, with your talk about the police." His eyes narrowed. "You were thinking about the effect on Dr. Hawa of the news, which the police for their own protection would feel bound to pass on to higher authority, that one of his precious industrial progress cooperatives was busy making explosives for the PAF. Am I right?"

He was partly right. I shrugged helplessly and he leaned back, satisfied. "It would be amusing, would it not, to hear Dr. Hawa trying to explain it away to his seniors in the government? Would he try to brazen it out, do you think? Would he perhaps ask what was wrong with a sincere Ba'athist giving a little discreet, comradely assistance to the front fighters of the Palestinian movement? Or would he protest abjectly that he knew nothing of this terrible affair and put all the blame on you? You know him better than I do, Mr. Howell. What do you think he would do?"

I played along with him, sighing ruefully. "Probably he would announce it to the press as a mew pilot project for the manufacture of munitions."

His lips twisted. "If he thought the Minister of Defence would let him get away with that he might try, I agree. But more likely, I think, he would put the blame on you. However, since the police will not know, *he* will not know. So you really have nothing to worry about, have you?"

"I suppose not." You could ask an atheist standing on a gallows with a rope around his neck whether he had anything to worry about, and receive the same reply.

"Then let us talk seriously." He waved at us impatiently to sit down as if our standing before him had been an unnecessary deference on our part. "I have for some weeks had plans for extending the Agence Howell's cooperation with us. However, your intrusion here this evening makes it necessary for me to change those plans slightly. As I am sure you realize, you now know more than you would otherwise have known."

"Yes."

"Well, we can remedy that. But so that there are no misunderstandings I will put plainly what I hope is now obvious to you. There will be no changes made here unless I say so. Specifically, Issa will not be dismissed. Nobody will be dismissed. I shall continue to use these facilities as a rear echelon headquarters. Is that clear?"

I nodded.

"I asked you a question. I require an answer."

"Yes, Mr. Ghaled."

"Miss Malandra?"

"Yes, Mr. Ghaled."

"Good. Now, I am going to take you some way into my confidence. You referred to Issa's work, Mr. Howell, as amateur bomb-making. I realize that you were angry at the time and that your intention was to humiliate him. However, you were both right and wrong. Right, in that the processes we are obliged to employ at present are primitive. Wrong, in that we are concerned here with bomb-making. Our present concern is for the production of detonators of a certain kind, and in quantity. Lacking the proper apparatus, equipment for temperature control, and regulation of flow tables, for example, we must, having due regard for safety, do the best we can without it. You follow me?"

"I follow."

"But why, you must be wondering, do we need detonators so urgently? Of what use are detonators without the explosives to detonate? The answer is that we have the explosives, but that our supplies of the means to use them have been cut off by our opponents in Cairo and elsewhere. Even some of our so-called friends have attempted to obstruct and control our operations in this underhand way. Weapons are delivered, but the necessary fuses, though promised, are unaccountably lost or delayed in transit.

And when they do arrive, as often as not, they are unfilled, of the wrong type, or for some other reason useless. It is deliberate sabotage."

An ingenious and wholly admirable form of sabotage, it seemed to me, but I nodded sympathetically.

"So," he went on, "we must create our own sources of supply. That, Michael Howell, is where you will be coming in."

"I, Mr. Ghaled?"

"You have knowledge and skills and resources at your disposal which can be of great value to us. Would you not agree?"

My smile must have looked sickly. "It seems to me, Mr. Ghaled, that you are already utilizing my resources, and Issa's knowledge, to excellent effect. You have created a source of supply for the material you were lacking. My knowledge and skills, such as they are, don't appear to be needed."

"There you are quite mistaken," he said firmly. "However, I shall not explain now. Naturally, I was not expecting this meeting with you this evening. If I had known about it in advance I would have been better prepared. As it is we shall have to postpone discussion of your work for us until tomorrow. I will be able them to tell you exactly and in detail what is required." He stood up and we stood up, too. "Shall we say nine o'clock in the evening? Miss Malandra had better come, too. You may wish to take notes."

"Very well."

"There is one other matter to be dealt with." He snapped his fingers loudly and the gunmen came in from the hall. "This man and this woman will be here again tomorrow night," he told them. "They are to be treated as comrades." He glanced at me. "Did you hear that, Mr. Howell?"

"Yes."

"But do you understand? I used the word 'comrades.' "

"I heard it. I hope they remember."

"I see you don't understand. Surely you cannot suppose that, after your discoveries here tonight, and our frank conversation, I can allow you to leave without, shall we say, making sure of you?"

I shrugged. "You have already made it abundantly clear that I have to be discreet, and why."

"I am not talking of discretion now, but of loyalty and good faith."

"I'm afraid I still don't understand."

"It must be obvious. You are a foreigner here, but in a privileged position. You are free to come and go more or less as you please. That is a situation which I may find it useful to exploit in the future, but in the meantime it permits you to have second thoughts. If, say, you were to decide that instead of meeting me tomorrow you would prefer to be in Beirut or Alexandria or Rome and withhold your cooperation, I would be forced to take steps that I would regret."

He paused to make sure that I understood the threat. "As. I say," he continued, "I would regret the necessity for such action. It would be expensive because we might have to go a long way to find you. Besides, we prefer to have you alive and working with us. You must see that there is only one solution to the problem. You and this woman here must become loyal and committed members of the Palestinian Action Force and subject to its discipline."

"But we are foreigners," I protested idiotically, "we could not... we..." I began to stammer.

He silenced me with a gesture. "Other foreigners have been granted membership, foreigners of both sexes." He paused and then added coldly: "They consider themselves honoured to serve - *honoured.*"

I mumbled something about it all being so unexpected, which he ignored.

"You are not a Jew. Neither, I think, is Miss Malandra. There is therefore no obstacle. You will take the oath of loyalty in the Christian form, of course. Have you your passports with you?"

I had mine in my pocket. All Teresa had was her identity card. He took both passport and card.

"These will be photocopied for our files and returned to you tomorrow," he said. "At that time you will also complete some paper formalities. However, the oath of loyalty can be administered mow. I don't suppose you keep a Bible in your office?"

"No."

"Well, it is not absolutely necessary. You first, I think. Raise your right hand and repeat after me: *I, Michael Howell, a Christian, swear by the Holy Trinity and on the scared book of Antioch, that of my own free will, with a whole heart and without inner reservation, I pledge my life and property to the service of the Palestinian Action Force, and swear ...*"

He was speaking in Arabic and in that language the words sounded odd. The reference to Antioch made it a Maronite oath, and as I was technically Greek Orthodox I suppose it didn't really count for me; but my mother, who is a practicing Christian, would have had a fit I don't remember the exact wording of the rest of the rigmarole, but the substance of it was that I promised total and unquestioning obedience in perpetuity and recognized that the least faltering was punishable by death. The penalty for betrayal of the cause, described in rather sickening detail, was more complicated but had the same end result.

"In the presence of these fraternal witnesses," Ghaled demanded finally, "you swear this?"

The fraternal gunmen looked at me expectantly.

"I swear it"

"You are accepted."

He went through the whole thing again with Teresa. I thought that as a Catholic she might boggle at some of it, but she went through it briskly and impersonally, rather as if she were reading back from shorthand a letter that I had just dictated.

"I swear it" By then she sounded slightly bored.

"Yon are accepted." Ghaled got rid of the gunmen with another snap of the fingers and gave us a long look.

"Congratulations, comrades," he said. "It is proper now for you to address me, respectfully, as Comrade Salah. Will you remember that?"

"Yes, Comrade Salah."

He nodded graciously. "Until tomorrow night, then."

We were dismissed.

It was not until we were in the car again that I realized how tired I was. My back was still painful. It had been a long day. I could try hopelessly to think of ways out of the predicament we were in, but I did not want to talk about it.

Unfortunately, Teresa did.

"What are we going to do?" she asked. There was more excitement than anxiety in her voice.

"I haven't the slightest idea. At the moment all I want to do is go home and sleep."

She drove in silence for half a minute.

"Shall you speak to Colonel Shikla?"

"No."

I did not elaborate. Colonel Shikla was head of the Internal Security Service and an unpleasant man with a revolting reputation. I had met him socially, and in an effort to conceal my fear of him I had beam too affable. He must have been accustomed to that sort of reaction, for it had clearly amused him. The last thing I wanted was to meet him in his official capacity, even if it had made sense to do so.

But Teresa persisted. "You could talk to him privately, unofficially."

"Unofficially about Ghaled? Don't be silly. That sort of thing is Shikla's business."

"Officially, then. If someone else were to find out, we'd be covered if you had told Colonel Shikla."

"We'd more likely end up in one of his interrogation rooms."

"Why, if we'd told him the truth, everything?"

She was exasperating. "Because," I said loudly, "that sort of man never believes that you've told him everything, even when you have. And let's assume that for once he does believe. What then? The ISS has to do something about Ghaled. They may not want to. I may have told them something that they would rather not have known officially. But let's also assume that they decide, reluctantly or not, that they have to act on our information. Where does that leave us?"

"We've covered ourselves."

"With what? Transparent plastic? Yon don't think they're going to move against Ghaled without tipping him off first, do you? He'll have plenty of time to put our names at the top of the next purification list. You call that covering ourselves? Talk sense, comrade."

She actually giggled. "It's a funny feeling, isn't it, being a member of the PAF?"

"Funny?"

"Creepy, then. I wonder who those other foreign members are, what they're like. He said they were of both sexes."

"One of the women is almost certainly Melanie Hammad."

"She had an article in one of the French fashion magazines this month - about kaftans. Nothing terrible seems to have happened to her."

"She isn't in Syria making explosives."

"It's Issa who is making them, not us."

"But an our works." I suddenly lost all patience. "My God, woman! Don't you realize how serious this is, how dangerous?"

"Of course I do, Michael, but it's no use getting upset. You're tired now, but tomorrow you'll think of a way of dealing with the situation. You always do."

I wasn't flattered by her confidence; I knew that it was misplaced. She thought that because I was usually able to solve business problems, outwit competitors, get around difficulties, bargain shrewdly, and cope with men like Dr. Hawa, I could handle Ghaled and the situation he had created. What she did not understand was that business skills are not always transferable, that when the commodity is violence and the man you are dealing with is an animal, they don't work.

I have not often been frightened. As a child I used to have nightmares and wake up screaming, but of the nightmares from which there is no escape through waking up I have had little experience. There were some bad moments, of course, during the Cyprus troubles of the fifties, but most of them were shared with the rest of the community, and the dangers, though real enough, usually went away as suddenly and unpredictably as they had arrived. Ghaled, however, was not going to go away. For over twenty years he had dealt in death and violence, and would, presumably, go on doing so until he himself died violently.

Meanwhile, he frightened me. I admit it He would always frighten me. I knew even then that the only way for me to "deal" with Ghaled would be to kill him. I didn't think, though, that I was going to get a chance to do so; nor did I believe that, given the chance, businessman Howell would ever consider taking it. I am not a man of violence.

A few hours' sleep helped. When I woke up, my back was sore but no longer very painful. I was able to review the position more or less calmly.

Ghaled had said that he had plans for me and had spoken of exploiting my freedom to come and go as I pleased, which suggested that he meant to use me as a courier or go-between. But he had also talked about utilizing my "knowledge and skills and resources." Until I knew what that meant there was no point in trying to make plans of my own.

I could, however, survey my defences, such as they were, and take a few obvious precautions.

I had to recognize that a time might come when I would have what Ghaled had described euphemistically as "second thoughts." In other words, I might one day feel that, murder squads or no murder squads, I had to run for it. To do this I would need a passport, plenty of ready cash, a packed bag, and a place to go to ground.

The cash presented no problem and neither did the place to go to ground, though I would have to be desperate to use it. The doubtful quantity was the passport. If Ghaled could take my passport from me once "to make sure of me, he was perfectly capable of doing so again. Clearly, Teresa and I would both have to have second passports to put in our packed bags. Western consular officials in the Middle East are generally helpful about providing second passports for business people who need them; those going to Israel, for example. An Israeli visa stamp invalidates a passport in the Arab countries, and although the Israelis are very good about not stamping if asked not to do so, travellers sometimes forget to ask until it's too late.

I told Teresa to see about getting a second passport from the Italian consul. Getting mine would be more complicated. Although Cyprus has diplomatic relations with Syria, there was no Cypriot consul in Damascus at that time, so I telephoned our Famagusta office and instructed them to take the necessary action.

That done, I ran a security check. What Ghaled had done at the battery works he could also have done at the tile factory and the hardware, furniture, and electronic assembly plants. I could unknowingly be playing host to other PAF cells. If so, I wanted to know the worst. I gave Teresa the job of checking the purchase records for unusual items. I tackled the personnel records myself.

First, I got out Ghaled's employment file to see who had recommended him to us under the name of Yassin. The recommendation, I found, had come attached to the usual Ministry of Labour and Social Welfare docket and was signed by a staff captain in the office of the Internal Security Service.

So much for Teresa's bright idea about "covering" ourselves with

Colonel Shikla! The Internal Security Service not only knew about Ghaled's activities but was also giving him assistance and protection.

Next I went through the files on some of the other men we employed to see if this same ISS captain had recommended anyone else. I didn't bother much with those actually engaged in production, bench workers and craftsmen; there were, in any case, too many of them for a thorough check Instead, I concentrated on the night staffs and employees with keys in their charge.

I found two; one a maintenance man, the other a storekeeper. Both had been recommended by the ISS captain. Both worked in the hardware factory. They had been taken on at about the same time as Ghaled.

My first impulse was to get on to the works manager and tell him to fire them, but Teresa quite rightly objected. She must have slept better than I had.

"What reason will you give?"

"I'll find a reason."

"If they really are Ghaled's men he will make yon take them back, and then you will look foolish."

"And your way I only *feel* foolish. All right. But I mean to know what they're up to. Has there been much theft of materials there?"

"No, but there is one unusual purchase item. An order came through from hardware for a set of screw taps and dies of a type that doesn't exist"

"How do you know?"

"The tool suppliers wrote a letter, copy to us, that taps and dies for cutting the threads in question were not stocked by them, and, as far as they knew, not made. They suggested politely that there may have been a clerical error in the order."

"Let me see the order."

She showed it to me. I could see at once why the suppliers had thought that a mistake had been made. A machine shop apprentice in his first year would have known what was wrong with that order.

I ran over in my mind the various items of hardware we manufactured and tried to think of a process or operation *to* which this attempted purchase of taps and dies might, however crazily, be linked. I could think of none.

The order had been signed by the works office chief clerk, so I telephoned him. He could not remember that particular order offhand but would consult his files and call me back. It was late afternoon before he did so, and he had nothing helpful to tell me. The order for tools had been one of a batch of orders presented for his signature by his assistant No, the assistant did not remember who had put in the requisition; he was consulting his files. Meanwhile, the chief clerk informed me solemnly there was a note on the order saying that the suppliers were temporarily out of stock. I told him that they would be permanently out of stock and hung up. It was hopeless. I had to console myself with the thought that, if any hanky-panky was being attempted at the hardware factory, it was unlikely to succeed. Issa had at least known enough to order correctly the materials he needed. His counterpart at the hardware factory was obviously incompetent.

The other defensive measure I took began with a call to Dr. Hawa's Chef de Bureau.

After some preliminary chitchat I referred to the report on the Italian car-battery project which I had delivered to Hawa the previous day, and asked whether the Minister had had time to read it.

"It is on his desk, Mr. Howell, but he has not yet completely studied it, I think. There have been distractions, a finance committee meeting."

"Naturally," I said, "I would not expect the Minister to have already reached a decision. I ask only because I find that I omitted to include with the report a supplementary memorandum concerning the possible location of the new plant, It does not in any way change the maim conclusions of the report, but contains additional information and suggestions which the Minister may find useful. If

I were to send yon copies of the memorandum today, could it be attached to the main report which the Minister is studying?"

He made difficulties at first so as to give his eventual consent the appearance of a big favour, but that was normal. I promised that he should have the memorandum within the how.

I dictated it to Teresa in ten minutes. At the end she gave me a worried look.

"Is this wise, Michael?"

"It gives us a card to play."

"Ghaled won't like it."

"I don't suppose he will - if I show It to him. I may not, but I want to have it up my sleeve, just in case it could be useful. Date it three days ago and show it as having been written in Milan. Make am extra copy with an Arabic translation."

After the memorandum had gone off I tried for a time to concentrate on real work. Our agent in Athens was bidding on an important tile contract, and, faced by penalty clauses, was asking urgently for firm guarantees from us on the delivery dates. I could not afford to be careless or casual in replying to him, yet I found myself being both. It was Teresa who suggested finally, and to my relief, that I delay replying for twenty-four hours and then cable him to make up for lost time.

That I should have been more concerned at that moment with my involvement in the PAF than with my obligations to the Agence Howell, its shareholders, and its faithful employees was no doubt most regrettable. The responsible, seasoned man of affairs should be able to put first things first and keep a cool head. Obviously, them, I must be irresponsible and unseasoned. So be it. I am not much interested in the devil I know, but the devil I don't know gives me a pain in the neck. I *knew* what my obligations were to the business; what the PAF wanted from me I still had to find out.

We had martinis, as usual, but no wine or brandy. For one thing, I didn't want us to go to the meeting breathing evidence of what might be interpreted as an attempt to fortify ourselves; nor did I want to have to excuse myself to go to the lavatory while I was there. I don't know why I bothered. Probably, at that stage of the game, I was still, instinctively, thinking like a businessman in terms of bargaining sessions at which small psychological gains and losses counted. The idea that I was a member of the PAF pledged to do as I was told without argument took some getting used to.

It was a beautiful night, warm and still. The air in the courtyard was heavy with the scent of plants and there were bats flying. Suliman, the gardener, opened the gates for us. I told him that we might be late and not to wait up. He thought we were going to a party and wished us a happy evening.

We reached the battery works a little before nine and left the car outside as we had done the night before. This time the postern was unlocked, but as soon as we were inside, the two gunmen came out of the darkness by the loading bay and shone a light on us. We stopped.

"Greetings, comrades." It was the man with the broken teeth who had hit me in the back.

"Greetings," I said.

He came forward slowly and then suddenly thrust forward the flashlight in his hand. I thought he was trying to jab it in my face and started back.

He tutted reproachfully. "This light belongs to you, comrade. You left it behind last might. The glass is broken, but it still works."

Thank you, but I have another." I switched on the flashlight in my hand. "You see?"

"You do not want this one?" He sounded hopeful.

"Not if it is of use to you, comrade." I decided that it was time to start winning friends. "But, as you say, the glass is broken. Why not take this light, which is unbroken, and I will use the broken one. Tomorrow I can get a new glass."

Thanks, comrade, many thanks." We exchanged the flashlights.

"My name is Ahmad," he said. His breath stank.

"And mine is Michael."

"This is Comrade Musa," he pointed to his companion. "He cannot speak because he has no voice box."

Comrade Musa grinned and pointed to a big scar on his neck.

"A war wound?"

"Yes," said Ahmad, "but he can hear the smallest sounds. He heard you last night before I did. What time were you ordered to report, comrade?"

"Nine o'clock."

"Comrade Salah does not like to be kept waiting."

"I'm sure of that."

"Go on then, comrades," he said affably. "You know the way."

For a moment I thought that we were to be left to go on alone; then, as I started to turn, Ahmad chuckled and prodded me with his carbine. "March, comrades," he said. It was not a hard prod but firm enough to let me know that a flashlight did not buy indulgence and that he was still in charge there.

When we got to the steps of the office building he told us to wait while he went in to report our arrival. Musa grinned at us while we waited but kept his finger on the trigger of his gun. There were lights on in the laboratory, but I could hear no voices. My office was in darkness. Ahmad had gone through to the back of the building.

After half a minute or so he came back onto the terrace and beckoned us up. When we reached him he told me to raise my arms above my head and frisked me. Then he took Teresa's handbag from her and peered inside it. Satisfied that we were both unarmed he returned Teresa's bag.

"Follow me, comrades."

We went along the passage to the storeroom area. Changes had been made there that I hadn't known about. The larger of the two rooms was now Ghaled's command post. The rolls of zinc sheet-*my* zinc sheet-which should have been set out carefully in rows to keep the different gauges separate had all been stacked against one wall to make room for a trestle table, some chairs, and a bed. The place had a lived-in look, as well it might It had been months since I had time to bother with the battery works storage rooms. I had left them in Issa's care. Perhaps it was the sight of him sitting there at the table and giving me a superior little smile as I entered the room that made me so angry.

For me that anger was dangerous. Since there was no immediate way of giving expression to it I had to bottle it up. As a result, I became for a while less afraid of Ghaled and so less careful of what I said. I made mistakes.

It was all very formal to start with, rather like the first board meeting of a newly formed company.

Ghaled said, "Good evening, comrades." Teresa and I said, "Good evening, Comrade Salah," and were invited to sit down,

There were two other men besides Ghaled and Issa already seated at the table. Ghaled introduced them.

This is Comrade Tewfiq. This is Comrade Wasfi. They are Central Committee members."

Tewfiq was a sallow, pockmarked man with a heavy moustache and a paunch. Wasfi was a wiry young man with a very short upper lip and an unhappy half-smile which seemed permanent. I knew that I had seen both men before and could now guess where I had seen them. Tewfiq and Wasfi are fairly common names in those parts, but they also happened to be the given names of the hardware factory storekeeper and of the maintenance man whom I had marked down as suspect earlier in the day. It was reasonable to suppose that these were those same men.

They both gave me impersonal nods. They did not need telling who I was.

"Now," Ghaled was saying briskly, "we have much work to do. Last night I described our supply problems and special needs in general terms to the new comrades. Tonight we will detail our requirements and make the necessary plans for their fulfilment. I must impress upon you the need now for the utmost urgency in carrying out assigned tasks. Every task, I repeat, *every* task must be completed within the next thirty days. Is that understood, comrades?"

There was a murmuring of, "Yes, Comrade Salah," in which I didn't join. Ghaled looked at me sharply.

"I did not hear you answer, comrade."

"Because I have *not* understood. I have no knowledge of these tasks you mention."

"You will have. But I have told you of the urgency. That you can understand, and will accept."

"Very well."

He stared at me for a moment. I was being insufficiently respectful, but he wasn't quite sure that I realized that I was. I returned his stare with one of my own, innocent but expectant. He gave me the benefit of the doubt and turned to a paper in front of him.

"First," he said, "the matter of detonators, those for electric firing. I will hear reports. Comrade Issa?"

"We have powder for five hundred, Comrade Salah. Samples have been tested in the laboratory and are satisfactory."

"Comrade Tewfiq?"

"The copper tubes are on order, Comrade Salah, but not yet delivered."

"Why not?"

Tewfiq spread out his hands. "They were promised for last week and the week before. I am in the supplier's hands, Comrade Salah."

Ghaled looked at me. "Perhaps Comrade Michael can help us. Fifty meters of one centimetre diameter copper tubing are required. It must be a hard grade of copper."

"Who are the suppliers?" I enjoyed asking that question because I was sure that the truthful answer would have been that the hardware cooperative and I were the suppliers. After all, we would be paying for the stuff.

Of course he gave me the name of a metal wholesaler. It was the firm with which we normally dealt.

"There is a special government control on nonferrous metal purchases," I said. "Was a quota number given with the order?"

Tewfiq was sweating now. "I do not know, comrade."

"Why not?" snapped Ghaled.

"Because, Comrade Salah . . ." He foundered for a moment. "Comrade, you know that I do not actually issue the orders myself," he went on, pleading for understanding with his eyes. "I am only the..."

"Yes, yes," Ghaled waved him into silence and sat brooding. I knew what was going through his mind. If Tewfiq explained that he was only a storekeeper and that a works office clerk did the actual ordering, I would put two and two together and Tewfiq's cover would be blown as far as I was concerned. Ghaled was trying to decide whether or not to take me into his confidence. He decided against doing so.

"You must press for early delivery," he told Tewfiq severely.

"Yes, Comrade Salah."

"Continue your report"

"We have the insulated connector wires, the tin caps, and the packing material. However" - he hesitated and then went on with a rush - "I regret, Comrade Salah, deeply regret that there is still difficulty in obtaining the chrome-nickel alloy wire. It is not a material that I can reasonably order. I have tried. Comrade Wasfi will bear me out."

"That is true, Comrade Salah." Wasfi's anguished smile stretched until it became clown like. "We said that it was fuse wire for electrical maintenance use, but they ordered fuse wire. I think they may not be the same thing."

Ghaled looked at Issa. "Are they the same?"

Issa took refuge in some papers in front of him. "The specifications call for chrome-nickel alloy wire of thirty gauge," he said.

That is not an answer to my question. Are they the same?"

"I do not know, Comrade Salah"

Ghaled looked at me.

"No," I said, "they are not the same. Chrome-nickel alloy, nichrome as it is called, is a resistance wire. It is used in electrical heating elements because it can get hot without melting or oxidizing. Fuse wire melts when it gets hot. What is the chrome-nickel wire needed for?"

"Show him," said Ghaled.

Issa pushed a sheet across the table to me. He hated doing it, I could see. He was the technical authority there, not I.

A drawing on the paper showed how the detonators were to be made. A six centimetre length of one centimetre copper tube was to contain five grams of mercury fulminate held between plugs of cotton wool.

One end of the copper tube was capped with tin; the other end had a wax seal holding the two insulated firing leads. The ends of these two leads were in the middle of the fulminate powder, where they were connected by a small loop of fine chrome-nickel wire. That was the firing circuit. All you needed then was a six-volt battery and a switch. When the circuit was closed, the chrome-nickel wire, no thicker than a hair, would become white-hot almost instantly and the fulminate would explode, blowing off the tin cap and detonating any high explosive with which it had been placed in contact.

It was a simple design but a practical one. If you followed the instructions it could be counted upon to work. I continued to study the drawing to give myself time to think. I was tempted to sabotage the whole detonator project by advising them to use the fuse wire, but decided that it would be too risky. Issa had said that the powder samples had been tested. They would certainly test the completed detonators. If the test sample didn't work, any modification I had suggested would certainly be blamed.

I looked up.

"Well?" said Ghaled.

"A very thin fuse wire might get hot enough before it melted to ignite the powder charge, but I don't think you could rely on it. I think you must have this fine-gauge chrome-nickel."

"*We* must have it, comrade," he admonished me. "The question now is, where do *we* get it?"

Issa saw a chance to regain lost face. "If it is used on electric heating elements," he said, "we can obtain it easily. Only four or five meters are required. We can get a few of these elements and strip them."

Ghaled looked at me again.

"We could toy," I said, "but I don't believe that heating elements are ever made using such a fine gauge. Indeed, I am sure they aren't. It will have to come from a radio dealer who does repair work and has wire-wound hundred-ohm resistors in stock."

"Comrade Salah!" Wasfi burst out excitedly. "I know such a man. He has a shop in the souk."

But Ghaled motioned Wasfi into silence. His eyes were on me.

"Do you not use these resistors in your own electronic assembly work?" he asked.

"None of the resistors we use are wire-wound, Comrade Salah."

"Not even in the Magisch communications transceiver which you assemble for the army?"

That made me jump a little. The Magisch was supposed to be on the secret list.

"Especially not in the Magisch transceivers," I replied. "They use miniaturized circuit units which we get from East Germany already sealed in plastic. We merely assemble the units. There are no individual components of the ordinary kind."

He gave me a silent handclap. "Good. Very good." His eyes were mocking. "A little test, Comrade Michael, that is all Fortunately you have passed it with credit. My own electronics expert gave me the same advice."

I made show of being disconcerted, which seemed to please him. Identifying the "electronics expert" would not, I knew, be difficult. The reference to the Magisch had been the giveaway. I already had a short list of two suspects in mind and another look at the employment files would tell me which of them was guilty.

"Very well. Comrade Wasfi shall buy the wire resistors. Meanwhile we have another urgent matter on which you may be able to assist us, Comrade Michael"

"Of course, Comrade Salah, I shall be glad to do anything that I can."

He seemed not to hear me. He had risen to his feet and crossed to the bed. On it were two large metal objects which he brought back and placed on the table.

"Do you know anything about ammunition, Comrade Michael? I mean about such things as heavy mortar bombs and artillery projectiles."

"No, I don't."

"Then I will explain. Heavy projectiles have three main parts. The main explosive charge and the fuse you must know about, in principle anyway."

"Yes."

"In between those two parts there is a third. We call it the booster or gaine. High explosives of the kind used in large projectiles are insensitive staff, and a small detonator is not enough. So we place this large detonator, the gaine, in the middle of it and let the fuse explode the gaine. "This"- he picked up the larger of the metal objects- "is the gaine."

It was a bronze-coloured cylinder about thirty centimetres long and five thick with a heavy steel collar at one end. The collar was threaded on the outside, for insertion into the "projectile," I assumed, and there was a hole in the top, also threaded.

Ghaled pointed to the hole. "That is where the impact fuse should go." He picked up the smaller object, which was painted gray and shaped rather like an oversized spark plug. It was threaded at one end with hexagon facings just like a plug. "And this is the fuse," he said. "Now, Comrade Michael, take the gaine in your left hand. It is filled with tetryl, but do not be afraid. There is no danger. Now take the fuse. A little more care with that is advisable. It has a setback safety mechanism but should not be dropped or struck hard. Now try to fit the fuse to the gaine."

What he was getting at was immediately obvious. The threaded hole in the gaine was slightly bigger than the threaded end of the fuse. The two threads were also of a different pitch. I examined both more closely and had a revelation. I looked across at Tewfiq.

"So that's what you wanted those taps and dies for," I said.

There was a short silence. Tewfiq and Wasfi appeared to be stunned. Ghaled leaned forward.

"Explain yourself, Comrade Michael."

"To make these two fit together you need an adapter ring with an outer thread to fit the gaine and an inner one to fit the fuse. The threads are both standard metric by the look of them, and you have to cut them by machine. Taps and dies in those diameters are only made for pipe threads, which have completely different profiles. Comrade Tewfiq did not know that. He thought that the adapter rings could be made by hand with taps and dies, so he ordered them. The suppliers wrote back saying that the order could not be filled."

Ghaled had a very unpleasant expression on his face. "How long have you known that Tewfiq and Wasfi were our comrades?" he asked quietly.

"Not for certain until this evening, but I had my suspicions earlier in the day."

"Why did you have suspicions?"

I told him.

He sighed and glanced at Issa. "You see now why it was so necessary to make sure of him last night?"

And then to me: "What excuse have you to offer?"

"My curiosity was natural, I think, Comrade Salah. You did not tell me not to exercise it"

"Then I tell you now."

"Surely no harm has been done."

"That is for me to decide. The comrades in the field, the front-fighters, must know one another, but those who work in cells under cover must know only those with whom they have to work directly. So, there will be no more looking into records, Comrade Michael. You understand? I am giving you an order."

"I understand." I didn't see how he would know whether or not I obeyed the order, and, since he had now made it plain that there were other members of the PAF on my payrolls, I had every intention of disobeying.

Anger was still at work in me. I think he had sensed it, because he stared at me long and hard before adding: "I hope you do understand, Comrade Michael You would not like any disciplinary action I was forced to take."

"I understand."

"Then let us get back to work. How is this adapter ring to be made?"

"There is only one way to make it, on a screw-cutting lathe."

He looked at Tewfiq. "You have this machine in the factory?"

"No, Comrade Salah."

"Then you must obtain one."

"That" I said, "is impossible."

"Why?"

"Government permission has to be obtained for all machine tool purchases and the need for them justified. We would have no valid reason to support this purchase."

"Then invent a reason."

"It would take weeks, even then, to get delivery. We would also need a skilled machinist to do the work. Besides, it is unnecessary."

"You have just said that it is essential."

"The use of the machine is essential, yes, and a machinist to do the work, but if I needed this part or one like it for something we were manufacturing I would subcontract the job to a machine shop in Beirut."

"That is out of the question, obviously. Do you not yet

understand the need for secrecy?"

"There would be no breach of secrecy. I have used this machine shop several times. A draftsman makes proper drawings of the part to be machined. The material to be used and permitted tolerances are specified, the quantity we need is given. We do not say what the part is for. That is our business, and the subcontractor is not interested anyway. He does what the drawings and specifications tell him to do. He submits a sample for approval. If we approve it he completes the order and delivers."

He thought for a moment "The draftsman would have to know what the adapter is for."

"In this case I would do the drawings myself."

"Here?"

"No. There are no drawing-office facilities here. A rough sketch will not do. There must be clean, accurate machine drawings."

"These parts cannot be taken away."

"There is no need to take them away. All I need take are the necessary measurements and particulars.

I can do that here. There are callipers and a micrometer gauge in the laboratory. Issa knows where they are."

Ghaled nodded to Issa, who scurried away. I began to examine the gaine and the fuse again, more carefully this time. There were Chinese markings on the fuse, I noticed.

"I take it," I said, "that this is one of the wrong size fuses you mentioned last night?"

"Yes."

"Have you one of the right size?"

"Yes. Why?"

"When the fuse is inserted it has to be tightened, I assume, with a wrench."

"Yes. That is done just before firing."

"You realize that with a plain adapter ring the wrong-size fuse will only be tightened when the wrench forces it up against this disk inside the collar of the gaine? It could fracture it. Would that matter?"

"It would matter very much. There must be no forcing."

"Then we need a flange on the ring which will allow the wrong-size fuse to penetrate only as far as the right one."

"I do not understand."

I reached for Teresa's note pad and drew a sketch for him.

He nodded. "Yes, I see. But we need a hundred of these rings. This is more complicated to make."

"Not really," I said. "Turning the flange is easy. The difficult part is cutting the threads. But I must have the right fuse to measure for depth of penetration. It is no use trying to guess."

"Very well.

He went to a gray-painted wooden box which was under the bed. He had to pull the box out to raise the lid and I saw that it had Russian lettering stencilled on it. He tried, too late, to conceal the lettering. I pretended not to have seen by busying myself with the things Issa had by now brought in from the laboratory.

Meanwhile, I could draw conclusions. Although I knew nothing about ammunition, some things were obvious. The length and thickness of the gaine suggested that the projectile that contained it was a fairly hefty weapon. It wouldn't be an artillery shell because guerrillas like the PAF did not have big guns. It seemed likely, then, that what Ghaled had was rocket-launchers from Russian sources. The friendly Russians, however, had, intentionally or through negligence, failed to deliver enough fuses to go with them. The Chinese, or persons with access to Chinese supplies, were trying to help him out.

"That is the right fuse," he said.

It was practically the same as the wrong one. The only basic difference was in the diameter of the threaded section. I took all the measurements I needed from it and Teresa jotted the figures down as I called them out. Then I turned my attention to the wrong fuse. Ghaled watched intently as I used the gauge.

"You take each measurement twice," he remarked.

"It's as well to be certain."

That is very thorough.'"

In fact, I wasn't being particularly thorough; I couldn't be because I hadn't all the needed measuring tools, but it didn't matter. I knew that these were standard metric threads and that, as long as I got the diameters and pitches exactly right, I could get the other details from a metric series table in the drawing office. I wasn't going to explain all that, though.

"If I am not thorough," I said, "the adapter ring will not work properly and I shall be to blame."

Tewfiq chuckled - he was obviously delighted to have been relieved of this responsibility - but Ghaled did not answer immediately.

He watched me in silence for almost a minute before he said: "I do not think so, Comrade Michael."

"I would *not* be blamed?"

"I do not think that it is fear of blame that drives you at the moment. Nor do I think that it is loyalty to our cause."

I didn't like the sound of that, so I pretended to be absorbed in re-counting threads and checking the figures with Teresa. Another half minute went by.

"I think that it is pride," Ghaled continued thoughtfully. "The pride that makes it difficult for a man to permit work, *any* work, to be done poorly when he knows how to do it well."

That sounded better. I put the Russian fuse down. Ghaled picked it up and weighed it in his hand as he went on.

"And you know how to do many things well, don't you, Comrade Michael? You are a merchant as well as an engineer, a manager as well as a successful capitalist exploiter. You have so many sources of pride to inflate your conceit. No wonder you so easily become arrogant."

He said the last word very deliberately and for a moment the heavy fuse became still in his hand. He was waiting for me to answer the charge.

"I am sorry," I said mildly, "that you should think me arrogant, Comrade Salah. You said that you wished to make use of my knowledge and resources. I have been doing my best to comply."

"But not without reservations. You see, your arrogance leads you into giving yourself away, Comrade Michael. For example, you concealed your prior knowledge of Tewfiq's and Wasfi's cover occupations. But when a moment came when you could show them to be, in your eyes, ignorant men, you did so. You could not resist the temptation."

He got up and put the fuse back to its box under the bed before turning to me again.

"I told you last night that I had other plans for securing your wholehearted cooperation. They would have involved damage to your company's bank balances rather than to your personal conceit. Perhaps that would have been more effective."

I said nothing.

"Well, we can still find out if it becomes necessary. Agence Howell ships constantly use the ports of Beirut, Latakia, and Alexandria. We have cells in all those places. The cargo fires and engine room explosions we had arranged for can easily be reordered. Meanwhile, remember that you have been warned." He sat down again at the head of the table. "How soon will the drawings of the adaptor ring be ready?"

"It will take me some time, Comrade Salah. As a draftsman I am a little out of practice. The day after tomorrow I should have it finished."

"And how long then to make the rings?"

"Ten days to two weeks for the sample. When that is approved a week should be sufficient to produce a hundred."

"Very well." He looked around the table. "Comrades Tewfiq and Wasfi have their assigned tasks. They are now excused. Comrade Issa will get the print maker." He waited until they had left the room, then opened a folder - one of my office filing folders - which was lying on the table in front of him. On top of the papers inside were Teresa's identity card and my passport. He looked at us. "For you two, before your other duties are assigned, there are membership formalities to be completed." He selected two papers from the folder and glanced at them before pushing them across the table to us. "Read them carefully before signing, both of you."

What I read was this:

I, Michael Howell, a British Commonwealth citizen resident in the Democratic Socialist Republic of Syria and subject to its laws in all respects, do hereby confess, freely and of my own will, to having transgressed those laws by illegally transporting arms and explosives for the use and on the orders of the Zionist secret intelligence service.

It then became more specific. I had, with others whom I could name, conspired to blow up the house of one Hussein Mahenoud Saga'ir in the Lebanese village of Bleideh on the night of the fifteenth day of Murharram in that year. I had actually manufactured the plastic bomb which had destroyed the house of this Palestinian patriot, killing him and all his family. The name of the Zionist secret agent who had recruited me for this filthy work was Ze'ev Barlev, and I had been contacted by him during one of my frequent visits to Cyprus.

In the hands of the Syrian police such a confession would be tantamount to a death sentence - after torture to extract the names of my co-conspirators. The Lebanese police might omit the torture and commute the death sentence to life imprisonment, but that would be the best treatment I could hope for in any of the Arab League countries.

I glanced at Teresa. Her face was pale and still. I reached for her confession and read it. She had been my confederate in the murder of the Saga'ir family and also a courier for the Israeli intelligence service. Her father had been a Jew. The two confessions were more or less the same.

As I finished reading I saw that Ghaled was watching me for signs of a reaction. I forced myself to appear unmoved.

"As a matter of interest," I asked, "who is - who *was* - this man

Saga'ir?"

"A traitor who was executed."

"And why am I supposed to have helped to execute him?"

"All the comrades sign confessions. In that way all can feel safe."

"I must say, Comrade Salah, that this confession does not make me feel safe."

"Your confession is for the other comrades' safety. Their confessions are for your own. Any comrade who thinks of betraying us must think again when he remembers what the cost to him will be. So do as you are told without further argument. Sign. You will not leave here alive unless you do so."

Teresa and I signed. As we did so Issa came back into the room carrying a small wooden box which he put on the table.

Ghaled looked at our signatures, then handed the confessions to Issa. "Those comrades who cannot write their names sign only with a thumb print," he said. Those who can write, however, give a thumb print, too. It is better so. Signatures can be denied, but not prints. Issa knows the way. Follow his instructions."

The box contained a portable fingerprinting outfit of the kind used by the police. Issa rolled ink onto the metal plate and went to work. He obviously enjoyed giving me orders. He declared my first print insufficiently clear, inked my thumb again, grasped my forearm, and pressed the thumb onto the paper with his other hand. He did the same with Teresa.

Ghaled took the papers from him, satisfied himself that the prints were clear, and then handed me my passport. Teresa received her identity card.

That is exactly how our much-publicized "terrorist confessions" were obtained. We neither wrote nor dictated them and there is not a word of truth in the admissions they contain.

I have been asked repeatedly if we knew what we were doing when we signed, and I answer again - of course we knew, dammit! What we did *not* know was how to avoid signing. We signed under duress; we had no choice.

In the circumstances I can't blame Teresa for misunderstanding what I did then. To her it seemed that I was merely trying, ill-advisedly and even childishly, to hit back at Ghaled in the only way I could think of on the spur of the moment.

In fact, there was nothing impulsive about my move. I wasn't trying to hit back at Ghaled, but to needle him into hitting out at me. A man with his kind of secrets is always under pressure. Anger him suddenly by goosing him with bad news, and, nine times out of ten, he will overreact. Then, in his desire to demolish you and dispose of your bad news, he tends to forget discretion and give himself away. Of course, it was a dangerous game to play with a violent man like Ghaled, but I desperately needed information and the risk seemed worth taking.

As I put my passport back in my pocket, I said casually: "By the way, Comrade Salah, there is something that I think you should know."

"What?"

"You said last night that there were to be no changes made here, that there were to be no dismissals and that you would continue to use these premises as a headquarters."

"What of it?"

"I am afraid that the matter will shortly be taken out of my hands."

"Why? By whom? What do you mean?"

I told him about the projected switch to car-battery manufacture. I went on: "This place has been running at a loss for months. The original plan was to close it down altogether and build a new factory at Homs for the Italian operation. Later it was felt that would be a wasteful proceeding and that this works should be changed and extended to accommodate the new plant. This building, for instance, will be modified and enlarged for use as offices. The laboratory and storerooms will be accommodated in the new factory extensions which have been planned."

"He is lying," Issa shouted excitedly, "I work here and I know nothing of these plans."

"Comrade Issa knows nothing about a great many things," I retorted. "I am reporting the facts."

"Why did you say nothing of this last night?" Ghaled asked quietly.

"Because it didn't occur to me to do so. I accepted your orders then without question. Understandably, I think. I didn't realize until tonight that I should have warned you that my ability to obey those orders might have a time limit."

"What time limit? How many weeks?"

"That will be for the Minister, Dr. Hawa, to say, I am afraid."

"But he will base his decision on your advice."

"Unfortunately, my advice has already been given." I drew from my pocket the copy of the memorandum I had written and handed it to him.

As he read it his mouth tightened grimly. That didn't surprise me. The moment that what I had proposed in the memorandum was agreed to, his snug little headquarters, hard by the Der'a refuges camp where his goon squads hid out and conveniently near the Jordanian and Lebanese borders, was going to become the centre of a building site, swarming with outsiders and about as secure from his point of view as a floodlit frontier post.

He stared at me bleakly and for so long that I began to think that he had seen through my ploy.

"I thought that you should be aware of this situation," I said to break the silence.

"Quite right, Comrade Michael. And now you will think of a way of changing it."

"Unfortunately - "

He held up his hand. "No excuses. You will change your advice, you will do whatever is necessary. Just understand that under no circumstances may this headquarters be disturbed in any way for the next six weeks."

"I will do my best."

"Of course you will. But make certain that your best succeeds."
He paused. "Have you any other surprises for me, Comrade
Michael?"

"Surprises?"

He frowned. "Come now. I have already warned you once
against trying to play your slippery little businessman tricks with
me. What else have you to reveal?"

"Nothing, Comrade Salah. I am merely trying to be open with
you, not to play tricks."

"I hope so, for your sake. But to make quite sure, I am going to
tell you what will be required of you in our forthcoming operation.
In that way you will have ample time to overcome any difficulties
you may foresee, or pretend to foresee, in carrying out your tasks.
You will have no excuses for failure."

"I have already said that I will do my best for you, Comrade
Salah."

"I have heard you say it. I hope you are to be believed. We shall
see." He paused. "Your company owns a motor ship, the *Euridice
Howell.*"

It was a statement, not a question, but I nodded. "Yes, Comrade
Salah."

"Carrying mixed cargoes regularly between five major ports of
call - Famagusta, Iskenderun, Latakia, Beirut, and Alexandria. Am I
right?"

Those are her most usual ports of call, yes, but she goes where
the business takes her - Izmir, Brindisi, and Tripoli - Genoa and
Naples sometimes."

"Nevertheless her captain acts on your orders."

"He acts on our agents' orders. I don't give the orders
personally."

"But you could do so."

"I could instruct our agents to do so, but that would be an
unusual interference on my part. There would have to be some

feasible commercial justification for it. If you could tell me what sort of orders you have in mind, Comrade Salah, I would be better able to assess the possibilities."

"Finding the commercial justification, as you call it, is your affair. I want the ship to sail from Latakia on or about July the second and to be on passage to Alexandria in the vicinity of the thirty-second parallel during the evening of the third before midnight. That is all."

"Carrying what cargo?"

"A normal cargo. The nature of it is immaterial. She will, however, be required to take on four passengers in Latakia. During the night of the third the course and speed of the ship will, for a short time, be those dictated by the passengers."

I shook my head. "You must know, Comrade Salah, that no ship's master is going to take orders about the course and speed of his ship from passengers."

"Not even if those orders are transmitted to him by the owners before sailing?"

I hesitated. "That would depend on the orders. No captain is going to hazard his ship or his crew, and on that coast no Agence Howell captain would take even the smallest risk. In particular, he would take the greatest care," I added meaningly, "not to enter territorial waters."

"He would not be required to enter territorial waters, nor to hazard his ship. The course would take him very slightly out of the normal shipping lanes for a period of two hours at reduced speed. Nothing more."

I thought for a moment about the captain of the *Euridice Howell*. He was a middle-aged Greek, a dignified, highly respectable man with a plump wife and seven children. Ashore as well as afloat he was a strict disciplinarian. The prospect of having to persuade this valued employee that Ghaled's orders about course and speed, however innocuous they might appear, were to be obeyed without question was not one that I cared to contemplate.

"Have you any special reason for using the *Euridice?*" I asked.

"Only that this is a normal passage for her to make and that she is known to make it regularly."

"We have other ships making it all the time. You said, Comrade Salah, that finding convincing commercial Justification for this sailing at this precise time and with passengers is my affair. I must tell you that with the *Euridice Howell* it would be difficult to find convincing justification. It is really a question of how discreet we have to be. If discretion does not matter …"

"Of course it matters. There must be absolute discretion."

"Then we should not use the *Euridice.*"

"What ship, then?"

"I would like time to think about that, Comrade Salah." In fact, I had already thought, but in terms of amenable captains rather than suitable ships. The captain I had in mind was a swashbuckling Tunisian who had been a prosperous hashish smuggler until business rivals had shot him up in his fast motorboat off the toe of Italy. After some time on the beach he had come to work for us. Touzani was an efficient captain, but although he had kept his nose clean with us, I suspected that he was still in touch with his former associates. He wouldn't question strange orders, I thought, whatever he might think of them privately; and he would keep his mouth shut.

"Very well," said Ghaled, "but do not say that you have not been given sufficient time to make the necessary arrangements. As soon as you have the name of the ship you will inform me."

"At once."

"It must be an iron ship, you understand, and no smaller than the *Euridice Howell.*"

"She would be of about the same tonnage."

"Progress reports on your various tasks should be made through Comrade Issa, who will also transmit further orders."

"Yes, Comrade Salah."

"Then you may go now."

We went. Teresa, tight-lipped, was obviously seething with

various suppressed emotions. I assumed that the predominant ones would be a sense of outrage and indignation directed against Ghaled. It wasn't until Ahmad and Musa had left us at the gate that I found that I had been mistaken. Her quarrel was with me.

"You think that he's insane, don't you?" she said abruptly. There was accusation in her voice.

The question disconcerted me. Until then I had thought of Ghaled as a violent and dangerous animal. It hadn't occurred to me to think about him in terms of sanity or insanity. I am not a psychiatrist.

I said as much.

"But you have been treating him as if he were insane, haven't you? Insane or stupid?"

"I certainly don't think he's stupid."

"Hearing you this evening one would never have guessed it."

"You mean I humoured him too obviously?"

"I mean that you humoured him one moment and challenged him the next. Worse, you pretended to be afraid of him and then demonstrated that you weren't."

"Well, I am, dammit! I *am* afraid of him."

"You concealed the fact too well. Now, he doesn't know what to make of you. Are you to be trusted or aren't you? That's what he's wondering. Your attitudes weren't consistent."

I sighed. "I'm not used to dealing with Ghaled. What would you have done?"

"Given in on all points. Created no obstacles. Agreed to everything."

"And then what?"

"Run. At least we can still do that. Get out as soon as we can."

"And hide from his killer squads?"

"He was bluffing. What could he do to us in Rome?"

"Our businesses are in the Arab countries, and he knows it. We're also foreigners and vulnerable. There's no bluff about that."

"Then liquidate the businesses, Michael. Sell the ships. Your family wouldn't care. You'd all still be rich."

I stared at her in amazement. She made a performance of shoving the key into the ignition, but wouldn't look at me.

"Liquidate because of Ghaled?" I demanded. "Are you serious?"

She paused before answering. "You've thought of it yourself," she said. "You know you have. And not just because of Ghaled and the PAF. You don't think the Agence Howell has a future in the Middle East. You think that it has had its day. I know, Michael. I know very well."

"Splendid! May I know how?"

"It's no good taking that tone with me, Michael. You must know that I, at least, am not stupid. What is all this business you are doing here but a process of liquidation? You won't admit it, but getting out is what you really want-on your own terms, of course, and in good order-but soon. The Howells have had a good run for their money, but for them there is no longer security of tenure in this part of the world. Your mother knows it, I am quite sure."

"Mama?" I laughed.

"Certainly. She as good as told me so once, before I became *persona non grata*. She must have told you. The best suites in five-star French hotels, plenty of bridge with good players, and remote control over the upbringing of her grandchildren-that's her plan for the future. Monaco in winter, Evian in Summer, a Rolls-Royce and chauffeur and her Lebanese personal maid. You know it's true, Michael."

"And you think I share my mother's tastes?"

"No," she said, "you'll always work. But not here. You don't often give yourself away, but you did this morning."

"I did?"

"That one place where we could go to ground quickly and be absolutely safe from the PAF."

"What about it?"

"It was Israel you were talking about, wasn't it?"

"It was. Naturally, that would only be a last resort."

"Naturally. The presence of Michael Howell in Israel, as soon as it was known about, would make the trading position of the Agence Howell extremely difficult. Liquidation would no longer be a matter of choice. It would become involuntary."

"I'm well aware of that. As I said, a last resort in an emergency situation."

"But you did consider it. Bad for business, yes, but not out of the question even so. You see, Michael?"

I wasn't prepared to listen to much more. "Do you want to run?" I demanded.

"Alone, you mean?"

I said nothing.

She persisted. "Alone, leaving you to explain my defection to Ghaled?"

"You can if you want to."

"That, Michael, is either unkind or silly."

"I'm tired. Let's go home."

"Very well."

It wasn't until we were reentering the city that she spoke again.

"What did Ghaled mean by the thirty-second parallel?" she asked.

I was thinking about metric thread tables and did not reply for a moment.

"Michael?" She started to repeat the question, when I answered her.

"Thirty-two degrees north is the approximate latitude of Tel Aviv," I said.

Chapter 5

Teresa Malandra

May 18 to June 10

The reason why Michael is so difficult to understand - especially for journalists - is that he is not one person but a committee of several. There is, for instance, the Greek money-changer with thin fingers moving unceasingly as he makes lightning calculations on an abacus; there is the brooding, sad-eyed Armenian bazaar trader who pretends to be slow-witted, but is, in fact, devious beyond belief; there is the stuffy, no-nonsense Englishman trained as an engineer; there is the affable, silk-suited young man of affairs with smile lines at the corners of wide, limpid, con man eyes; there is the mother-fixated managing director of the Agence Howell, defensive, sententious, and given to speechifying; and there is the one I particularly like, who . . . but why go on? The Michael Howell committee is in permanent session, and, though the task of implementing its business decisions is generally delegated to just one of the members, the voices of the others are usually to be heard whispering in the background. Ghaled certainly detected the faint sounds of those prompting voices, but to begin with he positively identified only the engineer. About that member of the committee, at least, his judgment was correct; the Englishman's professional pride borders on the obsessional.

In the days that followed that second meeting with Salah Ghaled there seemed to be no more enthusiastic and devoted adherent to the cause of the Palestinian Action Force than Comrade Michael. Within forty-eight hours the drawings and specifications of the fuse adapter ring had been completed and sent to the Beirut machine shop. A day later, after a telephone discussion, a price had been agreed and work on the sample ring put in hand. Meanwhile, the probable Howell shipping movements for the months of June and July had been analysed and a number of projections made. Then the possibilities of change and manipulation were explored.

It was like a mad chess problem.

On July 2 the M. V. *Amalia Howell* (4,000 tons, Captain Touzani) must sail, possibly though not necessarily in ballast, from Latakia bound for Alexandria. Problem: bring this sailing about in not more than three moves, none of which may be observed by your opponent (in this case your own shipping agents) or, if observed, not recognized as moves.

Michael thought about it on and off for days. In the end he found a solution requiring only two moves: first, the contrived, temporary withdrawal of the *Amalia's* Deratization Exemption Certificate (required under Article 17 of the International Sanitary Regulations) which would hold her idle in port for three or more days; second, a consequential rearrangement of Howell freighter sailings which would send the *Amalia*, when released, to Ancona to pick up a cargo for Latakia. His eyes gleamed with pleasure as he went over the mechanics of it with me.

"Tell Issa to pass the news on," he said finally. "No details, just the name of the ship. You can tell him, too, that the sample ring will be in our hands on Monday next. Ghaled will want to see it. Request orders. We want to appear to be cooperating one hundred percent."

"Why do you say 'appear' to be?"

"What do you mean?"

"Well we *are* cooperating, aren't we?"

He frowned impatiently. "What else do you suggest we do?"

"Is this adapter ring going to work?"

"Of course it's going to work." He was indignant for a moment, then he shrugged. "Oh, I see. You think it would be better if the ring didn't work."

"Don't you think so?"

"Aren't we out to sabotage this criminal operation of Ghaled's, you mean? Of course we are. But how can we sabotage it when we don't know exactly what he's planning?"

"We know some things."

"Bits of things. Not enough. Anyway, messing about with the adapter ring wouldn't do any good. I considered changing the flange dimensions slightly.

Maybe that would have made a difference, but how could I be certain? I don't know enough about ammunition to say. Anyway, he's not going to take it on trust. He's bound to try it out."

We were in the villa office and he tried to change the subject then by opening the *Urgent* file on his desk and starting to go through it. I had already dealt with the really urgent things there and wasn't going to be put off like that.

"Michael, I've been thinking," I said.

"Yes?" His tone was a clear intimation that he wasn't interested.

"About those confessions we signed."

That caught him. "What about them?"

"We're both supposed to have been in touch with the Israeli intelligence service."

"Standard incriminatory stuff. Mandatory death sentence."

"They gave the name of an Israeli agent in Cyprus."

"I know. Ze'ev Barlev."

"Well, why *don't* we get in touch with him? He must exist or they wouldn't have named him."

Michael sat back. I had his attention. "Oh yes, Barlev exists. He was based on Nicosia."

'Well, then."

"I said was. He hasn't been in Nicosia for six months. There was a little trouble. He was blown."

"He must have been replaced by now."

"I daresay."

"Famagusta could find out about the replacement."

"You make it sound very easy, but let's say, for the purposes of your argument, that they could find out. One of us gets in touch with him? Is that your idea?"

"We've already confessed to being in touch with Barlev. Why shouldn't we really be in touch with his successor?"

"Be hanged for a fact instead of a fantasy?" The con-man was wrinkling his eyes at me now, roguish and extremely tiresome.

"I was hoping to avoid hanging," I said tartly. "I assume you are, too. Among the other things I am hoping to avoid is any responsibility, direct or moral, for whatever atrocity this Ghaled is planning. You say we can't go to the authorities here. In the case of Colonel Shikla and the Internal Security Service, that I accept. We know now that Ghaled has ISS sympathizers. But there are others who would listen to us. Colonel Shikla has enemies who would be glad of a chance to embarrass him."

"And you think Shikla would not know that we were responsible? Of course he would know. And so would everyone else."

"Yes, it would be bad for business. Poor Agence Howell"

"That is unfair!" The managing director had suddenly emerged from the committee room. "We have been over all this a dozen times. It is not a matter of business but of our personal safety. Any action, official or unofficial, that we initiate here against Ghaled will result in action, direct action, against us. I am not talking about cargo fires and engine room explosions in company ships, but personal attacks."

"We could demand protection."

"Against Colonel Shikla when Ghaled has passed him our confessions and they are sitting on his desk? You know better than that, Teresa."

"Very well. So we have a choice. We either run away or we sabotage Ghaled without his knowing it. And since you say we mustn't run ..."

"I have already accepted the policy of sabotage, providing that it can be carried out without personal risk. What more do you want?"

"Some assurance that the sabotage is going to be effective."

"We're going to get that by sticking our necks out with Israeli intelligence? Is that what you believe?"

"Our necks are already sticking out."

"There is a certain difference, as I have been endeavouring to point out," he said coldly, "between the words in a false confession and the deeds you are proposing. Do you think I haven't already considered the possibility of contact with the Israelis? Of course I have."

"Well, then."

"This isn't the time." He eyed me sullenly for a moment and then his forefinger shot out, pointing at my nose. "All right, my girl, let's say you're going to meet an Israeli agent tonight. It's all been arranged cutouts, the safe house, everything. What are you going to tell him?"

"What we know."

"Which is what? That Ghaled is planning something against them? That'll be no news to him. That he's got arms of a sort, rockets perhaps? No news again."

"What about the night of July the third?"

"What about it? An anniversary day in Israel. Did you think I hadn't looked it up? Tammuz twenty in the Hebrew calendar. Anniversary of the death of Theodor Herzl, the founder of Zionism. From Ghaled's point of view a symbolic day on which to strike. Yes, indeed!"

"There's going to be a ship, the *Amalia*, off Tel Aviv that night with some of Ghaled's men aboard. We know that much."

"A neutral ship outside Israeli territorial waters? What are these men of Ghaled's going to do? Spit in the sea? But go on. You also know that five hundred electrically operated detonators are being manufactured in our battery works. How are they going to be used? Do you know? You do not. How do you think this good Israeli agent is going to respond to your tidings? I'll tell you. He's going to say, "Thank you very much, Miss Malandra, this is all very interesting and suggestive. Will you please now go back and discover what this alleged plan of Ghaled's really is? That is, Miss Malandra, if you really want to help us as you say you do.'" He threw up his hands. "You see? You don't yet know enough to be useful. Why then run the risk of making this dangerous contact? Why not wait until the information you have - if you can get it - makes the risk worth taking? Why take useless chances?"

I should have mentioned another member of the committee-the hectoring Grand Inquisitor.

There was nothing I could say, of course; he was right. However, I didn't have to reply because letting off steam like that had started him thinking again. He pushed the *Urgent* file away from him and watched a fly that was circling the office. After a time he opened the deep drawer in his desk and took out the aerosol insecticide spray he always kept there. He shook it absently.

"Pressure," he murmured. "We must apply pressure."

He took the cap off the spray, waited for the fly to come around again, and then gave it a short burst.

When he was sure that the fly was doomed he returned the spray to the drawer.

"I want to speak to Elie Abouti," he said.

That was one of the last things I had expected to hear. Abouti was the contractor who had built the electronics assembly plant. He was completely unscrupulous and had been clever enough to conceal the depths of his infamy until it was too late for us to take countermeasures. He had made a fantastic profit on the job, which, thanks to his ingenious use of substandard materials, had become a major maintenance problem almost before it had been completed. Michael had vowed vengeance to the most bloodcurdling terms. If he now wanted to talk to Abouti it could only be that the hour of vengeance was at hand. I was carious to see what form it would take, and wondered what connection it could have with the Ghaled situation.

When Abouti came on the line you would have thought that he and Michael were the best of friends. I could hear Abouti's high voice quacking happily as they exchanged compliments, and Michael was oozing camaraderie. I waited patiently for him to come to the point, but when he did I could hardly believe my ears.

"My dear friend," Michael said unctuously, "I am most happy to tell you that I see a chance, a good chance, of our being able to work together again."

The quacking at the other end became slightly guarded in tone. Small wonder. Although the vengeance had been vowed privately, Abouti could not have been unaware of Michael's feelings on the subject of the electronics plant buildings.

"I am delighted to hear it, my dear friend, delighted," Michael was saying, and then he chuckled.

"But this time, my dear Abouti, I hope you will not take it amiss if I ask that I may be allowed a little personal share in your profit."

The quacking immediately became more animated. A man who wants to share with you in an illegal profit to be made out of a government contract cannot be seriously ill-disposed toward you.

"Have you still got Rashti working for you?" Michael asked.

Rashti was Abouti's overseer and as big a crook, if that were possible, as Abouti himself. He, too, had been marked down for vengeance.

"Good. Can he be made available at short notice with a survey team? Possibly next week? I ask because we may have to act quickly to secure this business without competition. Best to move in and occupy the site. There is an Italian interest involved. Yes, it will be a Ministry development contract. The Der'a area. But the foreign interest will try to exercise control unless the door is firmly closed."

He had lost me by then. Obviously, Abouti was not going to go to the trouble and expense of a move onto government land without the usual written directive from the Ministry. I did not see how Michael could possibly get one for the car-battery project at that stage. The joint venture with the Italians had still to be approved.

The conversation ended with expressions of mutual respect and goodwill and undertakings on Michael's part to produce the directive within a day or two.

He hung up at last and smiled spitefully at the telephone. "Hooked and loving every minute of it," he said.

"How are you going to get the directive?"

"Somehow."

"From Hawa?"

"Who else?" He looked at me apologetically. "I'm sorry, Teresa. I'm afraid it means having him to dinner."

He knew that I disliked those evenings; he disliked them himself. Like many other educated Syrians, Dr. Hawa was ambivalent on the subject of female emancipation. In theory he approved; in practice it made him uneasy. Although Michael had been allowed to meet Dr. Hawa's wife briefly he had always known that an invitation to the villa that included her would not be accepted, so none had ever been issued. Though I naturally thought that my presence and status in the household was the stumbling block, Michael had always denied this. Hawa wasn't a prude, he said; it was just that he was an Arab and felt more at ease on social occasions in all-male company. He also liked to drink alcohol and in that sort of privacy could do so. Being Dr. Hawa, of course, he also liked the other guests to be of subordinate status so that he could dominate the proceedings. He was most relaxed, however, in solitary tête-à-tête with Michael, who would always respond to his genial bullying with the kind of subtle impudence that Hawa seemed to find entertaining. He was the king, Michael the licensed fool.

Sometimes on these occasions I used to do what the Muslim women did in their homes; that is, listen in an adjoining room through one of the decorated grilles which had been put there originally for that purpose; but the conversation was mostly so boring, or, especially when a lot of brandy had been drunk, infuriating, that generally I went off to bed and left them to it.

This time, though, I was determined not to miss a word.

It was on the evening of the day on which we had received Ghaled's approval of the fuse adapter ring sample, and the order had gone to the Beirut machine shop for a hundred more. It seemed to me that we had just made it possible for a hundred explosions to take place, and the thought was depressing. I desperately wanted Michael to succeed with Hawa. So far, all we had done was help Ghaled in his plan to kill a lot of people, and though our putting a survey team into the battery works wouldn't be likely to stop him, at least it might hinder and obstruct him. It would be *some*thing. Besides, as Michael says, you never know about pressure. Just a little of it can sometimes do a lot - not perhaps directly, but by slightly changing the value of some small unknown in the equation.

The declared purpose of these evenings *à deux* was backgammon, to be played by two well-matched and practiced opponents; but Dr. Hawa's real reason for coming to the villa was to pick Michael's brains and pump him for information. Someone once said that if you want to know what is going on in Damascus you must inquire in Beirut. In a funny way it's true, and not only of Damascus. Information is an especially valuable commodity in the Middle East, and Michael's sources were not confined to Beirut The Agence Howell had fingers in a great many pies and representatives doing business in a great many places. Naturally, along with the credit reports, the trend assessments, and the accounts of competitors' activities, came much news - and gossip and rumour - that was political as well as commercial in character. Sometimes Dr. Hawa would ask specific questions, but usually, as the dice clattered and the pieces clicked, he would hint vaguely at the area of current interest to him and leave Michael to do the talking.

It began like that on this evening. Dr. Hawa was curious about Iran and the latest proposals of a Soviet trade delegation. He scarcely spoke at all, giving only an occasional grant to indicate that Michael still had his attention.

From Teheran they switched to Ankara and from there to the newly independent Bahrein. It was at that point that Michael fell silent.

The next thing I heard was a short laugh from Dr. Hawa and an exclamation of disgust from Michael.

There was another laugh from Dr. Hawa. "I have never seen you make such a mistake as that before," he crowed. "Didn't you see your chance?"

"No, Minister, I didn't see it."

Michael still called Dr. Hawa "Minister," even in his own house; it was a thing that had always irritated me. He sounded now as penitent as a schoolboy caught out by a feared master.

"You were not concentrating."

"No, I was not. I am sorry."

"Do not apologize. The dice were kind to you and you ignored them. They do not like such impoliteness. Take care, Michael, or I shall go home rich."

"Yes, yes. A little more brandy, Minister?"

"Ah, you wish to dull my perceptions. Very well. But you had better drink no more."

"The truth is, Minister, that I am not myself this evening."

"That is evident. The digestion perhaps? The liver?"

"I am, I must confess, a little worried."

"You, worried?" A scoffing sound. "I have yet to see this. Unless, of course, there is a new woman. That must be it. You Christians make such fools of yourselves."

"Not a woman, Minister. But I refuse to bore you with my

troubles." Bravely this. "You are here to be amused, not to talk business."

"True. Then let us play. Let me see the score. Ah yes, this is very good. Now watch yourself, Michael. I am in an attacking mood."

They played in silence for a minute or two. Then Dr. Hawa said casually: "This business that worries you - does it concern any of our cooperatives?"

"Oh no." Michael spoke quickly and then seemed to hesitate. "That is, I am not sure."

There was the sound of a dice cup being slammed down onto the table, by Dr. Hawa presumably and in exasperation.

"It is not often, Michael, that I hear you talk foolishly."

"What I meant was that none of the existing cooperatives is concerned, Minister. What I fear is threatened is the battery transition plan."

"That is quibbling. What is the matter with you?"

"The battery transition plan is still only a plan, Minister." Michael sounded desperately unhappy; the Armenian bazaar trader was wringing his hands in anguish. "Paper, nothing more. There are no firm commitments, it is not yet a living thing. The child may be stillborn."

"The plans are already with the Minister of Finance. What is this nonsense?"

"Alas, Minister." He really said "alas."

"What are you talking about?"

"I did not want to tell you."

"Tell me what?" The game was forgotten. Dr. Hawa's voice had a rasp in it now.

"The news I have had from Beirut, Minister. We are being betrayed."

"How betrayed? By whom?"

"It is the Italian."

"Which Italian? One of those to Milan you call your friends?"

"No, no. This is the one in Beirut. Remember, Minister, I told you. These people in Milan have long been trying to sell to our markets here. Unsuccessfully, but they have tried. They have a selling agent to Beirut, a scorpion named Spadolini. Well, this Spadolini - his mother was a Romanian - this scorpion has learned all about our car-battery project. How has he learned? Who knows? A spy to the Milan offices perhaps. Possibly, as a concerned agent of the Italian company, he was given some advance hint. We cannot be certain. But certain it is that the scorpion is preparing to strike!"

"Strike? Speak plainly, Michael, for God's sake."

"Fearing to lose this little agency of his, fearing to be bypassed, recognizing the business potential of this Joint venture of ours, he has put forward the proposal that the new plant shall be located not here at Der'a, not here to Syria, but in Lebanon."

"But how can he succeed to this? The proposal from Milan was made to us."

The Armenian, his duty done, shuffled off with a heavy sigh, and the Greek money-changer strode in briskly to replace him.

"These are hard-faced men, Minister. A proposal commits them to nothing. Production is all they care about because production is money. This little schemer in Beirut has found something to offer them that we as yet cannot - factory space."

"We would build."

"This is already built. Near Tripoli. Six thousand two hundred square meters of floor space and of recent construction. It was planned for production lines of typewriters and business machines, but there were licensing difficulties with the American parent company and the plan fell through. The buildings have never been used and are going for a song. They are not ideal for lead-battery production and alterations would have to be made, but the floor space is there and waiting. In Milan they are already thinking, already tempted."

"You know this for a fact?"

They are sending a senior manager and an engineer from Milan this week to inspect the place. I know because I have good friends in

Milan. But friendship will not override self-interest. We must show them that we have more to offer than this Spadolini and that we can move faster."

"But how?"

"That is what concerns me. We have good arguments on our side, but nothing to back them up. When their representatives arrive here and we sit down at the negotiating table they will have questions to ask. Among the first will be-when do we start to get a return on our investment, when can production begin? And, as we try to answer, we will know that in their minds there is the vision of six thousand two hundred square meters of factory floor space, unused and waiting for them, in Lebanon."

"You said that there would have to be alterations."

"Minor changes, Minister. Nothing. If we had work already in progress to show them it might be different. But..." He left it.

"What sort of work in progress?"

"Something to impress. Land allocated and surveyed. Bulldozers already clearing and grading. Plans on the drawing board. Evidence that we are serious."

"You know that is impossible, Michael."

"With respect, Minister, difficult but not impossible."

"You Know that I cannot authorize funds for speculative use. Finance would never approve this expenditure. Once the joint venture is approved, of course . . ."

"Of course. But by then it could be too late."

There was a silence. One of them rattled dice and again there was silence.

Dr. Hawa broke it finally. "I think that you have something to propose, Michael. What is it?"

"Agence Howell could finance this preliminary work."

"How would you get your money back? This cannot be a pilot project. You made that clear from the start. Do not tell me that you have become altruistic, Michael, for I shall not believe you."

"I want this venture to succeed, Minister, and to succeed here, because I want the agency for its products. I am prepared to pay to secure that agency. Call it an insurance premium if you will. There is nothing altruistic about that."

Short laugh. "I am much relieved. I would not like, after so long, to have to revise my ideas about you, Michael."

"Never fear, Minister."

Then what you want from me is a directive, eh?"

"Yes, please. It should cover our occupation of three hectares of land adjoining the present battery works. The precise details of this parcel of land are set out in the supplementary memorandum I have already submitted. The directive should further authorize the Abouti Company to make a survey and carry out the preparatory work necessary for building, including the cutting of a new access road. In accordance with Agence Howell instructions of course."

"And at Agence Howell's expense?"

"Certainly. I cannot tell you, Minister, how much I would appreciate your help in this."

"Help in spending your money?"

"In removing the source of anxiety." The Armenian returned briefly to take a bow. "Minister, if this Lebanese scorpion, having injected his vile poison, had stolen this business away while I slept, I would never have been able to sleep again."

Dr. Hawa burst out laughing.

"Minister?"

"You and your business ethic, Michael! You cannot bear to lose, can you? Winning is all that matters, not just money. After all these years I can read you like a book."

"So easily, Minister? I must mend my ways." I could imagine him pretending to smile away a nonexistent discomfort.

"You never will, Michael. You can't." He chuckled. "Well, I will look at the papers again and think about it. Come and see me tomorrow. You may bring a draft directive if that will make you sleep better tonight."

"Thank you again, Minister. More brandy?"

After a moment or two the dice began to rattle again and the backgammon pieces to click.

When Dr. Hawa bad gone, Michael poured me a brandy and looked at the one he had been nursing himself.

"Well, so far so good," he said.

"This empty factory near Tripoli," I asked, "does it exist?"

"Oh yes. A white elephant. We were offered it six months ago. When the price is low enough we may buy it for a warehouse."

"And this man Spadolini? Does *he* exist?"

"Of course. He has the present agency. Hard worker. Not a bad salesman. If this car-battery business had been going forward with our participation I would have taken him into the Beirut office."

"*If* it had been going forward? Isn't it?"

He ignored the question. "Abouti will need copies of the factory layout and the specifications that I brought back from Milan. The land details, too. He should have it all in the morning."

"Are we really going to pay him for this work?"

"Pay Abouti?" He finished his brandy. "Not a penny. Let the fat thief whistle for his money."

It is almost unheard of for Michael to refuse to pay a debt, even when he believes that the creditor has cheated him. And there had been that "if." I knew then that he had at last decided to cut his losses, and that, in Syria anyway, the days of the Agence Howell were numbered.

Later that week the survey team moved into the dry-battery works and the land adjoining it.

"What do you think Ghaled will do?" I had asked.

"Nothing at first A few men with theodolites, rods, and measuring chains won't disturb him much. Wait until the earth-moving starts, though. Then it'll be different. Heavy machinery all over the place and men to stand guard on it at night! That'll soon cramp his style."

But Michael was wrong. The pressure began to work immediately and, while it did not change any of the factors in the equation, it was the means of converting one of the unknown ones into a known.

Michael spent most of that day out at the tile and furniture plants. He did not tell me what he was doing, but I could guess. With the end of the Agence Howell's Syrian operations just around the corner the more goods he could ship out before the corner was reached the smaller the final write-off would be.

The call from Issa came at four thirty in the afternoon. Issa seemed to be Ghaled's local chief of staff now as well as works manager, and his tone was peremptory.

"Where is Howell?"

"I don't know, but I expect him back soon. I can ask him to return your call."

"No. Give him this message. You will both report here tonight at eight o'clock."

"Mr. Howell may have made other arrangements."

"Then he will cancel them. You both report here at eight o'clock. That is an order."

Michael was thoughtful when I told him.

"You read the directive carefully, Teresa. There was nothing in it about the Agence Howell paying Abouti, was there?"

"Not directly. His costs are to be charged to Green Circle. There's no way of Issa's knowing that isn't the government. No way of Abouti knowing, either. Anyway they would assume it was a government expenditure because of the directive. So would Ghaled."

"Well, perhaps it isn't that he wants to see us about."

But it was.

We were received by Ghaled in Michael's office and he had a copy of the Ministry directive in front of him. We were not asked to sit down.

Ghaled waved the papers under Michael's nose. "What do you know of this?" he demanded angrily.

"Of what, Comrade Salah? May I see?"

Ghaled threw the papers at him. Michael retrieved them from the floor and studied them solemnly.

After a moment or two he made a clucking sound.

"Well?"

"I did warn of this possibility, Comrade Salah."

"And you were at the same time warned to prevent it. Why did you not obey?"

"Even if I had known that this directive was about to be issued, which I did not, there are limits to my powers, Comrade Salah."

"Limits that you determine."

"I cannot give orders to the Ministry."

"You do not have to. The Minister listens to your advice and requests, doesn't he? Answer me. Doesn't he?"

"When he has asked me for advice, yes, he listens. About this directive he did not consult me." Michael peered at it again, his lips moving as if he were having trouble in understanding the words. "It orders a survey to be made of this and the adjacent land in accordance with an earlier policy decision. Your orders, Comrade Salah, were that your headquarters here were not to be disturbed. I cannot believe that a few more men working here during the daytime will disturb you." As he spoke he turned the page and then gave a theatrical start of surprise. "Ah yes. I see the difficulty."

"You do, eh?"

"An access road is to be engineered."

"That is part of the work ordered, yes. What else do you see, Comrade Michael? If you are having trouble reading it, I can tell you. The contractor is empowered to erect temporary buildings for fuel dumps and other purposes, and night-shift work is authorized. The contractor is to work in cooperation with the Der'a police, who will furnish special patrols."

"This is very bad, Comrade Salah." Michael looked genuinely shocked.

"It *would* be bad," said Ghaled, "if any of this work were to be done. Your task is to see that it is not done, or, if it must be done, that the start of it is delayed until the end of June. There must be no inconvenience. You hear me?"

"Yes, Comrade Salah, I hear you."

If he had left it at that the next half hour might have been less frightening, but Michael could not leave it at that. Having gone to considerable trouble and at least some expense to create a *force majeure* that should have driven any sane leader in Ghaled's position onto the defensive, he was affronted by Ghaled's cool dismissal of the threat as no more than an avoidable inconvenience. For once a committee spokesman lost his temper, and none of the rest of the members was quick enough to cover up for him.

"Unfortunately," he went on nastily, "although I hear, I am not omnipotent, Comrade Salah. Any more than you are. The ability to hear an unrealistic order is no indication that the hearer is capable of carrying it out. I will do what I reasonably can without exciting suspicion. No less, but certainly no more."

It was a pity that Issa had come into the room while Michael was speaking, to be a witness of this act of insubordination. Even if he had wanted to do so, Ghaled could not have ignored it with Issa there. As it was, Issa gaped, started to say something, then stopped and waited for permission to speak.

He did not get it. Ghaled was staring hard and curiously at Michael, reassessing him. The reassessment made, he looked at me.

"Do you remember the oath you swore?" he asked.

"Of course, Comrade Salah."

"Do you believe that your employer remembers? Be careful how you answer. Your loyalty here is to me, not to him."

"Comrade Michael has certainly remembered his oath," I said. "He has done everything he can to carry out his assigned tasks. In fact, he has seriously neglected his own business in order to do so."

I knew that Michael was looking at me balefully, but I kept my eyes on Ghaled.

"When did your employer last see Dr. Hawa?"

I was afraid to lie. It was always possible that Ghaled already knew the answer. "A few days ago, in the evening."

Ghaled looked at Michael again. "And he told you nothing of this directive about which you profess to be so surprised?"

"Our meeting was a social one." Michael shrugged. "We played backgammon, as a matter of fact. No business was discussed. In any case the issuance of this directive would not have been a subject for discussion. As I said when I first raised the question, the policy decision about this works had already been made."

"The policy decision which you had been ordered to reverse or modify?"

"The decision which I had hoped to be able to modify. These things cannot be done by edict, not my edict anyway. It is easier to make policy decisions than to reverse or modify them. One needs time. I thought I had time. Obviously I hadn't enough." The committee had recovered its composure and was all lined up again behind the managing director. "As for my surprise, I have no reason to profess it. I *am* surprised. The explanation, presumably, is that, since the Agence Howell is not a principal in this affair, it was not thought necessary or appropriate to consult us before issuing the directive."

Ghaled thought for a moment, then nodded. "Very well Pending my own inquiries, I will accept your explanation, your excuse for your failure. But" - he leaned forward - "for your disrespect there can be no excuse."

"No disrespect was intended, Comrade Salah. I was merely stating the situation as I saw it."

"So you say now. I warned you before against your arrogance. I also warned you that it would be punished. Did I or didn't I?"

"You did."

"Then having ignored my warnings you must be punished. Who are you to question orders, to decide whether or not they are realistic? We must teach you humility, Comrade Michael, the meaning of discipline. The punishment, therefore, must be one that you will remember. Do you find that reasonable and realistic?"

Michael was looking blandly impassive. I tried to, but less successfully.

"*Do* you?" Ghaled persisted.

"That depends on the punishment, Comrade Salah."

"Yes. Since you have other assigned tasks to complete, an Action Force punishment, the kind that comrades Ahmad and Musa are used to inflicting for lapses in discipline, would - what is the phrase?"

"Defeat their own object, Comrade Salah?"

"Yes." Ghaled smiled unpleasantly. "So you must not be hurt *too* much, comrade. Perhaps not at all if you are lucky. We shall have to see." He looked at Issa, who had been listening avidly. "Are you ready for the demonstration?"

"Yes, Comrade Salah. All is prepared."

"Let us go then."

Ghaled rose and led the way from Michael's office, along the passages to the zinc storeroom.

Waiting there was a man I had not seen before. Though neither he nor Michael said anything by way of greeting I saw an exchange of glances which said that they knew one another.

Ghaled addressed him as Comrade Taleb. He was in his thirties, tall and thin with a Nasser moustache and a very clean drip-dry shirt. He wore a tie. When he smiled, showing his teeth, two gold inlays were visible. He was standing behind Ghaled's trestle table, which had been moved to the centre of the room.

My mind had been running sickeningly on instruments of torture, so that the two objects I saw standing on the table in front of Taleb were, though surprising, also reassuring.

The most prominent was a big clockwork music box of a kind that I had not seen since I was a small child. There had been one like it on a side table in my grandmother's house in Rome. That one had played four or five different melodies from the operas - arias. This was slightly smaller than the one I remembered and fitted into a battered, black leather carrying case with a purple plush lining; but the box itself was much the same, an oblong casket made of highly polished mahogany with a narrow glass window in the top. Through the window you could see the big metal cylinder with the tiny pins bristling all over it and the long steel comb which sounded the notes. There were levers in front and, at the end, a brass key for winding the clockwork. A worn gold-leaf inscription just visible on the front panel said that this was *La Serinette* made by Gerard Frères of Paris and that the Tonotechnique Design was protected by patents.

Beside *La Serinette* on the table stood, incongruously, a Pakistan International Airlines plastic flight bag.

Ghaled looked with amused interest at the music box.

"Does it still play?" he asked.

"Certainly it plays, Comrade Salah." Taleb was obviously proud of his work, whatever that was. He touched one of the levers, the cylinder revolved, and the box began to play Mozart's Minuet in G. After two bars he switched it off.

"We must conserve the spring," he said.

"Of course. Then let us proceed with the demonstration."

"Yes, Comrade Salah."

Taleb reached inside the back flap of the carrying case and pulled something out of the plush lining. It was a narrow strip of metal rather like a steel tape measure and about twenty centimetres long. He left it sticking up in the air above the box. Obviously it was not part of the original *Serinette*.

"That is all?"

"That is all, except for the controls, Comrade Salah. The new ones are on what was the musical change lever here. The first stop now deactivates the speed regulator. The second stop allows the cylinder to revolve freely. The third stop engages the clutch which . . ."

Ghaled broke in. "Yes, comrade, we know what the third stop should do. That is what we are to test. Now, Comrade Taleb, I think that this test demonstration would be more convincing if the target were to be moving. Do you not agree?"

""Moving or stationary, it makes no difference, Comrade Salah."

"For me," Ghaled said firmly, "a moving target would provide a much more satisfactory test. And since Comrade Michael has volunteered to assist us ... That is correct, Comrade Michael, isn't it? You have volunteered?"

"If you say so, Comrade Salah."

"I say so."

"Then I'm glad to be of assistance."

Michael spoke easily and his apparent calmness clearly irritated Ghaled.

"Let us hope you will continue to be glad," he snapped and pointed to the airline bag on the table. Pick that up."

Michael reached out for the bag and his hand was about to touch it when Ghaled spoke again.

"Carefully, comrade. It is not heavy, but handle it as iff it were."

Taleb started to make a protest. "Comrade Salah, we do not know exactly - "

"No, we do not know exactly," said Ghaled quickly. "That is why we are making the test."

"It really is not necessary for the target to move."

"That is for me to decide." He turned to Michael, who now had the bag in his hand. "Comrade, you will walk out of here slowly. When you are outside walk in the direction of number one work shed and go past it to the boundary wall. We will follow you as far as the outer door. When you reach the wall, turn and start to walk back toward us, slowly so that we can keep you in sight all the time. You understand?"

"I understand."

"Then go. Issa, you follow him with your light so that we do not lose sight of him in the shadows. Don't get too close. Taleb, I will give you the word."

"Yes, Comrade Salah."

My heart was thumping and the sweat on my face was ice-cold. I followed them out to the door.

The guards, Ahmad and Musa, had come to see what was going on. Ghaled told them to stand to one side. From the passage just behind Ghaled I could see Michael walking away across the yard with the bag and Issa stalking him with the flashlight. They might have been playing some sort of child's game.

As he reached the corner of number one work shed Michael stumbled on an uneven patch of ground and Ghaled shouted to him to be more careful. Michael was about a hundred meters away now and nearing the perimeter wall. When he began to turn Ghaled spoke to Taleb in the storage room behind us.

"Get ready."

"Ready, comrade."

"All right *Now!*"

From the storage room came three notes of the Minuet in G, then that sound was cut off and a whirring noise took its place, a noise that suddenly began rising in pitch to a whine.

Almost at the same moment there was a flash of light across the yard - it seemed to come from Michael's right hand - and a muffled bang. Then the flight bag burst into flames and Michael flung it away from him.

He was obviously hurt because he was doing something to his right wrist with his left hand, tearing a scorched shirt sleeve away from the skin I know now, but that did not stop him satisfying his curiosity. The bag, still burning, had landed near the wall and Michael immediately went over to look at it.

He and Issa reached the bag at almost the same moment. Ghaled called to Taleb an order to switch off and went to join them. The whole incident had taken only a few seconds, but I noticed that, even before Ghaled's order to switch off, the pitch of the whining noise had begun to fall.

Taleb came out of the storeroom.

"You saw it work?" he asked.

"I saw it. The bag caught fire."

He looked across the yard. Issa was stamping out the remaining flames. Ghaled was carefully examining Michael's wrist

"It was stupid of Mr. Howell to carry it," said Taleb.

"You'd better tell Comrade Salah that. It was entirely his idea."

"Oh." He waited no longer and went out to receive the congratulations and words of praise which were no doubt due to him. From Issa they were effusive, but Ghaled's were more perfunctory. By then he was more concerned with Michael. Ghaled had for a moment become Sir Galahad, solicitously shepherding a stricken opponent from the field of honour. With me the reaction had set in, and, though I was hating Ghaled totally, I did not find Michael's brave smile particularly endearing. I made no attempt to return it as they approached.

"Is it bad?" I asked.

"No. Just a bit of a burn."

"All burns are bad," said Ghaled severely. "They easily become infected. This must be treated at once."

You would have thought that I had proposed not treating it at all.

In the storeroom Ghaled ordered Michael to sit down and produced an elaborate first-aid kit. He then proceeded to cut away the scorched shirt sleeve with scissors.

The burn area extended about halfway up the forearm. There was reddening, but it did not look serious to me.

"First degree only," remarked Ghaled as he examined the arm. "But painful no doubt."

"Not as bad as it was at first."

"It must still be treated with care. I did not realize that plastics were so flammable."

"A lot of substances are if you raise the temperature high enough."

"Well, I did not realize."

It was nearly an apology. He busied himself now with pouring water from a jerry can into an enamel washbasin and stirring into it a white powder from the first-aid kit. When it had dissolved he began very gently to swab the bum with the solution.

"Did you know that I was trained as a doctor?" he asked chattily as he worked.

"No, Comrade Salah."

"Yes, in Cairo. I have practiced as a doctor, too, in my time. And on worse wounds than this, I can tell you."

"I'm sure of that."

Taleb came in with Issa and stood watching. Ghaled took no notice of them until he had finished cleaning up the arm. Then he looked at Taleb and nodded toward *La Serinette*.

"Your masterpiece can be put away now. Comrade Issa knows where it is to be stored. It will be safe there until we conduct the long-range tests."

"Yes, Comrade Salah."

The music box was secured in its carrying case and taken away. I saw Michael watching the securing process out of the corner of his eye.

Ghaled had been rummaging in the first-aid box. "The treatment of burns," he said briskly as he turned again to Michael, "has changed much in recent years. The old remedies, such as tannic acid and gentian violet, are no longer used. In this case penicillin ointment will be the answer." He looked at me. "Have you an analgesic at home? Codeine, for example?"

"I believe so."

"Then he may take that. But no alcohol tonight. A warm drink, tea would be suitable, and a barbiturate for sleep. That and the codeine."

"Very well."

I watched while he applied the ointment and then strapped on a gauze dressing. It was done neatly and without fuss. I could believe that he had once been trained.

"There," he said finally. "Is that better?"

"Much, thank you." Michael dutifully admired the dressing. "What was to the bag, Comrade Salah?" he asked.

"Haven't you guessed?"

"Some of Issa's detonators presumably."

"Of course. With two kilos of high explosive for the detonators to work upon we would have shaken a few windows in Der'a."

"So I imagine. But what fired the detonators? I heard nothing before they went off."

Ghaled looked pleased. "No, you would hear nothing. It all worked well, didn't it?" He considered the arm again. "It should feel easier tomorrow. If it does not, let Issa know. It may be necessary for me to put on a fresh dressing."

"I'm sure it will be all right."

"Well, if it is not, you know how to communicate with me." He paused, and then a strange expression appeared on his lips. It was very like a simper. "I, too, like to play backgammon, Comrade Michael."

For a moment I could not believe my ears. He was actually asking for an invitation to the villa.

Michael managed to conceal his surprise by beaming fatuously. "I am delighted to hear that, Comrade Salah."

"And perhaps better than Dr. Hawa. Does he win or do you?"

"I am more lucky than skillful."

"You would not rely upon luck, I think. Are you a cautious player?"

"Almost never."

"Good. There is no sport in cautious play. We shall have a good contest. But that is for another day. Now you must go to bed and rest. You have work to do tomorrow."

"Yes, indeed, on the directive, Comrade Salah." Michael held up his bandaged arm and again looked at it admiringly. "No hospital could have done better. I am deeply grateful."

Another simper. "We look after our own, Comrade Michael."

They were both sickening.

In the car I said: "So much four pressure."

"What do you mean?" Michael sounded surprised.

"All you get is a burned arm."

"Nonsense. But for the directive we would not have been there tonight. We would certainly not have witnessed that demonstration. As it is, we at last know what sort of thing it is that we are up against."

I was too disgusted to argue.

As soon as we got home Michael, in defiance of "doctor's" orders, poured himself a large brandy. Then, instead of going to bed, he told me to get my book and take notes.

"The weapon that Ghaled intends to use against the Israelis," he dictated, "is an explosive package consisting of two kilos of high explosive, detonated electrically by a system of remote radio control. The quantity of detonators available to him is in the hundreds. Allowing for wastage, misfires, and the use of two detonators for each package, we must still assume that a large number, fifty or more, of these charges will be placed. It also seems likely that the intention is to explode them simultaneously."

"How?"

He was thoughtful for a moment, then shrugged. "I don't know much about electronics."

That was true. It was the main reason for his dislike of the electronic assembly plant. Though it did not make much of a profit it did not lose money. When he hated about it was not knowing exactly how everything they made there worked. Worse, when he asked for explanations, they would usually be given in technical language that he only half understood; and, although he was good at framing his questions in a way that made them sound as if he knew what he was talking about, all he could do with most of the answers was to nod sagely and pretend to be satisfied.

"Who is this Taleb?" I asked.

"The foreman in charge of the Magisch stuff for the army and air force. We knew that Ghaled had an electronics man somewhere in the background. I thought it might be our Iraqi, but Taleb was always a possibility. They're both German-trained. Tell me what happened after I left with the flight bag. What did they do with that music box?"

I told him.

"You say that the bag exploded almost as soon as the noise started?"

"Yes, but the sound went much higher afterwards." I gave him an imitation of the whine I had heard.

"I see. Well, I may not know much about electronics, but we can be pretty sure about what's been built into that old box of tricks."

"Can we?"

"Isn't it obvious? First, a high-frequency oscillator with tape antenna. Second, a small generator which can be driven at high speed and full power for a few seconds. That's done by suddenly disconnecting the ordinary speed governor and bypassing the main gear train. A little dog-clutch would do it. Those things have hefty springs in them. Let one go all out for a moment or two and the torque would be terrific. And a moment or two is all you need. Just long enough for the oscillator signal to trip the relays."

"The what?"

"Electronic relays wired to the detonators. There was a relay in that flight bag. I saw the remains of it afterwards. It looks like the inside of a small pocket transistor radio - or a burned-up Magisch unit component. I expect we'll find when we go into it that there are some shortages in that department. Of course, they may not be down as relays on the stock sheets. Taleb may have had to adapt or modify something else to make it work as a relay, but that's what they would need - a small, simple device that responds to a radio signal by closing a firing circuit."

"I see." I did see, dimly.

"Now put this down. Range of system is unknown, but there are some suggestive pointers. Demonstration range was only one hundred meters or so. On the other hand the relay was tripped several seconds before full transmitting power was achieved. What is more, there was a thick concrete wall between the transmitter and the relay. Effective range at full power, with some line-of-sight assistance - e.g. the transmitter operating from a ship at sea to activate relays ashore is probably to be measured in kilometres. Got that?"

"Yes."

"We'll check the electronic plant stock sheets in the morning for shortages. Then I'll want a sample or samples of whatever components they're short of. Taleb mustn't know, of course."

"Anything else?"

"Not for the moment. Don't make any copies of those notes, just the top. I'll be adding to them, I expect"

"All right Michael, about the directive..."

"Yes, we shall have to think about that But not now, my dear. Now, I think, I really will go to bed."

"Shall I get you some codeine?"

"Is that the stuff the dentist gave me that time?"

"Yes."

"It made me feel sick. Aspirin will do."

When we were in bed I asked a final question.

"Michael, what are those notes for, and why do you want samples of this component?"

I hoped I knew the answer, but he did not give it for a moment Instead, he turned over so that he could rest his bandaged arm outside the sheet.

Then he said slowly: "I think we know enough to make sense now. I think it's time we stuck our necks out."

Chapter 6

Michael Howell

June 14 to 29

Three days later I went to Cyprus; first to Famagusta and then to Nicosia. It was then mid-June.

I was a fool. I admit it By going at that moment I was making the very mistake that I had warned Teresa against: I was jumping the gun. I thought that by then I knew enough, and I didn't I should have waited.

I offer no excuses. The trouble was that, in working to put pressure on Ghaled so as to make *him* do stupid things, I had made insufficient allowance for the pressure that the situation was exerting on me. I don't mean things like Ghaled's sadistic little game with the flight bag - though I daresay that helped to distort my judgment - but the psychological pressures. It was easy enough for Teresa to talk of liquidation, but a family business like the Agence Howell isn't a street-corner shop. You can't just sell off the stock, put up the shutters, and walk away - even if you want to, even if you don't mind tossing a three-generation going concern into the gutter, even if you'll accept a nil valuation on the goodwill and can ignore the gloating of your competitors as they hasten to get their sticky hands on the pieces. What is being "liquidated" is an organism, an organism of which you are a part and which is as much a part of you as your stomach and intestines.

I am not going to describe here how I got in touch with Israeli intelligence in Cyprus; I am still hoping that the Israelis will be gracious enough to acknowledge publicly that I did so. The personal risks that Teresa and I ran in order to warn those people of an impending terrorist attack were considerable, and we cooperated with them in every way we could in order to avert a catastrophe. I don't see why they should be so close-mouthed about it. I am not asking for gratitude; I never expected to be clapped on the back and given a public vote of thanks in the Knesset; I do not ask them to commend me. But a nod, even a very cool and distant nod of recognition would be a help. It would relieve me of at least some of the "Green Circle Incident" odium which now clings to me, and from which both Teresa and I have to suffer.

As I say, I still hope.

It is for that reason, too, then, that I am not giving a description of Ze'ev Barlev's successor which would permit him to be identified and so "blown." I will say only that he lacked charm, that his manner toward me was patronizing, when not offensive, and that the whole experience was thoroughly disagreeable.

My meeting with the successor - I may as well call him Barlev - took place in a house near Nicosia. We spoke in English; he had a "regional" British accent. All he offered me in the way of refreshment was a revolting bottled orangeade.

I began by explaining who and what I was, but he cut me short. He already knew all he needed to know about me, he said. What had I to tell him that I thought he didn't know and should?

I started with my discovery of Issa's private work in the laboratory, which seemed to amuse him, and went on to the appearance on the scene of Ghaled. That, I was glad to see, he found less funny. Ghaled had killed a lot of his people over the years and was taken seriously. The details of Teresa's and my recruitment intrigued him and he wanted the exact wording of the oath we had sworn. When I told him about the bogus confessions we had been forced to sign, he nodded.

"Yes, I'd heard they were doing that. Awkward for you."

Awkward, I thought, was an understatement, but I didn't pursue the matter. He wasn't really interested in Teresa and me as persons, only in what I knew. So I went on to tell him about the fuse adapter rings. He stopped me again.

"Hold it" We were sitting at a desk and he pushed a note pad across to me. "How about drawing that gaine you saw?"

"All right"

I made a rough sketch. When I started to put in the approximate dimensions, he stopped me again.

That'll do, Mr. Howell. We know all about those things."

"What is it?"

"You guessed right. It's from a rocket. The hundred and twenty millimetre Katyusha. Has a fifty-kilogram warhead and a maximum range of around eleven kilometres. Quite a lot of the terrorist gangs have them. Good for hit-and-run work. They attacked a hospital with one a few weeks back. A single round killed ten people. The launcher is a simple affair, easy to make with angle iron. They don't mind leaving it behind them when they run."

"Where do they come from?"

"Is that a serious question? Oh, I see what you mean - how does Ghaled get them? Well, he could have brought a few with him from Jordan. More likely the Algerians let him have them. Those Chinese fuses were probably smuggled in by the Turkish liberation underground. Or maybe - " He broke off. "I thought you were here to tell me something I didn't know."

"I was just curious."

"Well let's get on. There's nothing in this for us so far. I'd be surprised if Ghaled didn't have a few Katyushas."

So then I told him about the ship thing and about the remote-control radio detonators. I described the test firing and gave him the notes I had made on it.

He read the notes carefully enough; in fact, he read them twice, but of course he pretended to be unimpressed.

"This doesn't tell us much, does it? Did you get a sample of this electronic component, this part you think may have been used?"

"Yes, I did." I got it out of my briefcase. It looked more like a bar of toffee than an electronic component - very hard toffee with red, yellow, and green nuts embedded in it. Metal connector tags stuck out from one end.

He put it on the desk in front of him and peered at it "Does it have a name?"

"No, just a part number. It's stamped on the end - U seventeen."

"U for *Ubertragen,* do you think?"

"I don't know."

"Didn't you find out exactly what it was?"

The person to ask would have been Taleb. That didn't seem a good idea."

"Pity. Nothing was said about the radio frequency they're using?"

"Nothing that we heard. I assumed that your people could find out by examining that thing."

"It's possible."

"Well, there you are. All you have to do then is jam their transmission."

"Do what?"

"Jam their transmission."

"And detonate all their bombs for them? Are you kidding?"

"I'm not am expert. But surely with that knowledge you can do something."

He regarded me pityingly. "Look, Mr. Howell, unless this thing is operated by a coded signal - that is, a combination of signals acting like the wards of a lock which won't turn unless you use the right key - any jamming on the frequency it responds to is going to have the same effect as that music box gadget you saw. This relay, or

165

whatever it is, doesn't look complex enough to me for the kind of circuitry you need for an elaborate coded arrangement. As you call it in your notes, a small, simple device. Why, it could be set off accidentally."

"Accidentally?"

For a moment he did not reply. He was gazing into the middle distance, rather as if he had lost the thread of his argument. Then he seemed to recover it.

"I'll give you an example. A few months ago in Tel Aviv they had trouble with a new apartment building. The architect was an American and he had installed one of those fancy remote-control openers on the garage door. Each of the tenants was given a little thing with a press-button on it to keep in the glove compartment of his car. Press the button and the door opened, press again and it closed. Everything was fine except that the door would open and close sometimes when nobody pressed a button. In the end the door did its closing act while a tenant was actually driving in and the roof of his car got crushed. They had to do something then. It took time, but they solved the mystery eventually. There's a hospital two blocks away. One piece of apparatus in the physiotherapy department was sending out a radio signal every time it was used. Not a very strong signal, but it was on the same frequency as the door opener and just strong enough to do the trick. See what I mean?"

"Yes, but

"Let's go back to this ship business."

It was a very abrupt change of subject, and I didn't understand the reason for it until very much later. At the time I made no attempt to resist the change.

"What about the ship?"

"Tell me again what was said."

I told him.

"These four passengers - I take it that Ghaled will be one of them - are to be allowed to give orders about the ship's course and speed. I've got it right?"

"That's right."

He frowned. "Why speed? Why course *and* speed? See what I'm getting at? If all this speculation of yours is correct - and it is only speculation - someone, let's say Ghaled, wants to be a few kilometres offshore in the Tel Aviv area on the night of the third. There he's going to press the button on the music box and set off some bombs planted ashore. That's your idea, isn't it?"

"Yes."

"Well, a simple change of course would bring him into a position to do his button-pressing. He doesn't really have to nominate the course for that matter. All he has to do is ask what time the ship will be passing Tel Aviv and ask the captain to go in a bit closer so that he can see the pretty lights."

"He'd have to be sure that he was within range."

"All right, I'll accept that. But it still doesn't explain why speed matters."

"Timing? The Herzl anniversary?"

"He stipulated the evening of the third before midnight, according to you."

"Yes."

"What other timing is involved? The charges to be exploded - certainly if there are to be as many as you think - will have to have been placed much earlier. You've no idea where he plans to have them placed, of course?"

"No."

He sipped his orangeade. "It's all very scrappy," he complained. "Nothing solid."

I pointed to the Magisch component "At least that's solid."

"It may tell us something, it may not. The question is now, what are *you* going to do?"

"Me? I'm here talking to you, aren't I? I've done all I intend to do. It's up to you now."

"To stop Ghaled playing with that music box and pressing buttons? How do you suggest we do that, Mr. Howell? The *Amalia*

Howell is your ship, not ours."

You would have thought that he was doing the favours, not the other way around. The nerve of it took my breath away.

"You're not suggesting that I stop the ship sailing, I hope. Because iff so..."

"Perish the thought, Mr. Howell You'd be in trouble with Ghaled then, wouldn't you? Miss Malandra, too, I shouldn't wonder. He'd twist your arms right off, and that would never do. No, I'm not for a moment suggesting that you actually run any risks in defence of your high moral principles."

The sarcasm came with a tight little smile. He was a good hater that one.

"Just talking to you is for me a risk," I retorted. "If your people can't work out am effective counter to this relay device, if that means that Ghaled's going to have to be stopped physically from pressing the button, you'll have to do the stopping. I'll cooperate passively, if I can reasonably do so, but that's the limit."

"What do you mean by cooperate passively?" He made it sound like cyanide of potassium.

The *Amalia is* going to be in Ancona until Friday of nest week, when she sails for Latakia. I could arrange to take on a man of yours, a trained agent I mean, as an extra crewman."

"One man against Ghaled with an armed bodyguard? What use would one man be in that situation?"

"Send two then, do-or-die boys."

"Armed with what? Hand grenades? Our people are not that expendable."

"All right, then, use superior force. You've got a navy. Send out an armed patrol vessel and intercept the *Amalia* before she gets near enough for Ghaled to do any damage. Board her and take him off, and his bodyguard. What's wrong with that?"

"You're asking me?"

"That's right."

"You, a shipowner? You're asking *me* why we can't board a

merchant ship flying a British Commonwealth flag on the high seas and kidnap some of her passengers?"

"A state of war exists."

He gave me a long-suffering look. "You want to read up on your international law, Mr. Howell. A state of war may exist, even though there's a cease-fire in force. What does not exist is a proclaimed blockade with some pretensions to being effective. Stopping and searching neutral vessels on the high seas without the justification of a recognized blockade is totally illegal. As for the kidnapping bit..." He threw up his hands.

"I assure you that the owners of the *Amalia Howell* would not complain."

"Will the owners of the *Amalia,* or you as their representative, be on board the ship at the time?"

I saw the trap opening and backed off at once. "I most certainly will not be on board."

"Then the captain of the ship would undoubtedly complain. He would have to, and rightly. The Defence Ministry would never authorize such an action."

"Well, if the Defence Ministry don't want Ghaled pressing that button in the vicinity of Tel Aviv, they'd better authorize something."

He ignored that "Distances and the appearance of things can be deceptive at sea," he said thoughtfully. "Couldn't Ghaled's plan go a little wrong?"

"How?"

"Well, you will be passing on Ghaled's orders to the captain. Supposing you changed them a bit. Couldn't the *Amalia* find herself in the vicinity of Ashdod instead of Tel Aviv at the appointed time?"

"Yes, and in near-zero visibility that might work. But Ghaled is no fool. In the sort of weather we can expect at this time of year, he would have to be half blind as well as stupid to mistake the lights of Ashdod for those of Tel Aviv."

"Then perhaps the *Amalia* could stray accidentally into territorial waters farther north. Say, somewhere just south of Haifa?"

"Stray! Did you say stray?"

"These things happen."

"The *Amalia* isn't a fishing boat with a clapped-out compass. She's a four-thousand-ton freighter with a competent captain and crew sailing in familiar waters."

"You said that you wished to cooperate, Mr. Howell. You ask for an Israeli patrol vessel and a boarding party to deal with Ghaled. All I'm asking is some slight assistance from you in creating the conditions in which we can oblige you."

"You're not obliging me. I'm trying to oblige you."

"Why can't the captain simply radio requesting assistance?"

"On what grounds? That he has a man with a music box on board that he doesn't like the look of? No, the initiative will have to come from you."

"But what sort of initiative?"

"As you've pointed out, distances at sea can be deceptive. Let's say your coastal radar makes a slight error. He's really a mile outside, but your people insist that he's a mile inside. Anyway, he's acting suspiciously. So you order him into Haifa as a suspected smuggler or for verification of ship's papers. Under protest he agrees to obey. You could always apologize later."

"Is that the best you can do, Mr. Howell?"

"Yes. The ball's in your court. If you people are too fussy to bend the international rules a bit, I'm sorry. Mind you, I don't think you are too fussy. You're just hoping that I'll do the bending for you. Well, I won't. I have enough bending of my own rules to keep me busy, my own company rules. The captain of a ship may be an employee of the owner, but he's not going to behave like an incompetent just because the owner starts issuing foolish orders. The captain is still responsible."

"Even if the owner is on board and willing to take the responsibility?"

"Even then. And anyway, this owner will not be on board."

He sighed theatrically. "Cooperation? Ah well. Let's add up the score. We don't know the radio frequencies Ghaled's going to be using. We don't know the course changes he's going to give you to pass on to the captain. Correction! The course *and* speed changes. We don't know why speed comes into it. We don't know where ashore these charges are going to be placed or how. Don't know, don't know. When will you be given these course and speed changes? Don't tell me, let me guess. You don't know."

"That's sight As soon as I do know I'll get in touch again."

"Not with me you won't Don't even try."

I got a beady stare with that, so I gave him one back.

"Okay. That suits me. Well just forget the whole thing."

"I understood that you were offering passive co-operation. Are you now regretting the offer and now withdrawing it?"

That's up to you. Let's say that I find your reception of the offer discouragingly unattractive. Yes, I wouldn't mind withdrawing it."

He snorted. "Bullshit, Mr. Howell! You just don't like plain speaking. You came here to get something off your conscience. What did you expect? Bouquets of roses?"

"Ordinary courtesy would have done."

"Oops! Sorry. We're very grateful indeed, Mr. Howell, believe me. Very, very grateful for all this information and non-information you've brought us. Will that do? Now have some more orangeade and cool off."

"No thank you."

He refilled my glass anyway. "It's full of vitamin C. Don't like it? All right, don't drink it I'll tell you, very courteously if I can, what I'm going to do. First, I'll have this component analysed. Maybe we'll find something, maybe not Another don't know, but what's one more among so many? Second, I'll propose this interception you suggest Mind you, I can't do more than propose. Other people will make the decisions. Third, whatever is decided about interception and, if there is to be one, the manner of it, I've got to have those course and speed changes well in advance. What do you say about that?"

"Ghaled is shrewd and always suspicious. He doesn't trust anyone completely."

"How far does he trust you?"

"He can't quite make up his mind. If you're suggesting that I might just casually ask for the information and get it, I can tell you now that wouldn't work. The initiative will have to come from him. I can prod him, of course."

"How?"

"*Amalia* will be three days in Latakia discharging and loading cargo. I could convincingly argue that in order to get the captain to accept the passengers in the first place and then to acquiesce in the course changes wanted, I will have to work on him a bit."

"*Will* you have to?"

"Not much."

"So it will still be last-minute information."

"I'll try and figure out a way of getting it earlier, but I'm not going to promise. And while on the subject of promises, you'll have to understand a couple of things very clearly."

"You're wagging your finger again, Mr. Howell What do I have to understand?"

"My private orders to Captain Touzani of the *Amalia* are going to leave him with a lot of discretion. I don't yet know how much I'll have to tell him, but he's an experienced man and can be relied upon to act sensibly. If the course which Ghaled dictates will, with a slight modification, make it easy for your people to intercept the ship near Haifa, Touzani will make that modification. But if, unavoidably, he is obliged to steer a course feat will take him directly into the Tel Aviv area, then my orders will impose restrictions."

"Such as?"

"Ghaled proposes to operate this transmitter of his from somewhere just outside the six-mile limit, say seven miles. At a guess that probably means that its extreme range is eight miles or nine.

My orders to Captain Touzani will be to keep at least ten miles offshore - *if* he cam do so without arousing suspicion, You might expect to get away with a three-mile position error with the ship out of sight of land. But close offshore, where there are charted lights on which bearings can be taken, that's not so easy,"

"So?"

"So you have to face the fact that, if the *Amalia* gets within tern miles of Tel Aviv, your people will have to be ready, rules or no rules, to take instant action. What's the range of fee Tel Aviv coast radar? Fifteen, sixteen miles?"

"About that."

"Well, then, there you are. Touzani may or may not be able to keep his distance. Your lot have got to be watching, and prepared to move in to intercept if he can't."

"Supposing he can."

"Then, presumably, there'd be no explosions ashore that night and, presumably, Ghaled would soon know that something has gone wrong. Maybe he'd come back and try again another night. He'd certainly be looking for scapegoats. Captain Touzani's orders will be to see feat there is no risk of his being among them. My people are not expendable either"

"What about you?"

"As far as Ghaled is concerned I will have carried out my orders. Don't worry. I intend to be in the clear."

"But you'd still like us to pick him up for you, if we can."

"Don't you want to pick him up, for God's sake?"

"All right Point taken. Intercept early if practical to do so, or later if he looks like getting too close. We'll do what we can for you." For *me!* He was insufferable. "Now, Mr. Howell, about communications. As I said, nothing direct from you."

"My Famagusta office could handle it indirectly."

"Don't you know that Colonel Shikla's people monitor everything you send out?"

"I could make a change of course look like a price quotation."

"That's hanky-panky. We don't want any mistakes. I'd sooner you used Miss Malandra."

"How?"

"She goes to Rome every so often to see the lawyers for her family estate. About all that unusable land in the *mezzogiorno* that they're still trying to unload for her, right?"

He waited for me to ask how he knew about that, but when I only nodded he went on.

"The moment you have the information, put her on a plane for Rome with it. Then send a wire to your Famagusta office authorizing the payment of her hotel expenses in Nicosia if she stops over on the way back. No more. I'll know."

"Will she stop over?"

"No. We'll pick up the message from her in Rome. She always stays at the Hassler, doesn't she? We'll contact her there, giving your name. Right?"

"Supposing Ghaled objects. Don't forget, we're supposed to be under PAF orders."

"He's really got you locked in, hasn't he? I should have thought it was easy enough. Don't tell him, and don't wire Famagusta until she's on the plane. Then play innocent if you have to. That shouldn't be too difficult"

"Supposing I don't get the information, supposing there's some last-minute change of plan."

"Send Miss Malandra to tell us. Same routine."

"It's all very chancy."

"Whose fault is that? You're the one with access to the information."

"You could shadow the *Amalia* and get the course change yourselves with what I've already told you."

"Do you know the size of the Israeli navy?"

"Yes."

"Well, talk sense, Mr. Howell. One fast patrol boat to make an interception, that's feasible. We might even send a destroyer at a pinch. But let's keep this thing in proportion. We're not the U. S. Sixth Fleet and we have plenty to keep us busy as it is. Shadow one unarmed merchant ship all the way from Latakia? If I proposed that they'd think I'd gone round the bend."

"Well it's your skin, not mine. I just think we're leaving a lot to chance and introducing unnecessary complications."

"Why? You send that innocent little wire to your office here and we'll act on it. We'll get your message then, in clear and with no possibility of error, within hours, very little more than the air-time from Damascus to Rome. What's complicated about it?"

I didn't answer immediately because I was by then confused as well as annoyed. What was annoying me, of course, in addition to the man gazing smugly across the desk, was the realization that the Palestinian Action Force was not the only underground organization to have infiltrated the Agence Howell without my knowing it. The source of the confusion had to do with Teresa. The thought of her being safely out of the way in Rome when the Ghaled thing became operational was more of a relief than I would have expected. Naturally, I assumed that there must be something wrong with the idea.

But I couldn't see what In the end I nodded.

"Okay," I said, and without thinking drank some more of the orangeade.

Barlev smiled his approval.

"Full of vitamin C, that stuff," he said again. "The right kind of sugar, too. Good for you, Mr. Howell."

Although I had been away three days and had no time to waste on travelling, I went to Beirut by air and returned to Damascus by road.

The truth was that, while I didn't just then feel up to going through the airport VIP routine, I was uneasily aware of the fact that if I arrived by air at Damascus without having given the usual advance notification, Dr. Hawa might wonder why. That is the way in which contact with intelligence people affects me; I start looking over my shoulder, I become furtive. In their line of work I wouldn't last five minutes.

There was the usual backlog of office work waiting for me, but I made no attempt to tackle that with Teresa. Our extracurricular activities had precedence now.

I told her, more or less, what had happened with "Barlev." She listened calmly enough until I came to that part of the discussion which had concerned her. Then she became indignant.

"You mean to say that those Israelis have been prying into my affairs?"

"They pry into all their enemies' affairs, Teresa."

"I am not their enemy."

"Here we are all enemies. So they keep dossiers on us. It's no use getting cross."

"But I *am* cross."

"Not too cross to go to Rome, I hope."

"Oh, I will go if I must, but these are private things. How could they know about them?"

"Land ownership, wills, and trusteeships are matters of public record. They only have to look."

"Well, I do not like it."

"If the worst that's going to happen to us is some slight invasion of privacy, we won't be doing badly. So stop fuming and tell me *your* bad news."

"First, you are to report to Issa. That is very urgent. Second, you are to call Abouti. That is also very urgent. Third, you are to speak at the earliest possible moment with Dr. Hawa's Chef de Bureau. These are all connected urgencies, I think."

"The battery works directive?"

"Yes, but I could get no details. They will only talk to you."

"I'll start with the Chef."

He was his usual long-winded self, but we got to the point in the end. "Concerning the new surveying and clearing work being carried out at your Green Circle site, Mr. Howell, some questions have been raised."

"By whom, Chef?"

"By, ah, that is to say in - ah - certain Quarters."

Certain Quarters was the accepted euphemism for Colonel Shikla and his merry men of the Internal Security Service.

"Questions?"

"As to the, ah, security arrangements and allocation of responsibilities to the local police. I understand that the questions have been raised particularly to connection with the night work."

"Would it be convenient if night work could be suspended until these questions can be resolved at the appropriate level?"

"Yes, Mr. Howell, it would indeed. I realize, and the Minister realizes, that the work is urgent, but if, without undue inconvenience, there could be am accommodation, a temporary easement...?"

"I understand, Chef. You need say no more. It shall be attended to immediately."

He was grateful. Life could be made very unpleasant for a chef de bureau when Certain Quarters did not get what they wanted from him.

I was encouraged by one thing: Ghaled, it seemed, had decided to accept my plea of impotence in the matter of the directive, and had applied to his allies in the ISS for protection. I was not, at any rate for the moment, unduly suspect.

However, I would have to act.

Abouti was inclined to be obstructive at first. As he was charging treble for the night work, and paying out for it, at best, time and a half, my instruction to him to stop it was not well received.

"My dear, you asked for the utmost speed," he wailed. "I have allocated my best men to the job at the expense of other work. I must plan in order to do this for you. I cannot chop and change."

"The difficulties are only temporary, my friend, only temporary, I assure you."

"They are not difficulties, my dear, only *bêtises*. I know all about

177

it. I have Rashti's reports. An argument or two with your watchmen who are exceptionally stupid. An absurd dispute with the driver of your truck. That is all."

I nearly said, "What truck?" but a warning bell rang in my head just in time.

I said instead: "Which truck? Which driver?"

"Which? You have so much night business, so many loadings from that place? Does it matter? Wait, Rashti is here. I will ask him."

Ever cautious, he put his hand over the telephone while he spoke to Rashti. Then he came back on.

"He says the truck is a Mercedes diesel and that the driver is a little cockroach whom he will crush with two fingers of his left hand if you will authorize him to do so."

"Unfortunately, my dear friend, it is not so simple. As I said, the difficulties are only temporary. But the incidents to which you refer are not the difficulties we are concerned with now. These, which I think it better that we do not discuss on the telephone, have been created in certain quarters. There are matters of border security and police jurisdiction involved."

Even Abouti could not shrug off Certain Quarters.

He was silent for a moment and then said, "Ah," three times in three different and highly expressive ways. After that he waited for me to cue him.

"A little patience?" I suggested.

"Yes, yes, my dear. In such circumstances one should not be hasty."

"Good. We shall keep in touch, them. But for the present no more night work. Agreed?"

"Agreed. I do not wish ..." He did not say what he did not wish, which was to be involved in any way with Certain Quarters. "Yes, we will keep in touch," he ended and hung up.

"When were the fuse adapter rings delivered?" I asked Teresa.

The day after you left for Famagusta."

That meant that somewhere - most probably in the battery works - the adapter rings were now being married by night to the Katyusha rocket bodies.

I didn't have many tracks in the Damascus area. There was a transport pool, based at the tile factory, which served the various cooperatives as and when needed. I used mostly Fiats. The biggest vehicle I had was a Berliet van generally used for handling the furniture shipments. I hadn't one Mercedes diesel The "little cockroach" - Issa by the sound of it - was utilizing some other unfortunate's transport to convey the Katyushas to their secret destination.

I didn't give the matter any more thought then. Barlev had said that it would have been surprising if Ghaled had not had a few Katyushas. It was no concern of mine where they were going; or so I thought in my innocence. I did, however, bear the Mercedes diesel truck in mind. That, too, was a pity.

"What about Ghaled?" Teresa asked. "And reporting to Issa. They know you're back."

I made up my mind. "Tell Issa that there will be no more night work."

"Just that?"

"No. Tell him also to convey a social invitation to our master.

"Do we really have to?"

"Yes. I've got to get him off his own ground and onto ours. Dinner and backgammon the day after tomorrow, or, if that doesn't suit him, any other evening he chooses."

"When will I be going to Rome?"

"That's why we're asking him to dinner - to see if we can find out."

The following morning I drove to Latakia and saw our agent there.

His name was Mourad, Gamil Mourad, and if I speak of him in the past tense it is because he has recently severed all connection with the Agence Howell.

A shipping agent like Mourad is rarely the employee of a single company; generally he is in business on his own account, finding cargoes for and serving the interests of several owners, and handling all the paperwork involved with discharging and loading: cargo manifests, bills of lading, insurance, and so on. He is a sort of traffic manager.

I don't blame Mourad for disowning us. I didn't level with the old man and he has grounds for complaint; although, to be frank, I never knew a time when he did not complain. He was the complaining kind; it was his way of doing business. My father thought highly of him.

He was very fat, suffered from bronchial catarrh, and always carried in his right hand a large bandanna square. This he used as a fly-whisk, a fan, and an expander of gestures as well as a handkerchief.

When I saw him he was still brooding over the rearrangement of schedules which had followed the, for him, extraordinary delay of *Amalia* in Tripoli.

He made downward flapping motions with the bandanna to signify his displeasure.

"I did not realize," he wheezed, "that those Libyans had become so difficult"

By "difficult" he meant "more than reasonably venal."

"Now that they have oil," I said, "they all expect to become rich."

"Oil! Ah yes." In Syria, the only Arab country with no oil of its own, you can blame almost any commercial misfortune on oil. "But such petty harassment is new."

It was not only new but had also proved extremely expensive to me personally. I had had to employ a man I knew to be a crook as intermediary and pay him five hundred dollars of my own money; this in addition to the Libyan bribes. He would keep his mouth shut for the time being because I had promised him further similar commissions, and because he would still be trying to figure out why

I was sabotaging my own ships; but eventually he would talk. Even if he were not wholly believed, his tale would leave a certain smell in the air.

"This delay has cost us money," Mourad persisted.

"Perhaps this will make up for it. Here." I gave him a list of the shipments I would be making from the cooperatives in the *Amalia*. They were substantial.

He shook his head over the list "Is this all?"

"What have you got for her?"

"A hundred tons or so of scrap iron-briquettes. She will be half-empty."

He never described a ship as being half-full; unless loaded to the gunwales she was always half-empty.

"She will also have passengers."

"Passengers!"

If I had said chimpanzees he could not have been more astounded.

"That's right For Alex. Four of them."

"Paying deck passengers?"

"Deck passengers, of course." As there was no passenger accommodation on the *Amalia* they couldn't be anything else. "As to whether they will be paying or not, I don't know."

He was looking at me oddly and I don't wonder. "Mr. Howell, this is a new departure."

"As you well know, Mr. Mourad, we have become steadily more involved here with government business."

"Yes, yes." It was a wheezed lament for the Agence Howell's lost virginity.

"And that this involvement has brought us many business advantages."

"Many, you think? I would say a few, only a few."

"Few or many, advantages have sooner or later to be paid for."

"Ah!" Doom-laden.

"Having received certain favours we must expect that we will sometimes be asked to repay them."

"That is always the trouble."

"And in ways that we ourselves cannot choose, Mr. Mourad. We are not consulted, we are told, instructed."

"By whom?"

"In this case an agency of the government of which few approve. It is a branch of the security service."

He hawked loudly and raised his right hand to his lips. Phlegm neatly disposed of, he slightly rearranged the folds of the bandanna.

ISS, you mean?" No Certain-Quarters nonsense, no beating about the bush for Mr. Mourad.

"I'm afraid so."

"Who are these passengers?"

"I don't know yet."

"Why must they go by ship to Alex?"

"I think we should not ask that question, Mr. Mourad. It is possible that Captain Touzani may be given certain orders. There may be a rendezvous with another vessel off Haifa, something of that kind."

"You are willing to tolerate this sort of thing?"

"It has been made plain that I have to."

Touzani may have other views."

"I will speak to Touzani."

"No doubt." He brooded for a moment. "Your father had a somewhat similar situation to deal with in '46."

"Oh?"

"Yes, very similar it was. He dealt with it"

"How?"

"He knew the right man to go to in the military administration."

"Which military administration?"

The British, of course. The French had gone. Are you too young to remember? Perhaps. Well, British or French, whoever ruled the roost, your father always knew the right man to go to and the right things to say. He would never tolerate interference. He knew whom to pay and how much, and he would always get his way. He had a high-handed way with politicos. Troubles were brushed aside."

It might have been my mother speaking. I was tempted to point out that times had changed, that the "right man" in this case was Colonel Shikla, and that anyone in my position attempting to high-hand him would have to be out of his mind; but then I would have had to explain about Ghaled and other things, and frightening old Mourad would not have helped. He might have started fumbling things because he was scared. As long as he did as I told him without fuss, I didn't care if he thought me a weakling.

"I prefer to handle this in my own way, Mr. Mourad."

He floated his bandanna horizontally in a brief gesture, as though drawing a line under a column of figures. He had given his advice and it had been rejected, unwisely rejected in his opinion, but so be it.

"I shall want the names of these passengers, Mr. Howell, for *Amalia's* muster roll."

"You shall have them, Mr. Mourad."

We spoke of other things for a few minutes and drank some more coffee. Then I went back to Damascus.

Teresa had had a reply from Ghaled.

"He will come tomorrow night at eight."

"What about transport?"

"He assumes that we will pick him up in the car, I think. I said that I would let Issa know."

"Do you mind fetching him? I want to be alone with him for a while when he gets here. When you've put the car away give us half an hour by ourselves."

"All right"

"Offer to pick him up at seven thirty at the works. When you speak to Issa tell him to pass on the news also that *Amalia* may be docking a day early, on the twenty-sixth."

"Is she docking early?"

"Not as far as I know. I just want him thinking that she may be. And I want the map put back on the office wall."

"Have we still got it?"

"We must have."

The wall map I was talking about was a big one covering the eastern Mediterranean and most of the Middle East, and had been specially drawn to display the Agence Howell organization. All the places where we had offices and main agencies were ringed in blue, and the principal tracks used by Howell ships were drawn in red. It was quit an elaborate affair. I had it taken down only because, one evening some months earlier, Dr. Hawa had made a nasty crack about it. Looking at the map he had commented acidly that Syria still seemed to be part of "the Howell empire." Was that how I saw it? He had called me Emperor Michael once or twice after that.

So the map had been put away.

But now I had a use for it.

One of the things most clearly marked on it was the main shipping lane between Latakia and Alexandria.

I had not expected to enjoy entertaining Ghaled, but I had not been prepared for quite such a ghastly evening. It was humiliating, too. Although I planned everything very carefully - and, I thought, rather artfully - I got what I wanted from him not because I was clever, but because he chose to give it.

I received him with full ceremony in the big room which opened onto a courtyard of its own. There was a fountain in the courtyard, and it was very cool and pleasant.

That evening was the first time I had seen him in "civilian" clothing; that is, without his khaki bush shirt He had put on a white shirt for the occasion, with tie, and was carrying a tatty-looking briefcase, the kind without a handle that the French call a *serviette*. I assumed at first that this was a prop carried to make him look respectable in the city, but when he refused to let the servant take it, and I had had a closer look, I realized that he was using it to conceal a gum. Even on territory that could be presumed friendly he was taking no chances.

I gave him a champagne cocktail with plenty of brandy in it, which he drank thirstily as if it were water. I gave him a cigar and lit it for him. He sat back in his chair and looked around. Though he was clearly impressed he seemed perfectly at ease. That suited me. I wanted him relaxed and in as expansive a mood as possible. All the stiffness was going to be on my side. I continued to address him respectfully as Comrade Salah, and fussed a little. As soon as he had finished his first cocktail I immediately gave him another in a fresh glass. Then I suggested that he might like to inspect the rest of the villa.

He agreed, indulgently, with a soggy little quip about viewing my "capitalist decadence" I invited him to bring his drink. He thus had a cigar and a drink in his hands. I thought that he was going to leave his briefcase behind, but, though he hesitated for an instant, he ended by taking it with him.

The object of the exercise, from my point of view, was to get him to the office; but I took it slowly, lingering over things that took his fancy - he was pleased to let me know that he knew a Feraghan carpet when he saw one - and drawing him into giving opinions. When, at last, I took him along the passage leading to the office suite I murmured an apology.

"Only offices here, I am afraid, Comrade Salah. Nothing of interest." I opened one half of a pair of double doors to prove it.

"Nothing of interest in Comrade Howell's office?"

It was exactly the sort of reaction I had counted upon. Immediately, I opened the other door and switched on all the lights.

The map was staring him in the face. It covered practically the entire wall, a splendid mass of bright colours all bristling with little yellow and green flags.

He had started toward it, heading straight for the Latakia-Cyprus area, and what I had hoped would develop into a revealing little illustrated chat about his plans for the *Amalia Howell;* he was almost within touching distance of the map, and then, maddeningly, he suddenly turned away.

He had seen the ship models.

They had been one of my father's few extravagances. This thing of his for scale models had started soon after he had bought the *Pallas Howell.*

Pallas was the first ship of over 1,500 tons owned by the Agence Howell She was also the first to have a modern funnel The narrow stovepipes of the older ships had always been painted black; but, with the acquisition of the *Pallas,* named after my mother, Father had decided that we must have a "company" funnel like the big lines. He had designed it himself: yellow with a black "boot-top" and a big dark green H on the yellow ground. Below the H, and seeming from a distance to underline it, was a transliteration in Arabic characters of the name Howell.

When he saw the *Pallas* newly painted, he had ordered a scale model made for his office. By the time he died there were eight Howell ship models, three in his office and the rest in the board room, all in big glass cases on mahogany stands. They were made by a firm in England and cost a great deal of money, but my father said that they impressed visitors and were good for business. Although there may have been some truth in that, it was only am excuse really; he just liked them. And why not? They are soothing things to look at There in the Damascus office I had three of the original eight: *Pallas, Artemis,* and *Melinda.*

They fascinated Ghaled. I tried to steer him back to the map, but it was no use. He put his glass and the briefcase down on my desk and returned to the models. Then he began to ask questions.

What was this and what was that? And then: "Which is the *Amalia"*

"We haven't a model of the *Amalia,* Comrade Salah. I can show you a picture of her iff you like."

But he was only interested in models. "Is the *Amalia* like any of these?"

"Very like the *Artemis*. That's this one. She's a three-island ship, too."

Three-island?"

"Well, that's what they're sometimes called. You see she has these big well-decks fore and aft. They have a comparatively low freeboard, so that when the ship is hull-down on the horizon, all you see are the bow and stern sections and the bridge superstructure sticking up. From a distance they look like three little islands."

"And where will we be on the *Amalia?* Which of these windows will we see from?"

"I'm afraid there's no regular passenger accommodation on any of our ships, but there's a saloon, where the officers mess, Just there. The *Amalia's* saloon has portholes. She's not quite the same." I made another attempt to steer the conversation into a more useful path. "I daresay Captain Touzani will try to make your party comfortable."

Touzani? Is he Italian?"

Tunisian."

"Oh." That did not please him. Tunisia tends to be lukewarm in the Palestinian cause.

Is he loyal, this Captain Touzani?"

"If you mean will he obey orders, yes, I think he will Providing, of course, that they do not endanger the ship." This was more like it, I thought. "And, naturally, providing that the orders he gets from me are clear and practical."

"You will give him the orders personally?"

"Oh yes, Comrade Salah. When I have them." I tried to pursue the advantage. "There is additional information that I will also have to have very soon."

"*Have* to have?"

"I shall want the names of the passengers to be carried. By law these must be entered on the ship's muster roll That is the list of all

187

on board when she sails."

He decided to make a joke of it. "I can tell you one name - Salah Yassin."

I smiled dutifully. "And no doubt Ahmad and Musa will be on the list, too?"

Those old men! No. They are good fighters and loyal certainly. For guard duties there are none better. But on operations we must have the younger men, the front-fighters. Why is it that this ship has two propellers and the others, not much smaller, have only one each?"

We were back to the models again. It was with difficulty that I persuaded him downstairs to dinner, and even then he kept on about ships. The different ways of measuring tonnage had to be explained. Teresa helped by asking sillier questions than his, but the going was heavy. He drank brandy.

The backgammon later was torture.

He played a reckless "Arabian" game and nothing else. He was out to slaughter me every time or die in the attempt Mostly, he died. Backgammon is a very difficult game to lose intentionally without letting your opponent know that you are trying to lose. He sees the dice you throw. You can's keep on making gross errors. With an all-or-nothing player like Ghaled you don't have to play even reasonably well to defeat him. You just make the conventional, flat-footed "back" moves and nine times out of ten he defeats himself. That was what Ghaled did, though naturally he couldn't see it It was the fault of the dice, then of my good luck, and, finally and inevitably, of my lack of imagination, of dash.

"You are too cautious. You play like a businessman."

"You force me onto the defensive, Comrade Salah."

"You must not allow yourself to be forced. You must hit out, reply in kind."

Play his game, in fact, and lose.

"Yes, Comrade Salah."

By playing so wildly that he was obliged for once to do the

obvious, I managed to lose two games in a row, but even that didn't please him.

"If you were a front-fighter," he nagged, "you would soon learn when to attack and when to hold your fire, when to assault and when to ambush."

He had had quite a lot to drink by then, much more, probably, than he was used to in one evening, and the effects were showing.

I gave some noncommittal reply and he glared at me. The suspicion that I had let him win those last two games was beginning to surface now. Someone had to be punished. He used Teresa to start with.

"You do not comment, *Miss* Malandra." The "Miss" was a sneer. "Would you not like, perhaps, to be a front-fighter, as some of the Zionist women are? Do you have no ambition to imitate them?"

Teresa replied coolly. "I have no particular wish to imitate anyone, Comrade Salah."

"Then-perhaps we can change your mind. Perhaps when you see what the Zionist women can do you will think differently."

He had reached for his briefcase and was plucking clumsily at the zipper. My guess that he carried a gun there had been right, but it was not the only thing in the briefcase. When at last he got it open I saw that it contained papers and a leather wallet as well it was the wallet he thrust at Teresa.

"Look and see for yourself. You, too, Comrade Michael. See what the Zionist women can do."

From what I saw during the next few minutes, and from later reading of Lewis Prescott's description, I am fairly certain that the photographs Ghaled showed us were the ones he produced at the Prescott interview. In other words, the same photographs shown to Mr. Prescott as evidence of Druse commando atrocities were shown to Teresa and me as evidence of atrocities committed by Israeli women.

As a former war correspondent, Lewis Prescott may, as he says, have found it necessary to become used to horrors. I am glad that he also found it possible. I had not, at that stage, found it necessary, with the result that I was not only completely unprepared for what I saw, but also when my nose was rubbed in it, quite unable to cope. I don't know, or care, who was really responsible for the things shown in those photographs. I thought at the time, insofar as I was able to think, that the "Zionist women" claim had to be false, and Mr. Prescott's account suggests that I was right. Obviously Ghaled would change his story about the photographs to suit his audience.

But changing the story didn't change the photographs. I wished I could have done what Teresa did. After one glance she just got up and moved right away, saying that she would get more coffee. She stayed away, and Ghaled took no more notice of her. But he made me sit there and look at the lot, not just once, but three times with no skipping, and all the time he watched my face.

The only defence I could think of was to take my glasses off as if to see better; he could not know that without my glasses everything blurred a bit But I had left it too late, because, having once seem what was there, I could not blur what was already clear in my mind's eye.

"Front-fighting, Comrade Michael, front-fighting."

He kept intoning the words as if they were an incantation. In the end I managed to break the spell I did that by straightening up suddenly, putting my glasses on, handing him back the wallet with one hand, and reaching with the other for the brandy bottle.

"Very instructive, Comrade Salah," I said as briskly as I could, and refilled his glass.

He smiled as he took the wallet I hadn't deceived him; he knew all right that he'd shaken me.

"Let us say inspirational, Comrade Michael," he corrected me. "You know now the kind of thing we, and you with us, have to avenge." He dropped the wallet back into the briefcase and took something eke out. "You were asking about your orders. Clear and practical you said they must be." He shoved a wad of paper at me. "Are those orders clear and practical enough for you?"

What he gave me was a copy of the standard British Admiralty chart number 2834. That number covers the eastern Mediterranean seacoast from Sour in the north down to El Arîsh. Tel Aviv-Yafo is about half-way up.

The cartridge paper on which it was printed was limp and grubby from much handling and it had been folded and refolded too often, but it was still readable. On it, someone had plotted, in purple ink, a course for a southbound vessel.

As far south as the Caesarea parallel the course was normal enough, about twenty miles offshore on a heading of 195 degrees in deep water. Then there was a twenty-degree swing to the east which continued as far as the hundred-fathom line. At that point the course changed again, running parallel to the coast on a 190-degree heading for about twelve miles. Just south of Tel Aviv it turned west again, rejoining the original open-sea course somewhere off Ashdod.

In the blank space above the compass rose, the plotter of the course had written out in Arabic a precise description of the change sequence and the timing of it. The description ended with this Instruction: *On 190° south heading from 21.15 hrs. until 23.00 hrs. ship's speed is on no account to exceed 6 knots.*

I didn't take all this in at once, of course, but I didn't want to display too keen an interest After a brief glance I refolded the chart

"Well?" he asked.

"No difficulty, I think, Comrade Salah. The instructions seem perfectly clear to me. I am not a seaman myself but this looks like the work of a trained navigator."

"It is."

"If the captain has any questions, answers can be obtained, I imagine."

There should be no questions. Just see that the captain understands that he is to obey those orders strictly."

"Yes, Comrade Salah. The captain will have to choose his own sailing time, however. Otherwise he cannot be in the correct position on the evening of the third. In the port of Latakia all movement of shipping is prohibited between sunset and sunrise. Embarkation should probably take place, I think, before sunset on tike second of July so that departure can be very early on the third. But the captain must be consulted on these points."

"Very well, consult him and submit your proposals. But understand this. The timings of the course changes must be strictly adhered to."

"I understand."

Then I will thank you for your hospitality and ask you to drive me back. Before I cam sleep there is work to be done."

As he spoke he leaned forward with his hand outstretched. The briefcase was still open and for a moment I thought that he wanted to take the chart back. Then I realized that he was simply reaching for his brandy glass; but the movement had made me nervous.

"If you will excuse me," I said, "I will put these orders in my private safe."

He shrugged. "Very well"

I was gone several minutes because, before putting the chart in the safe, I scribbled out a copy of the sailing instructions written on it I was afraid, you see, that he might suddenly change his mind about letting me hold on to it The fact that I took this unnecessary precaution is a good indication of my own state of mind at the time - edgy, overanxious, reacting instead of thinking calmly, and all set to make crass errors of judgment.

They were already in the car when I went down, Teresa in the driver's seat, Ghaled in the back. He had his door still open as if expecting me to get in beside him, so I did so.

For a time he spoke only to Teresa. He was the worst sort of back-seat driver; he told her not only which way to go; even though she obviously knew the way, but how. "Slow, this comer is dangerous. Turn here, turn here! Keep right Now you can go faster. Are your headlights on?" Teresa kept her temper very well. Of course, she had had him earlier in the evening and so knew what to expect. Even so, her "Yes, Comrade Salahs" became quite curt. It was a relief when, on our reaching the Der'a road, he turned his attention to me.

"What experience have you with diesel engines?" he asked.

The question was so unexpected that I was off balance for a moment.

"Of using them, Comrade Salah?"

"Of maintaining and repairing them."

And then the penny dropped, or seemed to. I remembered what Abouti had said about the little cockroach who drove a Mercedes diesel truck. They must be having trouble with the thing. It was a natural enough conclusion to jump to. How was I to know that it was the wrong conclusion and that I had jumped too hastily?

"My only experience with diesel engines," I said, "is of what you must not do. That is to allow any untrained person, however resourceful he may be, to lay a finger on them. Diesel engines do not respond to semiskilled tinkering."

"If it were a question of repairing a fuel injection pump?"

"Don't try to repair it Have it replaced, and have the work done by the maker's agent."

"And if this is not possible?"

That puzzled me, because I was reasonably certain that there was a Mercedes agent in Damascus. Then, I thought I saw what the trouble was. The truck didn't belong to Ghaled, he was only "borrowing" it. Even if he had the owner's willing consent, direct dealing with the Mercedes agent might present a problem.

"You could order the replacement pump from Beirut and employ a local diesel fitter to do the work."

This answer obviously didn't satisfy him. "Why shouldn't the pump be repaired?"

I tried to explain that they were tricky things and that it was better to replace when they gave trouble. Thinking that it could be the expense that was bothering him, I suggested that it might be possible to exchange the old pump for a factory-reconditioned one. He listened, but obviously didn't care for what he heard. If I had been functioning properly and had been more perceptive, I would probably have suspected after a while that the wires had become crossed and that what I was telling him was, though true, for some reason irrelevant.

But I didn't suspect, and so failed to ask him the questions that should have been asked. As we neared the battery works he dropped the subject of diesel engines and returned to back-seat driving.

To me he said as we pulled up at the works gate: "You asked for a list of the special ship's passengers."

"Yes, Comrade Salah."

Then you had better report tomorrow night at eight thirty. I will give you the names then."

"Yes, Comrade Salah" I got out and opened the door for him.

Ahmad and Musa were already at the postern, waiting for him. They had the overhead lights on.

Once out of the car, he straightened up, tucked his briefcase under his left arm, and marched briskly to the gate, where he received and returned salutes. He had said nothing more to us and he did not look back. Presumably, we could go.

I shut the rear doors and got into the car beside Teresa. Abouti's men and machines had made a mess of the surface there and she had to be careful turning. We did not speak until we were on the main road again.

"Is everything yon wanted on that chart?" she asked then.

"I think it's all there. I hope it is."

"Were those pictures very nasty?"

"Very."

"I thought so. You looked as if you were going to be sick."

I'm surprised I wasn't."

"I told you he was insane."

I didn't answer. "Insane" was not the word I would have chosen. The only truly insane person I had known then - a man who worked for our company and who had one day tried to kill himself and his wife - I had pitied. I never pitied Ghaled. Nor do I now. On that particular evening, however, the last thing I was prepared to get into was a "mad-or-bad" argument with Teresa.

Later, in the office, I got the chart out again and put a scale ruler on it.

The written instructions and the track drawn in ink exactly corresponded. If the Israelis were going to intercept the ship, they would have to do so outside territorial waters, as I had suggested, and move in early, when the ship made her second course change south of Caesarea. They would also, I realized, have to bend the rules considerably, because if Touzani was able to follow the instructions I meant to give him, the ship was going to be even farther outside the six-mile limit than the track on the chart prescribed.

It was when I was considering this point that I noticed the second track.

It had been pencilled in and then erased, but the line was still just visible. It gave a course about half a mile west of, and running parallel with, that indicated by the ink track below Caesarea.

I only noticed it; I didn't pay it much attention. It could have been an alternative course pencilled in earlier and then rejected in favour of the one closer inshore. It could also have had nothing at all to do with the inked-in course. On that well-worn sheet of cartridge paper were other half-erased, smudgy pencillings, all clearly relics of past voyages.

I decided that I now had all I wanted.

"Is there a plane to Rome tomorrow?"

"Alitalia. Do you want me to try for a place?"

You'll get a place. Speak to Fawzi In the morning send the cables you would usually send to the hotel and to your lawyer."

"What about the one to Famagusta?"

I'll send that when you're on your way." I paused. "I don't want you back here until after July the third, Teresa."

She objected to that, of course, but I was firm.

"Supposing Ghaled gets suspicious."

"I don't see how he can."

"He can always get suspicious."

"Then I'll send you a cable ordering you back. You answer that you're catching the next plane, but you don't. Instead, you send another cable saying you're held up. Or go to Nicosia on your way back and get held up there. It's only ten days to the third. You can spin that out. If there's any trouble here I'll be able to slide out of it, but I don't want you involved unnecessarily."

"I don't like it."

"But I do. I'll have one thing less to worry about."

Thing!"

"Your being involved is a thing. No more arguments, please. I have to work out the message you're going to take,"

Teresa left for Rome the following afternoon.

I didn't go with her to the airport because I was known there and wanted no particular attention paid to her departure.

At four I called the airport to make sure her plane had taken off on time. I then drafted the warning cable, in the form agreed with Barlev, and told the clerk to get it to the Famagusta office.

After that I tried to put the whole business out of my mind I didn't quite succeed, but I worked until seven and gave the clerk his orders for the next day.

It was lonely in the villa without Teresa. If she had really been away seeing her lawyer, I would have had an early dinner and gone to bed. As it was, she was going to be away ten days instead of forty-eight hours, and I was due to report to Ghaled at eight-thirty. So, I had the early dinner and then sat wondering how soon the man calling himself Michael Howell would contact her for the message I had sent. Tomorrow morning would it be? The afternoon? If Barlev got it by tomorrow he should have plenty of time. Anyway I had done what I had said I would do. Now it was all up to him.

There had been thunder and even a few spots of rain, unusual for June; it was an unpleasantly sticky night. My shirt was clinging to me by the time I reached the battery works.

Ahmad let me in. It was the first time that he had seen me without Teresa and he wanted to know where she was. I told him that she hadn't been ordered to report, which was true, and he didn't ask any more questions.

Ghaled, however, did.

"You did not say last night that she was going to Rome."

There was no occasion to do so, Comrade Salah. She goes to meet with her lawyer on business. I expect her back on Thursday."

"You yourself reported, correctly, and obtained my permission before you went to Beirut on business. The same when you went to your Famagusta office."

"Miss Malandra's business in Rome is purely private. I gave her permission to go, I am afraid."

"As a comrade she has no private business, and you have no right to give such permission. The request should have been reported and permission obtained from me. What is this business?"

"Her father's estate. She was left some land which is being sold, I think."

"You mean she is rich?"

"There is some money. I don't know how much, Comrade Salah."

"Well, she shall tell us herself when she returns. Understand that, in future, permission to make journeys must always be obtained."

"Yes, Comrade Salah."

"Now. You wanted a list Here it is."

I glanced at the paper he handed me. There were four names on it. One of them was Salah Yassin, the others I didn't know. I looked up.

"One question I must ask, Comrade Salah."

"What question? You have the list."

"The port authorities may ask to see papers. Will the papers these persons carry have the same names as those on this list?"

"Of course. We are not fools."

"I only wish to be sure that all the arrangements I make will go smoothly, Comrade Salah."

"Quite right, Comrade Michael No, don't go. And don't stand there. Sit down."

I obeyed and waited.

"Since you are so anxious that arrangements go smoothly there is another matter you can help us with."

"Gladly, Comrade Salah."

For some reason my compliance annoyed him.

"Gladly, Comrade Salah." He mimicked my accent as he repeated it and added a servile whine. "How easily the words come and what a lot of thoughts they hide. I can almost hear them, Comrade Michael. I can almost hear them clicking away. What does he want now? What will it mean to me? Can I refuse? How much is it going to cost me? *Click, click, click!*"

I smiled amiably. "Force of habit, I am afraid, Comrade Salah. As you yourself said, I think like a businessman." No harm now in reminding him of those lost backgammon games. "And why not? That is what I am."

"And therefore superior to the stupid soldier, eh?"

Obviously he had needed no reminder from me about the lost games; they were still rankling. He probably had a slight hangover, too.

"I know nothing of the soldier's art, Comrade Salah."

"No, you only see the surface of the plan. A ship, an electronic exploder, charges laid ashore. The rest of the work you take for granted. The businessman thinks it all easy."

"Far from it I can imagine some of the difficulties."

He snorted derisively, so I went on.

The explosive for the charges, for instance. That had to be obtained and taken across the border into Israel. Not easy at all. Then, it had to be conveyed, disguised as something else no doubt, to a secret dump or dumps. Again not easy. The same is true of the detonators made here and the firing mechanisms. They, too, have had to reach their planned destinations, the right places at the right times. Then the charges have had to be assembled, and, once assembled, planted without discovery in carefully chosen places. Even a businessman can see the complexities."

"Very good." He seemed slightly mollified but he still couldn't let it alone. "You can imagine difficulties and complexities, but could you find solutions for them? If I ordered you to obtain a hundred airline flight bags, say twenty-five each of four of the airlines using the Tel Aviv airport at Lod, what would you say?"

"Is that what you wish me to do, Comrade Salah?"

"If I did wish it, what would you say? Bags from Pan-American, Swissair, KLM, and Sabena, for example, twenty-five of each. Well?"

"I would say that it would be difficult I would say that they would have to be stolen."

"Then you would be wrong." He was feeling better now. "Quite wrong. It required careful planning and much thought, but they were all obtained quite legally."

"To contain the charges, I suppose."

"Naturally. In all those crowded tourist coaches and hotels what could be more innocent than an airline flight bag waiting patiently for its owner to claim it?"

"I thought that all flight bags were searched at Lod."

He sighed at my ignorance and simplicity. "Flight bags are searched before Israel-bound passengers board the planes. Obviously ours will not be carried by arriving passengers. They are already in the country, ready to be armed and distributed to their final destinations."

"A most ingenious plan, Comrade Salah." It had, at least, the merit of simplicity. I wondered if Barlev had had the wit to deduce it from my account of the test Probably not. I wasn't even certain that I had used the description "flight bag." I could have just said "bag." It had been a Pakistani bag anyway, and the Pakistani airline didn't fly to Israel. If they had used a Swissair or El Al bag I might have cottoned on, but they hadn't; and in any case there was nothing I could do about it now. There was no way of getting the word to Barlev, even if it had been useful to do so. What could he have done at that stage? Banning all airline light bags wouldn't have been a very practical proposition.

"Can you see any weaknesses?"

"None, Comrade Salah, absolutely none." If his organization and planning were as good as he thought they were, it would be up to the *Amalia Howell* to inject the necessary weakness into the plan later.

"Unfortunately, not all our affairs go so well. Minor hitches occur. I was speaking to you last night about diesel engines. In that connection you can make yourself useful."

For a moment I had an absurd vision of myself haggling with the Mercedes-Benz agency in Damascus over the price of a reconditioned fuel pump. Then he went on.

"Do you know what a Rouad coaster is?"

"Yes, Comrade Salak."

"Good. We have the use of one of these vessels. It is used to bring in supplies from the north."

"I see." And I thought I did see. Barlev had said that the PAF received supplies smuggled through Turkey.

"It has a diesel engine."

"An auxiliary engine you mean?" The Rouad coaster is a schooner, a sailing vessel.

"An engine," he said firmly. "We cannot wait for fair winds in our work. It is with that engine that you will concern yourself."

"This is the one with the defective fuel pump?"

"It was. We are not the fools you seem to think. Your brilliant suggestion that a new pump should be installed had been anticipated. The new pump has already been fitted. However, the engine still does not work properly."

"What kind of engine is this, what make?"

"Sulzer."

"Where did the new pump come from?"

"Beirut."

"Who fitted it?"

"A local mechanic. He said he knows these engines."

"Local where? Latakia? Rouad?"

"Hareissoun. That is where the ship is berthed."

Hareissoun is a scruffy little fishing port just north of the Baniyas oil terminal The chances of finding a competent diesel fitter there would be remote. I said so.

"What solution do you propose?"

"Let the vessel go to Latakia under sail. There is a man there who will do the job properly."

"What man?"

"His name is Maghout. He is a foreman in the Chantier Naval Cayla by the South Basin."

"Our ship must stay in Hareissoun. This man of yours must go to her there and do the work."

"Unfortunately, he is not my man, Comrade Salah. I can't give him orders. I could make a request to Cayla."

"The matter is now urgent. Would they act on your request?"

"You can't expect them to release Maghout at a moment's notice. He'd have to drop everything to go and do a job like that. It really would be simpler to take the vessel to him."

"That is out of the question. I have already told you so. If this Cayla will not oblige you, he will oblige us. I have my people in Latakia, remember."

"I remember." They had once been going to plant bombs in Howell ships.

"All this foreman Maghout has to do is diagnose the cause of the trouble and tell the man in Hareissoun what to do. Am I right?"

"I don't know, Comrade Salah. The local man diagnosed a faulty fuel pump. He may have been wrong. The fault could be elsewhere. Other spares may be needed."

"Exactly. It is a problem of organization, a business matter. Go to Hareissoun tomorrow, Comrade Michael. Consult with Hadaya, the ship's master. Consult with this local incompetent if necessary. Ask your questions, decide what is best to be done, and coordinate the work. Report progress to me tomorrow night at this time. If you decide that you need this foreman from Latakia, let Issa know earlier so that Cayla may be approached at once. You understand?"

"I am not qualified to make judgments about engines, Comrade Salah."

"You are qualified to make use of those who can judge." He smiled maliciously. "Imagine that it is an Agence Howell ship in Hareissoun, one of those of which you have models. Imagine that this defective engine is costing your business money. The difficulties will very soon disappear, I think Don't you?"

"I don't believe in magic, Comrade Salah."

"No, but you always do your best That will be good enough." He paused. "Mr. Hadaya, the master, will be warned to expect you tomorrow and told that you are acting for me in this matter. When you report to me, Comrade Michael, I shall expect only good news."

Early the following morning I drove to Hareissoun.

It wasn't an easy or pleasant drive, but I didn't mind. Strange as it may seem, I was, in spite of everything, rather looking forward to that day. In a sense I was making a sentimental journey.

The Ile de Rouad is a port south of Latakia which used to have a small shipyard. In the latter part of the nineteenth century, this yard began building two-hundred-ton schooners and made itself something of a reputation in that part of the world. They were all wood but very sturdy, fully decked, and Bermudian rigged with two raked pole-masts and a heavy bow-sprit; useful little ships. Although no new ones have been built for years, there are still quite a few of them coasting in the Levant.

When I was a small boy the Agence Howell owned three of

these Rouad schooners and my father used to make a joke about them. He wasn't much given to making jokes about things we owned, so I have always remembered this one. It's a bit complicated, because you have to understand the background. All ships have to have their bottoms cleaned from time to time. The ordinary small coaster is hauled out of the water on a skid-cradle so that the job can be done. At Rouad, however, they used to careen the schooners; that is, pull them over onto their sides in the water by the masts. Then, instead of scraping them clean, they would drench the exposed bottom side with kerosene, set light to it, and burn off all the barnacles and muck. My father took me once to see them do it. That was where the joke came in. He said that the Agence Howell was "burning its boats." Not very funny, I admit, though it made me laugh at the time. The strange thing was that there were never any accidents; only the kerosene and the barnacles and the muck would burn. It must be harder to set a wooden hull alight than one would think.

So, I was looking forward to seeing a Rouad schooner again. On the outskirts of Hareissoun I left the car and walked down to the harbour. I saw her masts first. She was moored by the stern at the mole. I went along to her.

I had forgotten how small these boats were. Seventy feet on the waterline isn't much, and the high stem and massive bowsprit made it seem even less. She must have been over forty years old. There were traces of paint on her topside but not many; she was a work boat, and her paint - black, tarry stuff - was where it mattered, on the hull. She had no name of her own now. There was faded yellow lettering on her bow: JEBLE, the name of her home port, and the Arabic numeral *khamseh:* number five out of Jeble. Before being taken over by the PAF she had probably been sponge-fishing. Now she was back to carrying cargo and lying low enough in the water to suggest that she had a full load aboard.

The old man I could see on deck was dressed like a fisherman and could have been the skipper, but when I called up to him he shouted to someone below.

The person who came on deck then was not at all the fisherman type. Except for the suit of blue dungarees that he was wearing he might have been the young headwaiter at the Semiramis Hotel, an impression reinforced by the fact that he was holding a clipboard in his hand like a menu.

"Mr. Hadaya?" I asked.

"Mr. Howell?"

"Yes."

"Just a moment, please."

The old man shoved a rope ladder over the stern counter and I climbed up awkwardly. Hadaya helped me down onto the deck.

"A little inconvenient, I'm afraid," he said, "but we don't encourage visitors."

"That's all right."

He sounded like an Algerian. His shirt was unbuttoned to disclose a hairless chest and a gold chain with a gold identity disk on it. A flashlight stuck out of his breast pocket. His smile was affable.

"May I say how surprised I am suddenly to be conversing with Mr. Howell as a comrade."

"Have we met before, Mr. Hadaya?"

"No, but once I very nearly worked for you. There was a vacancy for a second mate. Your regular man had broken a leg. In Bône that was. I applied, but someone else got the berth."

"I'm sorry."

"It would only have been temporary." He flashed the smile again. "Like this one. Would you like to see the engine first or hear about it?"

"Hear about it, I think. What about this local mechanic? Is he still working?"

"No, I sent him away. He was well recommended and he had a kit of tools. I let him remove the old pump and install the new one. With the old pump the engine had worked unevenly, but it had worked. With the new one it does not work at all. I think the timing is all wrong."

"I see"

"I am only guessing." He grinned. "The mechanic suggested that the trouble might be with the ignition."

"Oh."

"Yes. That was when I got rid of him. I don't think he can have done any real damage, but after that I knew that he wasn't going to do any good. The fishing boats he is used to all have gasoline engines. I found that out later."

"What about the owners in Jeble? Won't they help?"

"We are the owners, or rather, Comrade Salah is."

"I had the impression that she'd been chartered."

"We bought her cheap. Too cheap." He tapped his chest "It is my fault entirely. I have told this to Comrade Salah. He is always tolerant of error when a comrade confesses it freely to him. I should have anticipated this trouble. She is the right size for the job, but that engine is twenty years old and we have overworked it."

"The trips north?"

He nodded. "Never under sail. Engine all the time. No maintenance to speak of, either. What can you expect? Of course, it would have to happen now, but better now than later. Do you want to see it?"

There was a separate hatchway and a ladder down to the "engine room." Originally, I suppose, it had been part of the after hold. A bulkhead had been added to make a compartment for the auxiliary, but it had been made as small as possible. There was scarcely room to move and the place stank; but although everything else was filthy, the engine wasn't. There may have been no maintenance to speak of, but there hadn't been total neglect.

"What did she give you?" I asked. "Before the pump started going, I mean."

"Six knots. Sometimes a little more." He pointed the flashlight beam. "There's the old pump."

It was on an oil drum chocked against the bulkhead. I wasn't really interested in the old pump, but I made a show of looking at it.

"Have you an engineer?"

"One of the crew knows enough to act as a greaser, but he's ashore now. Except for the old man on anchor watch they're all ashore. Comrade Salah's orders. One of them might have recognized you and started talk."

"You'd better send them ashore tomorrow, too. I'm going to try to get a foreman fitter down from Latakia to attend to the engine. It may be tomorrow or the day after, but you'll be kept advised. His name is Maghout"

"A comrade?"

"No, but he won't ask questions or talk. If the job's simple he'll just do it and go. I'm hoping it's simple, but he could still need odd spares, gaskets or something like that. He'll have been forewarned of the nature of the problem, but I'll take the type and serial numbers of the engine. They may give him an idea of what he ought to bring with him."

He turned his light on the clipboard. "I had expected that you would need that information."

"You have it there? Good."

He tore the top sheet off the clipboard and handed it to me with a little bow.

"I could not ask Comrade Howell to crawl about this engine room on his hands and knees looking for numbers."

"Very thoughtful of you, comrade."

I glanced at the paper and he shone the light on it. The information was all thesis - written in purple ink. I folded the paper and put it in my pocket before climbing back up the ladder.

Hadaya was behind me and stopped to close and secure the engine compartment hatch, so I strolled forward along the deck. Although I had seen the bottom-burning done I had never actually been aboard a Rouad schooner and I was curious. She had no wheel but an enormous tiller. I was remembering my father telling me that in heavy weather two helmsmen were not enough and that they had to rig relieving tackles to hold the ship on course, when I stumbled and stubbed a toe.

What I had stumbled over was a heavy bulk of timber which had been bolted to the deck. A meter away and parallel to it was a second one. Both were about two meters long and the work was new; the bolts that held them hadn't even begun to rust. And there were freshly drilled holes in them as yet unused. A shadow fell and I looked up.

"Bearers for deck cargo," Hadaya said.

He kept a perfectly straight face as he said it, so I just nodded. Forward of the cargo hatch I could now see a second pair of "bearers."

"There is a place in the town where we could eat if you wish," he went on.

"Is that wise?"

"Wise?"

"I was thinking of Comrade Salah's orders about my being recognized. No, it will be better if I go straight back, Comrade Hadaya. There is a lot of telephoning to be done and I have to report later to Comrade Salah."

"Then I must not detain you."

He walked with me to the car. I learned on the way that my guess about his being Algerian had been correct, that he had served as a cadet officer with Messageries Maritimes, and that none of his subsequent seagoing appointments had lasted very long. There was bitterness behind the smile. He had been recruited personally by Ghaled for the PAF gunrunning operation and was devoted to him; and, of course, to the Palestinian cause. A curious young man; not quite a mercenary but near to it.

As soon as I arrived home, I telephoned Issa and gave the necessary instructions on the subject of Maghout. Even if my newly formed suspicions were justified there was no way of stalling the engine repair. Ghaled already knew Maghout's name and place of work. If I didn't follow through promptly, he would do so himself, and I would have become suspect. I could not afford that. Unless I managed to retain some measure of his confidence during the critical days ahead I would be helpless.

After the telephoning I got out the chart he had given me and studied it again, along with the sheet of paper from Hadaya's clipboard.

The purple ink used was the same and so was the writing. The course changes, then, had been plotted by Hadaya.

That was point one. By itself there would have been nothing particularly sinister about it; things would have been no worse than they already were. But it was not by itself.

There was point two. The speed of .the *Amalia* while steaming close to the Israeli shoreline would be six knots. Six knots was the standard speed, when running on her engine, of the *Jeble 5*.

There was point three. The sort of deck cargo that it would be possible to load onto a small vessel like the *Jeble 5* could not conceivably need lengths of four-by-four bolted to the deck to support it. Therefore, they had been installed to support, or hold down, something else. What? The *Jeble 5* already had a full cargo in her hold.

Point four: there was that second track which had not been completely erased from the chart.

I remembered what Barlev had told me about the 120 mm. Katyusha rocket: fifty-kilo warhead, range of about eleven kilometres, the launcher a simple affair and easy to make with angle iron - "They don't mind leaving it behind them when they run."

Presumably they would not mind dropping it into the sea when they'd finished with it, either. All they would have to do would be to remove it from the "bearers" and heave it overboard.

I looked again at the second track and recalled then something that Ghaled had said when I had been arguing him out of using the *Euridice*. Speaking of the ship I would provide for him instead, he had told me, "It must be an iron ship and no smaller than the *Amalia*

Howell."

At the time, I had dismissed the "iron" qualification as an exhibition of ignorance. It had been years since the Agence Howell had owned ships made of anything else. Now, however, I wondered. It could have been a slip of the tongue, an indiscretion.

Jeble 5 was of all-wood construction. Unless she had one of those special radar reflectors that wooden yachts are beginning to carry now, she wouldn't show up clearly on a coastal radar screen. However, metal objects, particularly if they were carried on her deck, might act as reflectors. In that case, the best way for her to approach the Tel Aviv-Yafo area unobserved would be to use her engine to motor along on the same course and speed as, but just beyond and masked by, a larger iron or steel vessel. As far as the coastal radar was concerned *Jeble* 5 would then be invisible.

The Katyusha's range was eleven kilometres. From ten kilometres offshore *Jeble* 5 could do a lot of damage. I had no idea what the rate of fire might be, but there would be two launchers on her deck. I had made a hundred adapter rings, so there would be no shortage of ammunition. Even if each launcher fired only ten rounds before the schooner turned away and the crew began jettisoning the launchers, there would have been a thousand kilos of high explosive discharged.

According to Barlev, one Katyusha hit on a hospital had killed ten persons. Well, there were a lot of hospital-size buildings clustered along the Tel Aviv beaches. Some had names like Hilton, Sheraton, Park, and Dan, but there were apartment buildings as well as hotels, and all so thick on the ground that, even with rockets fired from a ship at sea, a high percentage of direct hits could be expected.

All this, of course, was to be in addition to the charges already set to be exploded ashore.

I had told Ghaled that his plan was ingenious. I hadn't really thought it so. There is nothing ingenious about a bomb in a suitcase or a flight bag. Killing or maiming noncombatants who can't defend themselves is an easy game. All that is needed to play it, apart from the high explosive, is a touch of megalomania fortified by the delusion that campaigns of terror can end in happiness ever after.

The novelty of Ghaled's plan was not in the nature of it, but in its size. A lot of bombs going off together in a number of locations would probably cause some panic as well as heavy casualties. A simultaneous bombardment from the sea would add confusion as well as further destruction. If the operation were even partially successful, Ghaled could count on international headlines. The smiles of the other Palestinian leaders might be forced, and their congratulations less than, wholehearted, but smiles there would be and congratulations, too. The PAF would have become a force to reckon with politically.

Meanwhile the Israelis would be burying the dead, and, no doubt, considering the nature of their reprisal.

I sat there for a long time, feeling sick and trying to think.

There was no way of letting Barlev know about this second part of the plan. In my anxiety to make sure that he knew about the first part, I had, by sending Teresa to Rome, closed down my only safe and clear channel of communication. I could send a cryptic wire to Famagusta and try to alert him that way; but in order to get past Colonel Shikla's monitors it would have to be very cryptic indeed. I could not be in any way explicit. The most I could hope to convey would be a hint that all was not quite as had been expected. I had no idea at that moment what form the hint could take.

And there was Captain Touzani to be considered. It was one thing to give a captain a rather unusual set of instructions and then tell him in confidence that if, as a result of his carrying them out, he got into a little argument with the Israeli navy not to worry; that he would under no circumstances be blamed or censured and could count on a nice bonus later. Admittedly, I had not been looking forward to telling him all that, but I had been prepared to do so. What I was not prepared to do, however, was, while giving him those unusual instructions, then neglect to warn him that in carrying them out he, a Tunisian, would find himself steaming in company with, and virtually escorting, an armed vessel all set to bombard Tel Aviv with rockets right under, or possibly right over, his very nose. That I could *not* do.

What I could have done, of course, was to tell Captain Touzani the whole truth and hope that, with a devil-may-care wave of his hand, he would relieve me of all the responsibilities created by the situation. I could have done that, but I didn't seriously consider it. Captain Touzani's early career may have been a trifle colourful, and under some circumstances I can see him cutting a corner or two, but he is a rational man, a realist. If I had wanted his instant resignation, taking him into my confidence would have been the way to get it; and his officers would have fully supported his stand.

So, I took the only other course open to me.

Ghaled was in a good mood when I arrived that evening.

Chantier Naval Cayla had proved accommodating. Maghout's immediate boss had very quickly sized up the situation and no overt threats had been necessary. The PAF squad leader in Latakia had reported that Maghout would go to Hareissoun the following day to attend to the fuel pump and would stay with the job until it was satisfactorily completed.

Ghaled was so pleased that he even praised me, and I had difficulty in getting him off that subject and on to the one that now concerned me. He mistook my air of gloom for modesty, and, when I disclaimed that, accused me again of arrogance.

"Comrade Michael does not need our praise," he told Issa. "His own self-praise is enough."

I was suddenly tired of his nonsense. I discarded the oblique approach and went at it crudely.

"One who certainly merits praise," I said, "is Comrade Hadaya."

"You found that young man interesting?"

I ignored the leer. "He has good judgment. He made a mistake about the local mechanic and when he realized that he had done so he acted to correct it. Some men would have tried to muddle through and cover up the mistake. I was glad to see that he didn't."

"He will be commended, never fear."

"One thing he said struck me particularly. It was about you, Comrade Salah."

That secured his attention. "Indeed?"

"He said you were always tolerant of error when a comrade freely confesses it to you."

"Concealment of error is despicable and can amount to betrayal Candid self-criticism earns respect."

"I am relieved to hear you say it, Comrade Salah."

He became jocular. "Why? Has the immaculate Comrade Michael something to confess?"

"Yes, Comrade Salah."

He looked at me sharply. "Well?"

"An error of judgment"

"What error?"

I glanced at Issa as if I were unwilling to let him hear of my shame. "It is in the matter of the Tunisian.

I eyed Issa again and Ghaled took the hint He motioned to Issa to leave.

"Now then, what is this? Speak up."

"I think that I underestimated the problem presented by Captain Touzani."

"What problem? The owner gives him his orders. He, your captain, carries them out."

"Regrettably, Comrade Salah, it is not as straightforward as that. There has been a development which I should have foreseen but did not."

"What development? Speak plainly."

I told him in some detail about the method I had used to delay the *Amalia* in Tripoli. His face cleared. I had used capitalist low-cunning; I had corrupted. He liked that.

"However," I went on, "there have been, unfortunate repercussions. I hear from Ancona that Captain Touzani has complained bitterly of administrative inefficiency in the Agence Howell, of blunders at the top causing delays and losses for which he is now being held responsible. Our agents in Tripoli and Ancona were not as tactful as they might have been. There has been ill-feeling and injured pride. Now, when Captain Touzani arrives in Latakia in two days' time he is going to be confronted with yet another unusual situation. He is going to be ordered to take passengers, and, en route to Alexandria, make a detour at sea which will obviously delay his arrival there. Almost certainly he will object vigorously to these orders."

"Then dismiss him. Get another captain."

"That is not practical, I am afraid, Comrade Salah. The mate on the *Amalia* does not hold a master's ticket, and even if he did there would be difficulties. Captain Touzani is popular with his crew."

"Are you telling me that this man will and can refuse to obey the owner's orders?"

"I am saying that he may accept them only under protest and with private reservations. These Tunisians cam be very stubborn."

His mouth thinned. "Stubborn? We have comrades who know how to deal with the stubborn, Comrade Michael. Give me your Tunisian for half an hour. He will not be stubborn after that, I promise you."

"Unfortunately, that is not a practical solution, either, Comrade Salah. Captain Touzani will remain in his ship with his crew. Besides, as a captain he has special legal powers and privileges that not even the police can ignore. Punishment of Captain Touzani might well result in the *Amalia* not sailing as planned. What we need from Touzani is not resentful submission but ready and willing cooperation."

"That is your affair. I warned you. You have had ample time. Yours is the responsibility."

"And I have accepted it, Comrade Salah. But in order to secure

Captain Touzani's cooperation I need authority from you for a slight change of plan."

"What change?"

"When the Amalia sails I must be on board."

He was silent for a moment. Then he said: "Impossible."

"May I ask why, Comrade Salah? Captain Touzani is in charge, but he must defer to me as owner. Nobody could censure him for delays occurring that I had sanctioned while we were at sea. With me on board at the captain's side there would be no question of his withholding cooperation, I assure you."

He was silent again. Then: "I do not like it."

"Without the captain's cooperation I can guarantee nothing, Comrade Salah. As you say, it is my responsibility. All I ask now is full authority to assume it."

There was another silence. At last he sighed irritably. "Why did it have to be this Tunisian?"

After talking so much rubbish and telling so many lies I was exhausted. When I got home I very much wanted to go to bed, but I knew that I wouldn't sleep until I had finished what I had started.

Late that night I drafted two cables.

The first was to Teresa ordering her back to take charge of the office in my absence. She would ignore it, as I had told her, but it was for Colonel Shikla's eyes and would cover the oddity of the second cable.

This was to our Famagusta office: **INSTRUCTED MALANDRA RETURN IMMEDIATELY TAKE CHARGE DURING MY ABSENCE. TAKING PASSAGE IN AMALIA TO ALEXANDRIA SAILING JULY 2. ADVISE ALEXANDRIA OFFICE. CONFER MALANDRA. ACKNOWLEDGE.**

HOWELL

They would think that I had gone raving mad in Famagusta. That was what I counted on. There was no chance of the news that I was going to travel as a passenger in the old *Amalia* being treated as routine. Barlev's informer in the office would be bound to let him know.

And when he did? Well, Barlev had twice suggested to me that I should be in the *Amalia* in my capacity as owner's representative when she was intercepted, and I had twice refused. For him, my sudden change of mind could only mean that the situation had changed radically in some way and that additional precautions were now necessary.

And, once on the ship clear of Syrian waters, I would have a radio channel at my disposal. True, I would still have to be fairly cryptic - merchant ships' radio traffic is listened to by many ears - but at least the ears of Colonel Shikla would not be among them.

I had done the best I could.

Chapter 7

Michael Howell

June 30 to July 3

I had spent a long time thinking over what I was going to tell Captain Touzani and had rehearsed it carefully. Although I never supposed that he would swallow the story whole - that would have been too much - I had hoped that he would find it politic to pretend to do so. So I did my best to make it easy for him.

It was wasted effort.

He is a barrel-shaped man with muscles like a stevedore and a big, bald head. He seems to wear a permanent and somewhat sarcastic little smile, but this is the result of a bullet through the lower jaw and the scar from the wound. When he really smiles the other side of his mouth moves and he shows his dentures.

He really smiled only once when I saw him in his cabin that morning.

He had rightly concluded that the trouble his ship had experienced in Tripoli had been contrived, but had not been able to discover who had done the contriving or why. Naturally, the failure rankled. Now, he was looking to me for the answers. Unwisely, I gave him the same ones I had given Mr. Mourad.

He shook his head. "I was there, Mr. Howell. I tell you that was a really funny business. Nobody had his hand out, nobody was saying anything, nobody knew anything. Then, suddenly, it was over. All a mistake. A mistake? With nobody having been paid?"

"Somebody was paid, Captain. You may be assured of that. There was a new cog in the machinery. It had been overlooked. Once it was greased, all was well. Let us leave it at that. These things happen."

I should have been less casual, less impatient to get to the matter I wanted to discuss with him. He became stuffy.

"Yes, Mr. Howell, these things do happen. But now, it seems, they keep happening to this ship, and that I do *not* like."

"*Keep* happening, Captain?"

"Mr. Mourad now informs me that this ship is to carry passengers to Alex."

I had meant to tell Mr. Mourad to keep quiet about the passengers and leave me to break the news gently, but I had forgotten. There had been too many other things on my mind.

"That is the main reason I am here to see you, Captain. About the passengers."

"I was wondering why I had been honoured, Mr. Howell. I had thought that perhaps it was because of Tripoli."

"Let's forget about Tripoli, Captain. I need your help in a rather delicate matter. It concerns these passengers Mr. Mourad has mentioned. What he did not tell you, because he doesn't yet know, is that I will be one of them."

He had small brown eyes. For the next few minutes they never left mine for an instant.

That is indeed a surprise," he said coldly, "although, of course, a very gratifying one. A voyage of inspection, I presume."

I sighed. "Captain, I don't make voyages of inspection, as you very well know. I said that I needed your help and I meant it"

"I'm sorry if I offend you, Mr. Howell, but after Tripoli..."

"And I asked you to forget about Tripoli. That's over and done with. This has absolutely nothing to do with it" His cabin was a hot-box. I mopped my forehead.

"A drink instead of that coffee, Mr. Howell. I have some beer on ice."

"Yes, that's a good idea."

But he still didn't take his eyes off me, even while he was pouring the beer. I waited until he was back in his chair and then said my piece.

"Even though you don't live in this country, you must be familiar, Captain, with the political situation. In particular you must be aware of the close but covert relationships which exist between some agencies of the government and the Palestinian liberation factions."

He nodded.

"Those agencies are powerful and have considerable influence in high places. No ministry, no minister is wholly immune from their pressure. With its considerable involvement in government-backed co-operatives, neither is the Agence Howell immune. You follow me?"

Again he nodded.

"So then, when we are asked by a certain agency to carry four passengers on a Howell ship bound for Alex, and also to arrange that during the voyage the ship departs slightly from her normal routing, I do not instantly refuse. I think first of the consequences of refusal. I don't have to tell you, Captain, that they would be unpleasant"

They dare to threaten you?"

There is no daring involved, Captain. They can threaten with impunity, and carry out their threats, too. I told you. Not even ministers are immune."

"Dogs."

"But with sharp teeth. When I raise objections - as, when I tell you what is required, you may do - I am insulted. When I persist, when I tell them that no captain of mine is going to take their orders, they make a further demand. So, you have five passengers instead of four. I am supposed to give you their orders and see personally that they are carried out"

He started to speak but I stopped him.

"No, Captain, don't say it There is no need. The only orders you will ever get from me are those that the representative of a ship's owner is properly entitled to give. I might make certain requests, but that is all they would be - requests that can be granted or refused at your discretion. That is understood."

He took a swallow of beer. "What do they want, Mr. Howell?"

I took the chart from my briefcase and spread it out before him.

"That's what they want"

He stared at it a long time. It was a relief to have him staring at something other than me.

I had expected an explosion of some sort, but none came. When at last he spoke it was to ask a question.

"Why six knots?"

I gave <u>him</u> what I thought was the safe answer. "I don't know, Captain. I assume - *only* assume, because I have not been told - that there is to be a rendezvous with a vessel from the Israeli coast."

To take off the passengers?"

"I don't know."

To take on others from the shore?"

I shrugged my lack of knowledge.

"Mr. Howell, if the intention were a rendezvous with a boat from shore, surely a position for the rendezvous would be indicated. There is nothing like that here. Instead, we are asked to steam at six knots for almost two hours."

Those are the orders as I was given them."

He reached for his beer again. "Who are these passengers?"

"Palestinian *fedayeen*. That much is certain. The name of the leader was given as Yassin. He is said to be an important man."

"Will these passengers be armed?"

"Probably."

"Will they be carrying other arms - arms to be put ashore?"

"Nothing was said about that"

There was a silence, then the brown eyes studied me again.

"You spoke of certain requests that you might make, Mr. Howell. What would they be?"

"First, that you make the course change indicated on the chart as far as the turn opposite Caesarea. Second, that, except for the slowdown to six knots, you ignore the rest of the orders and steer a course along the Israeli coast which will keep you not less than ten miles from it. No closer at any time. Third, that you do this without informing the passengers."

"Making them miss this rendezvous you spoke of?"

"That's right."

"I thought you said these dogs had teeth."

"With luck they'll believe that the shore boat was at fault. Anyway I'll worry about that later. Let's just say that I don't like being ordered about by thugs and having to impose on the loyalty of Captain Touzani."

He thought and then nodded. "All right, Mr. Howell. I won't refuse those requests. I can't say that I'm happy about the third one though, not informing the passengers. If there's a seaman among them and he knows what the original orders were, he'll know soon enough when they aren't carried out."

"I don't think any of them will be a seaman, but as a matter of interest what arms do you carry?"

"A few handguns, one rifle. The first mate has charge of the locker key."

"Would you consider issuing the handguns to the officers or having them available on the bridge?"

"In an emergency I'd consider that, Mr. Howell. This is not another request you're making, is it?"

"Only a suggestion, Captain."

"I'll bear it in mind." He emptied his glass and then put it down carefully in the middle of the chart. To speak plainly, Mr. Howell," he said slowly, "I don't think you're telling me all you know about this business. I'm not offended. Don't think that. I respected your father and I respect you. If you're not being open with me now I'm prepared to believe that it's because you think that the less I know the better off I'll be."

"Thank you, Captain." It was the least I could say.

It was then that he really smiled, briefly though.

"But," he went on, "if you don't mind my saying so, Mr. Howell, when it comes to dealing with the kind of men you call thugs, it's a mistake to let feelings get the better of you. I mean feelings like not wanting to be ordered about by people you despise. Naturally, a man has his pride and the Howells are a proud family, but if what you're asking me to do is just to satisfy pride, I'd advise you, for your own sake, to think again."

Arrogance was Ghaled's word for it. Captain Touzani was politer - pride.

"Good advice, Captain," I said. "I wish I could take it. But there's more than pique or personal pride involved here."

"I'm glad of that, Mr. Howell. Pride is a bad counsellor." He fingered the scar by his mouth. "I speak from experience. Another beer?"

"Thank you. Perhaps we should talk about accommodation for these passengers, or rather the lack of it"

"You will have my sleeping cabin."

That is good of you, but I don't think I'll be doing much sleeping. It's these four Palestinians I'm concerned about. If possible I would like their leader, Yassin, to be given a temporary cabin of some sort amidships and have the other three forward or aft. It might become necessary to isolate them."

"I will try to think of something, Mr. Howell."

"Good. Now, about embarkation and sailing. What will your orders be?"

We discussed those and one or two other matters before I said good-bye to Captain Touzani.

My call on Mr. Mourad was brief.

After the coffee had been served I handed him the passenger list for the *Amalia Howell.*

When he saw my name on it he hawked twice into his bandanna, but made no other direct comment. Perhaps, for once, words failed him. With his *"Bon voyage,* Mr. Howell" when I left, he washed his hands of me.

On the evening of July the first I reported to Ghaled at the battery works. It was the last occasion on which I was to do so.

That was when I heard about the "mishap."

Issa and Taleb were both with Ghaled when I arrived, and some sort of emergency meeting seemed to be in progress.

"But if we worked through the night, Comrade Salah," Issa was saying, "we could make good part of the loss at least and begin delivery tomorrow. With Taleb to help me I can . . ."

"No!" Ghaled cut him short decisively. "You must learn this, Comrade Issa. When we plan we make provision for things going wrong, for misfortunes and mistakes. That is what planning is for. So that when a setback occurs we can accept and absorb it. It is when hasty improvisations are made that trouble starts. Unacceptable risks are taken and a small misfortune is allowed to become the cause of major disaster."

"But Comrade Salah . . . "

"No more argument. You can make your replacements for future use, but there will be no last-minute foolishness on this operation. That is all, comrades."

They left. I got a weak smile from Taleb, but Issa ignored me. He looked very tired and close to tears.

Ghaled motioned me to sit down.

"A minor mishap," he explained to me. Two days ago, we have just heard, a hundred detonators were lost on the other side. Because he was the one who made them, poor Comrade Issa is naturally upset. What he forgets is that we made five hundred, and not merely three hundred, so that we could well afford to lose some. It is a pity, but I am not prepared to risk valuable couriers to send in replacements which would probably arrive too late for current use and are, in any case, not needed."

"The need being governed by the number of flight bags available and the manpower to distribute them?"

I wasn't really interested. If more detonators were *not* needed, that, as far as I was then concerned, seemed to be that I could not know that what I had just heard in that room had been the sealing of my own fate.

"Exactly, Comrade Michael. You are always quick to take a point. Meanwhile I have good news for you. The schooner engine has been tested and is now in excellent running order."

"I am glad, Comrade Salah. My own news is also favourable. Embarkation is still fixed for tomorrow at four in the afternoon. By then most of the cargo handling should have been completed. We sail early the following morning. There should be no difficulty after that in keeping to the timetable."

"The Tunisian is giving no trouble?"

"I will be at his elbow to see that he does as he is told. The arrangements for embarkation are typed on this paper." I handed it to him. "The agents are Mourad and Company. We assemble at four in their office to the Rue du Port. The ship is lying at the East Quay by number seven warehouse. The agents will take us to the ship and attend to the formalities."

"That is satisfactory."

"There remains the question of transport to Latakia, Comrade Salah, for you and your" - I fumbled slightly -"for you and the other comrades."

The front-fighters are already to our Latakia safe house waiting. I myself will join them there later tonight."

"You have transport arranged?"

"Everything is now arranged. All you have to do now, Comrade Michael, is to report to me yourself tomorrow at this Mourad office."

"Very well, Comrade Salah. If I may offer a suggestion?"

"Go on."

"Neither Captain Touzani nor the Mourad office is aware of your identity."

"What of it?"

"In that office and on board the ship we shall be among strangers. The use of a more discreet form of address might be advisable."

"Discreet?"

"Mr. Yassin would excite my curiosity. Comrade Salah might."

"What are the ship's crew? Arabs?"

"Mostly Greek Cypriots, but they speak a little coast Arabic, enough to understand."

"Very well. From tomorrow we shall play at being civilians again. I will give the necessary orders."

I stood up to go.

"One more task, Comrade Michael."

"Certainly."

"Bring a bottle of brandy with you. No, wait! Bring two bottles."

"With pleasure, Comrade Salah."

"We must be able to celebrate our victory."

I won't pretend that I did not sleep that night, but I had to take pills to make sure of doing so. If I had had any tranquillizers I would have taken those, too. I felt as if I were at school again with the threat of a beating hanging over me; no worse than that, true, but at my age it was a peculiar feeling to have.

In the morning I worked for a time with the clerk and then packed a two-night bag. That, I thought, would do me until I got to Alex - *if* I got to Alex. What might happen after that did not just then interest me.

I had borrowed a driver from the tile factory transport pool, who would return my car to the villa, and reached Mourad's office in

Latakia at three thirty. Mr. Mourad was out, and I found the task of dealing with the *Amalia's* passengers had been delegated to his assistant. The old man clearly wanted nothing to do with us.

Ghaled arrived punctually at four. He came, sitting beside the driver, in an ancient Citröen van with the *Serinette* in its carrying case resting on his knees. He would left no one else touch it when he got out. He was wearing his white shirt and the tie.

The "front-fighters" were unimpressive. The senior of the trio, the one to whom Ghaled gave his orders, was, according to the passenger list, Aziz Faysal He wore a crumpled suit, brown with black stripes, and a blue *Koffiyeh*. The others, Hanna and Amgad, wore *Koffiyehs* too, but had no suits, only khaki work trousers and grubby singlets. All three were youngish men with something oddly similar about their faces and physique. I knew from the names that they couldn't be brothers, and it took me a minute or two to identify the common factor. Consciously, or more probably unconsciously, Ghaled had chosen for his personal bodyguard younger men of his own physical type, earlier versions of himself.

In addition to the *Serinette* there were four pieces of baggage in the van. One of them, an old leather suitcase, belonged to Ghaled. Aziz carried that, along with a canvas hold-all of his own. I knew that there must be arms and ammunition as well as clothing in the bags, and wondered if the customs people had been squared.

They had. Mourad's assistant took us in the office panel truck to the ship, and we weren't stopped once. There was no customs examination. We were not even asked to show our papers.

The *Amalla Howell* was built in a Dutch yard in the late thirties. We bought her in 1959 and since then she has had two complete refits. Still, she does look her age. When we got out of the track on the quayside and Ghaled saw her for the first time, he stopped short and put down the *Serinette*.

"*That* is the ship?"

"Yes, Mr. Yassin."

"But it is old and filthy. The paint is coming off. It cannot be seaworthy."

"She is perfectly seaworthy, and the crew have been chipping off the old paint You can't judge by outward appearances, Mr. Yassin."

"You said that the *Amalia* looked like that model in your office."

"She does."

"Not to me."

"Models don't go to sea," I said shortly and walked away. He followed after a moment.

Mourad's assistant was waiting at the gangplank. I told him that he would not be needed any more and led the way on board.

They were still working cargo on the after well-deck but the first mate, Patsalides, had been warned of our arrival and came forward to receive us, or, rather, to greet me. He merely glanced at the rest.

"The Captain asks that you take your party to the saloon, Mr. Howell. The baggage can be left here for the time being."

Although he could speak some Arabic he used Greek now. I translated to Ghaled.

"We will keep our baggage with us," he announced firmly.

I could have done without that Patsalides understood, of course, and his mouth tightened, but he glanced at me for guidance instead of responding as he would have liked to.

"That's all right, Mr. Patsalides," I said hastily. "I can see you're busy. I know the way."

The saloon was immediately below the bridge and at the end of the alleyway serving the officers' cabins. It wasn't much of a place, I admit; just functional.

One one side was the table where the officers took their meals, on the other were some scruffy armchairs and a recently recovered leatherette sofa. There was a door to the galley and a second door opened onto a narrow strip of covered deck From there an iron companionway led up to the bridge. Inside, the smells of cooking oil and stale cigarette butts mingled with that of the new leatherette.

Ghaled looked about him as if he had been used to better things.

"A little different from the Howell villa," he observed. "I see you don't believe in pampering your officers."

The comment irritated me. "They don't have to be pampered, Mr. Yassin."

I didn't wait to see how he took the suggestion that front-fighters *did* have to be pampered; I went in search of the captain. I found him on the starboard wing of the bridge looking down at the quay.

"In the saloon?" he asked.

"Yes."

"Which is Mr. Yassin?"

The one in the white shirt How much have you told Mr. Patsalides, Captain?"

"That they are *fedayeen* and that we are to be cautious in dealing with them for the present I could scarcely tell him less."

"No. I am interested in their baggage, Captain. Not that strange-looking case with Yassin, I know what's in that, but their other baggage. I'd like to know what arms they have with them."

"So would I, Mr. Howell."

"Do you think Patsalides could organize a discreet search? Perhaps while we are at the evening meal?"

"I think so. I have arranged for a cabin for Yassin, as you asked. The other three will be in the special compartment aft."

There had been a time, before it became strictly illegal, when the Agence Howell had done a little business, mainly with American dealers acting for museums, in newly excavated Greco-Roman antiquities. The dealers said what they wanted; we had it shipped out of the area in which it had been found. Hence the special compartments.

"I had forgotten you had one."

"We still find uses for it occasionally." His expression was bland. "They will not be too uncomfortable. They can sleep on palliasses."

"What kind of door is there on the compartment?"

"It has a clip that is very difficult to move, unless you know how, and can also be padlocked. Perhaps I should now go below and introduce myself."

I had not been wrong in choosing Captain Touzani. It was almost a pleasure to introduce him to Ghaled.

"Mr. Salah Yassin, Captain Touzani."

They nodded, eying one another; two very different Arabs.

"And Mr. Aziz Faysal."

More nods. I didn't bother with the other two.

Captain Touzani smiled expansively. "Gentlemen, you are all most welcome aboard this ship. Mr. Howell will have told you that we do not normally carry passengers, so the accommodation I can offer you is limited. However, the second officer has offered to share another cabin until we reach Alexandria. His berth is therefore available to Mr. Yassin. Mr. Howell as owner will naturally berth with me. The other gentlemen will be accommodated aft." He pressed a bell-push. "The steward, Kyprianou, will show you where to go. Meals will be taken here. There will be separate sittings for passengers at times of which you will be told. I must ask you to observe certain rules. The bridge is strictly out of bounds to passengers at all times. You may walk anywhere on the main deck, that is the one below this."

The steward, a dirty little man in a clean white jacket, had come through the galley door in answer to the bell.

The captain pointed Ghaled out to him. "This is Mr. Yassin, Kyprianou," he said in Greek. "Show him and his companions to their quarters."

Ghaled was glaring at the captain. Clearly he hadn't liked being told what he could and could not do, but he wasn't quite sure how to go about registering his displeasure.

Touzani looked him straight in the eye. The weather forecasts are good, Mr. Yassin. I see no reason why we should not have a smooth and pleasant journey."

Then he turned and went back up to the bridge.

We sailed shortly after dawn.

I had dozed fitfully on a couch in Captain Touzani's office cabin. The results of the baggage search the previous evening had not been reassuring.

The front-fighters each had machine pistols. Ghaled had in his case, in addition to a new black suit, a Stechkin automatic in a webbing holster and a small transistor walkie-talkie set.

It was this set that worried me. When Patsalides told me about it I immediately asked if he didn't mean a pair of walkie-talkie sets. That's what I hoped he had meant, but he shook his head.

"No, Mr. Howell, just one."

When he had left us Touzani looked at me curiously. "Why should you mind about this set? If he has one that only means that someone on the boat coming from the shore has the other."

"Yes."

"What difference does it make? You can't use those things as direction finders, at least not effectively. A boat from the shore would be looking for our lights."

I didn't tell him what I was worrying about was not a boat from the shore, but Hadaya from the sea. It looked as if Ghaled intended to control and coordinate the whole operation from the *Amalia*.

I should have worried more about that walkie-talkie, seem the danger it really represented and so been better prepared to counter it. The trouble was that in my own mind at that moment I was quite certain that I knew what the Israelis were going to do. It wasn't just wishful thinking on my part; I had been using the ship's radio.

As soon as we had left Syrian waters that morning I had begun sending messages to Famagusta, a series of three. They could not be explicit; I had to wrap everything up in commercial jargon; but they made and remade three points.

First: that the information previously furnished had been found to be incomplete and that two ships were now involved in the transaction.

Second: that modifications to the announced routing would

have to be made.

Third: that, as a consequence, the steps to be taken already discussed should be taken not later than 21:15 hours in order to be effective.

They had been difficult messages to compose and one of them read like gibberish. The ship's radio operator had given me some odd looks. But I didn't care what he thought. From the fact that all three messages had been acknowledged without the bewildered demands for clarification that might have been expected, I concluded, rightly, that they were getting through to Barlev, and that my mad cable from Damascus had had the desired effect of alerting him. The final acknowledgment added what I took to be a personal assurance from him. Famagusta said that they would "proceed as planned."

To me that meant that the interception was going to be off Caesarea at 21:15 that evening. I felt that all I had to do now was wait.

Ghaled had kept to his cabin most of the day. The front-fighters preferred the deck - understandably, since the special compartment had no porthole. I stayed in the captain's quarters aft of the bridge until the late afternoon. This was with Ghaled's approval; I was supposed to be keeping an eye on the ship's progress. But around about five o'clock a message came, brought by Kyprianou the steward, that I was to report to him in his cabin.

With the message Kyprianou brought additional information. "Mr. Yassin is armed," he said dramatically.

"Oh."

"He is wearing his pistol on a belt, sir."

"I see."

"Shall I tell him to take it off, sir?"

"No, Kyprianou, it is perfectly all right."

He seemed disappointed. Touzani, who had been listening, added a further caution.

"You will pretend not to have seen the pistol. Just get on with your work in the ordinary way." He dismissed the steward. To me he said: "When you get back, Mr. Howell, it may be as well if we have a little talk."

I nodded and went down to see Ghaled.

He was sitting at the small cabin desk writing, and I stood in the doorway for several seconds before he turned.

"Ah, Comrade Michael. There was a small task I gave you on the day before we left."

"Task, Comrade Salah?"

"Two bottles of brandy."

"Oh yes. For the celebration. Would you like them now?"

"I would like one. And bring two glasses with you from the saloon."

I had to go back up to the captain's quarters to fetch the bottle. He watched in silence while I got it out of my bag. It was an eloquent silence. I would have preferred some spoken comment.

When I returned to Ghaled he had some papers in his hand.

"Sit down, Comrade Michael."

As he had the only chair I sat on the bunk beside the *Serinette.*

"You can open the bottle? Good. Then pour two drinks and let us talk about the future. We arrive in Alexandria tomorrow at what time?"

"Early afternoon I expect, Comrade Salah, but with the course changes ahead it is difficult to say exactly."

"My arrival will be kept secret, of course. It must not be known how I have arrived. The press conference I hold will be in Cairo."

"Is that already organized?"

"Everything is organized." He gave me a sheet of paper with mimeographed typing on it That is the preliminary statement in English which will be issued to the international news agencies in Beirut as soon as the first reports of our attack begin coming in."

The paper was headed *Palestinian Action Force Information Service* and datelined Beirut, July 4. The statement began:

At approximately 22:00 hrs. yesterday July 3, troops of the Palestinian Action Force under the personal command of their leader, Salah Ghaled,

*launched the most devastating attack yet seen on the Zionist pseudo-state
of Israel The target selected was that citadel of Zionist expansionism, Tel
Aviv. Massive bombardments by both land and sea forces of the PAF, though
directed primarily at military installations in the area, are believed to have
caused some civilian casualties. In a statement following the attack, PAF
leader Salah Ghaled said that, while such casualties were regretted, he
could not allow the presence of so-called innocent bystanders to influence
PAF war policy. "While we Palestinians must still fight for justice," he
said, "no bystanders are innocent. In the Palestinian liberation movement
there have been too many words and too few deeds. With this offensive the
PAF, representing the new militant leadership of all Palestinian forces,
begins the march to victory and ultimate justice."*

There was more of the same - Melanie Hammad's work
obviously - but I only pretended to read it.

"It is good English, Comrade Michael?" he asked anxiously. "I
can read English a little but not very well."

"Yes, it is to good English." I knew that there would be one
question expected of me and that I had better ask it quickly.

"It says here, Comrade Salah, that there will be a bombardment
from the sea. Can that be correct?"

He smiled contentedly. That is a surprise that I have been
keeping for you. Fill our glasses again."

So them he told me about the *Jeble* 5 attack.

I made the appropriate sounds of delight and amazement. In a
way he had made my task a little easier, because mow I did not have
to maintain quite so much of a pretence with him. On the other
hand, I now had more to conceal from Captain Touzani. Instead of
my own surmises and deductions to keep quiet about - and they just
could have been mistaken - I had confirmed information to withhold.
I would have to be careful when we had our "little talk."

The problem now was to get away from Ghaled. All he wanted
to do was talk about Cairo and the reception he .expected there.
Last time it had been cold. 'This time it would be very different. He
was looking forward to seeing Yasir Arafat's face as they embraced

for the photographers. He had been making notes of some of the questions the reporters would most likely ask him and preparing his replies.

I had to listen to them. He went on and on. After the third brandy I said that I must go and make arrangements for that evening.

"What arrangements?"

The first course change will be made at eight o'clock. When I am sure that all is well I think that we should have our meal, Comrade Salah, so that we are all ready for the next change at nine fifteen off Caesarea. I imagine the *Jeble 5* will be joining us soon after."

"Yes, you have work to do. Very well, go."

When I left he was pouring his fourth brandy.

Captain Touzani was drinking beer and not looking as though he was enjoying it.

"So," he said, "our armed passenger is now busy getting drank, Mr. Howell. As captain of this ship you cannot expect me to be pleased."

"He doesn't get very drunk. He gets nastier, but not drunk. I don't expect you to be pleased."

"But you have no change of plan to propose."

"None that we haven't already discussed."

"I take it, then, that you want me to issue arms to the watch officers."

"Yes. And when Yassin and the rest of the passengers go to the saloon to eat I would like the special compartment door locked. There's nothing we can do about Yassin's automatic, but we don't want the others armed as well."

They may be already armed."

"No. I checked. They're on deck forward, smoking."

"When they find the door locked they won't like it."

"Maybe they won't find out." I was still banking on the Caesarea interception.

"You mean they won't be going to sleep tonight?" The brown eyes were watching me intently.

"I mean that I expect the situation to change in our favour, Captain."

There was a long silence before he said: "I do hope you know what you're doing, Mr. Howell."

"I think I do, Captain."

When we made the first course change the sun was low in the sky. As soon as we were on the new heading I went down to the saloon and reported the fact to Ghaled. He didn't seem very interested. He must have gone on drinking steadily after I had left him. I sat down next to Aziz and forced myself to eat Kyprianou gave me disapproving looks; I was not conducting myself as an owner should. As soon as I reasonably could I left the saloon and went back to the bridge again.

Touzani had posted an extra man at the top of the companionway. Patsalides was on watch. They both had large revolvers stuck in their belts and were obviously self-conscious about them. They pretended not to see me.

Touzani was in his office. He carried his revolver in his right-hand trouser pocket. He had been staring out of the porthole when I came in, but now he turned.

He motioned toward the darkness with his hand, "There's another ship out there," he said. "She crossed astern of us a while back. Had the sunset behind her. A Syrian schooner motoring on her engine."

I sat down but said nothing.

"She wouldn't be the ship we're going to rendezvous with, would she?"

"Why do you ask?"

"When we change next time we'll be on convergent courses. I ask because she's running without lights."

"She can see our lights. I think you'll find shell stay clear."

"No rendezvous?"

"Not with her."

"Your orders are still the same, Mr. Howell?"

"My requests are, yes. Slow to six knots but stay ten miles offshore."

"Very well."

He left me and went to the wheelhouse. He was displeased with me and I didn't blame him. I was displeased with myself. He was trusting me and I should have confided in him. But it was too late now. I had begun to watch the clock.

Nine o'clock came and went. Then it was nine fifteen. From (She bridge I could hear the change being made. Patsalides rang down to the engine room for half ahead and then revolutions for six knots. The course change called for by Hadaya had been eleven degrees to starboard. Touzani ordered a change of fifteen. From that point on until he corrected again we would be moving away from the coast. After he had corrected we would be nowhere near territorial waters.

I had no idea what from a patrol boat interception would take. I presumed some form of flashing light signal - "What ship is that?" - followed by an order to heave to. I didn't know. I didn't care. I just stood by the porthole with my eyes glued to the darkness outside waiting for *something* to happen. I waited and waited.

I was still waiting when Captain Touzani returned to the cabin. He had a radio message form in his hand and he was clearly furious.

"Mr. Howell, a radio message has just been received. It is in English and for you." He thrust it under my nose.

It was addressed:

M. V. AMALIA HOWELL FOR M. HOWELL,

It read:

EMERGENCY PROCEDURE. STEER 170 DEGREES REPEAT 170.

YOU ARE CLEARED FOR ASHDOD.

It was signed: COAST GUARD HADERA

At least they hadn't forgotten me. I looked up into the angry brown eyes of Captain Touzani.

"It may be addressed to you, Mr. Howell," he said deliberately, "but I want to know what it means. I demand an explanation."

What it meant was that the radio warnings that I had sent earlier had not been fully understood, but I could scarcely tell him that.

"May we look at the chart, Captain?"

"All right. But I still want an explanation. I still want to know why, in my ship, you are getting navigational instructions from an Israeli coast guard station, and why we are cleared for an Israeli port for which we are not bound."

"Show me this course on the chart, please."

We went through to the wheelhouse and he laid a ruler across the chart to show me.

"There's one-seven-oh."

"On that course what would be our distance from Tel Aviv when we passed it?"

"Six miles about."

"What is our present course?"

"One-nine-two."

"Will you please radio back to Hadera? Say, please, in my name, that we are not, repeat *not*, able to carry out this emergency procedure, and that we are *compelled*, use that word, to maintain course one-nine-two."

"First, I want that explanation."

"We are trying to keep out of trouble, and keep a lot of other people out of trouble as well. That's all the explaining I can do now, Captain. Kindly send the message and mark it Urgent For Action."

He started to argue but I cut him short.

"This is an order, Captain Touzani, and I can assure you that it is a proper order from an owner to a captain."

"I'd like to be the judge of that."

"You will be, but just now you'll have to left me be the judge. Send the message please."

I left him before he could say any more. I had to think. The coast guard message could only have been dictated by Barlev's people in Tel Aviv and therefore was intended to have a special meaning for me. Since they had not understood my references to a second ship they were mow saying one of two things. The first was that they were still unwilling to intercept the *Amalia* far outside territorial waters and still asking me to make things easier for them. The second . . .

But I never really had time to think that one through. Something else distracted me.

The saloon door that gave on to the deck was held ajar by a catch, so that I was halfway down the companionway when I first heard it; a scratching noise and then, suddenly, very loudly, a voice.

I stopped and looked through the porthole.

Ghaled and the front-fighters were gathered around the walkie-talkie, and the voice coming out of it was Hadaya's.

I admit that I do not like recalling what happened during the next hour, but so much has been said, left unsaid, or half-said, or insinuated, that I must.

The range of those walkie-talkie things varies. That one I would guess was effective up to just over a mile. As Hadaya was over two nautical miles away then, we could not hear him very plainly at first.

There was sudden fading and then bursts of sound like the one I had heard from outside.

But his meaning was plain enough even then, and became plainer as the distance between the two sets decreased.

Ghaled looked up angrily as I came in. "You heard that?" he demanded.

"Was that Hadaya's voice, Comrade Salah?"

"It was. We are speaking to him on the *Jeble* 5. He says that we are off-course."

You didn't tell Ghaled he was talking nonsense, but I had the presence of mind to do the next best thing - make him suspect that he was.

"Comrade Salah, I have just come down from the bridge to tell you that the ship is now on course."

"Now? Why not before?"

"In a car, when one takes a corner, one turns the wheel and then straightens up. It is the same at sea. But we are not in a car, or a rowboat. This is a ship and, at the moment, a slow-moving one. It takes time to turn and time to straighten rap. Hadaya knows all this."

"He also says that we are out of position."

"With respect, Comrade Salah, that is not possible."

There was another faint squawk from the walkie-talkie. Hadaya said something about taking bearings and getting fixes. Ghaled did not understand it and I was glad to ignore it.

"You admitted yourself," he said accusingly, "that Hadaya is competent."

"I did, and I am sure he is, in port. However, he must be under some strain at present and perhaps overexcited. Has he been in action as a front-fighter before, Comrade Salah?"

"No, but all he has to do is steer to the right place. He does not have to fire a shot himself."

"He has the responsibility and is already in a position of danger. Perhaps he knows it."

"What danger?"

"Captain Touzani sighted the *Jeble 5* at sundown. She was running without lights, and on a collision course with this ship. What looks easy on the chart isn't always so easy when one is at sea and in darkness. Even the most competent officers can become confused."

"Hadaya can see our lights, and he says that we are out of position."

In Latalda Touzani had asked if there would be a seaman among the passengers on board and I had told him there would not be. But

Hadaya was a seaman and with that damned walkie-talkie he was as good as on board. What was more, his voice was rapidly becoming clearer with less fading. All I could do now was try to bluff, confuse, and play for time.

"Please ask him what course we are steering, Comrade Salah."

Ghaled pressed the transmit button and repeated the question.

A moment late the reply came back. "*Amalia's* course and ours is now one-nine-two, but..."

I tried to drown the rest. "Comrade Salah, that is the course called for in your instructions."

"Let him finish." To Hadaya he said: "Repeat that."

"We are on the right course but too far west."

"How can that be?"

"After the turn to starboard *Amalia* delayed too long before correcting. By my dead reckoning we are at least two miles west of where we should be."

"That is impossible," I protested. "Captain Touzani is a skilled navigator with modern instruments at his disposal. Hadaya must be mistaken."

Ghaled pressed the button. "Comrade Michael says (that you're mistaken. What do you say?"

"In a few minutes I should be able to take bearings on the Hadera and Tel Aviv lights marked on the chart. We will know then who is mistaken."

"How many minutes?"

"I could send a man to a masthead now, but I would sooner take the bearings myself. Give me five minutes, please, Comrade Salah."

"Very well."

Ghaled looked at his watch and then broodingly at me.

"I want to speak to this Tunisian of yours."

"On the bridge, Comrade Salah?"

"No, here. Send for him."

I rang the bell for Kyprianou. When he appeared I said: "A

239

message for the Captain. My compliments and would he please come down to the saloon." I was speaking in Greek and I added: "Tell the Captain that this is a request that he should ignore and that the whole crew should be warned to expect trouble."

He gave me a startled look and hurried out.

Ghaled turned to Aziz. "If this Tunisian has not carried out Comrade Michael's orders, we must see that he obeys ours. Arm yourselves."

"Yes, Comrade Salah."

They went aft along the alleyway.

It was a bad moment for me. The people on the bridge were armed and the rest of the crew would be alerted. Ghaled was also armed, true, but the odds, I thought, were in the ship's favour. They were not, however, in mine. So far Ghaled had appeared to trust me. We had had our cosy little drinking session in his cabin. Not even Hadaya's awkward revelations had seemed to cast doubts on my good faith. If the ship wasn't where she should be it was "the Tunisian" who was to blame, not Comrade Michael But at any moment now that was all likely to change. Ghaled might be ignorant on the subject of navigation, but he would know what a locked door meant. It meant that the Tunisian was being deliberately obstructive and committing hostile acts. And who was he taking his orders from? Me.

I started to talk my way out of the danger zone. "If the ship is a little out of position, Comrade Salah, that is not really very serious. The mistake can easily be rectified. Even at six knots we can make a two mile change of position well before zero hour. Hadaya is overanxious, that is all. Perhaps I am, too, now that we are really going into action. I am certainly getting forgetful I meant to bring the second bottle of brandy with me when I came down. If you will excuse me a moment, I will go back and get it."

He glanced at his watch again. I think that he was going to let me go for the brandy, but just then Captain Touzani came into the saloon.

I know now why he came. In spite of my suggestion that he stay put, he was afraid that the message about alerting the crew meant that I was in trouble over the special compartment door. He came to help me out Very generous after the way I had treated him, but it really would have been better if he had stayed on the bridge.

"You wanted to see me, Mr. Howell?" he asked.

I had no chance to reply.

"*I* want to see you," snapped Ghaled.

As he said it there was a pounding of feet in the alleyway and Aziz burst in.

"Comrade Salah! We cannot arm ourselves. We are locked out of our room." Then he saw the captain and pointed an accusing finger. "He has locked the room against us!"

Touzani smiled. "Nonsense, Mr. Faysal. That compartment is normally kept locked. I expect that the boatswain locked it without thinking when he was on his rounds. I'll give orders to have it opened."

"At once, please, Captain," said Ghaled, and I saw him as he said it release the flap of his pistol holster.

"By all means, Mr. Yassin."

Touzani had started to turn away when Hadaya's voice suddenly came through loud and shrill over the walkie-talkie.

"Comrade Salah! Comrade Salah!"

Ghaled reached for the transmit button.

"Yes?"

"Comrade Salah, I have taken bearings on the Hadera and Tel Aviv lights. We are three miles out of position, over ten miles offshore. Ten miles! On our present course we will be completely out of range."

"Are you sure?"

"Certain. We must immediately turn to port and steer one-six-oh. Immediately, Comrade Salah!"

Ghaled stared at Touzani. "You hear that?"

Touzani stared back mulishly. "I hear a voice, Mr. Yassin. I do not

241

know whose voice, but he is talking rubbish. Do you think I don't know my own position?"

"I think you know your position very well. That is why you are going to obey my orders from now on."

Hadaya's voice came bleating in again. "Steer one-six-oh, Comrade Salah. Immediately."

"And that's my first order," continued Ghaled. "You hear? Then obey."

"I'm not running my ship aground to please you, Mr. Yassin."

"She is no longer your ship. I have taken command. You hear?"

"I hear," said Captain Touzani, and went for his revolver.

It was in his trouser pocket and the hammer caught in the lining. He was still trying to free it when Ghaled shot him.

The heavy bullet knocked him backward against a chair. The chair went over and he with it, sprawling on the linoleum.

Ghaled shoved the automatic into Aziz's hand. "Up to the bridge," he snapped. "Take charge at once. Order the new course." He turned to me. "You go with them. Make sure the order is obeyed properly. Look at the compass yourself. Course one-six-oh. Move now!"

He went quickly along the alleyway to his cabin.

Aziz and the other two were already out on the deck and making for the bridge companionway, Aziz in the lead with the automatic. As he started up the companionway there was a sharp crack and I saw him swing around, clutching at the rail.

It was Patsalides firing down from the bridge. He had heard the shot in the saloon and was taking no chances. If the front-fighters had had their machine pistols it might have been a different story, but now they had to take cover by the companionway while the wounded Aziz sniped up at the bridge with the automatic.

I went to Captain Touzani.

Because he had half-turned when he tried to draw the revolver, Ghaled's bullet had smashed through his left arm and into his side. The blood was spreading on his shirt but more of it seemed to be coming from his arm. With the uninjured one he was still trying to get the revolver out of his pocket

I got it out for him, but kept hold of it.

He began swearing and tried to sit up. I told him to save his breath and lie still.

Then I went along the alleyway to Ghaled's cabin.

He had the *Serinette* out of its case and was setting it up on the desk The tape antenna was already extended by the open porthole.

He heard me and turned.

"I told you to go up to the bridge."

"Comrade Salah," I said, "nobody can go up to the bridge."

And then I fired at the *Serinette*.

I fired three shots from the revolver.

All were aimed at the music box, the *Serinette*.

I then went back to the saloon.

There, for a moment, I didn't quite know what had happened. When they had gone out to attack the bridge, the front-fighters had left the saloon door wide open. Now there was a blinding blue-white light blazing through it. It was the approaching patrol boat's searchlight, but when I realized that I paid it no more attention. Touzani was still swearing away. I told him again to save his breath. I heard the engine room telegraph and felt the vibration cease. We were stopping. I went to the walkie-talkie and pressed the transmit button.

"Hadaya, this is Howell. Do you hear me?"

"Yes. Is that a patrol boat attacking you?"

"I don't know, but we are stopping. I have orders from Comrade Salah. The operation is cancelled You understand? The operation is cancelled. You are to jettison your deck cargo and return to base. You hear?"

"Why doesn't Comrade Salah himself speak?"

"He is wounded. But those are his orders. Obey them immediately. You hear?"

"I hear. Is he badly wounded?"

I switched off the set without answering.

If the *Jeble* 5 had then headed straight for Tel Aviv she might still have been able to launch a few rockets before she herself came under fire from the patrol boat. Though I didn't for a moment think that Hadaya was the type to go in for suicide attacks, it was possible that the front-fighters in charge of the rocket-launchers were.

It was better, I thought, for them to believe that they were still answerable to Comrade Salah.

The lieutenant who commanded the Israeli patrol boat was a sharp-eyed, thin-lipped young man with sandy hair and freckles. I met him and his boarding party on the after well-deck. He gave me a formal salute and was very stiff at first. He had been briefed.

"Captain Touzani?"

"Captain Touzani is wounded. My name is Howell."

"Ah yes, the owner." His English was correct and only slightly accented. "I must ask you if you have requested assistance from the navy of Israel."

"Yes, I have."

"Why, please?"

"We were being hijacked by four passengers. One, the one who shot at and wounded the captain, is dead. Another was himself wounded by the first mate. That man has a gun but I think that he has now fired off all his ammunition. The other two hijackers are still loose but they have no firearms."

He seemed to relax. "You call them hijackers, sir. Did these passengers attempt to take over the vessel by force?"

They did."

"And intimidate the captain, compelling him to steer a certain course?"

"Yes, though they didn't succeed."

"Whether they succeeded or not is immaterial. By committing these offenses on the open sea these men are pirates, Mr. Howell."

"Whatever they are I'm glad to see you, Lieutenant."

But he had already begun snapping out orders in Hebrew.

It took only a few minutes to round up the unwounded front-fighters. Though they had managed to break the padlock on the special compartment door, they were still wrestling with the clip. They submitted sullenly. Meanwhile a trained first-aid man from the patrol boat had been attending to the wounded.

When he had made his report, Patsalides and I conferred with the lieutenant on the bridge.

The Faysal man's wound is not serious," he said. "However, Captain Touzani has a broken arm and at least one broken rib. The bullet is still in him. He should not be moved until we have proper medical assistance. I suggest that you put into Ashdod, where it can be waiting for him."

"What about the prisoners?"

"A vessel of amy nation arresting pirates on the open sea, Mr. Howell, is entitled to bring them to trial in the courts of her own country." He was reciting a learned lesson. "As they have been arrested by an Israeli ship they will go for trial in Israel."

"Very well."

"There is one matter about which I was to consult you, Mr. Howell, that of a second ship. We saw what looked like a fishing schooner about a mile away from you and under power, but no second ship."

"I doubt if it's of much interest to you now, Lieutenant. The schooner was the second ship, and I'm sure you could easily catch her if you wanted to. But she won't ask for assistance. You'll have to stop her and ask for her papers. She's Syrian, but they'll be in order. There'll be no incriminating evidence. That's overboard by now. I'll tell your people all about it when I see them. By the way, you had better take the dead man with the live prisoners."

"Very well, if you wish."

"He's down in the ship's papers as Yassin, but his real name is Salah Ghaled. I'd like him off the ship."

"Oh." He looked nonplussed. His briefing hadn't covered

245

everything; but he recovered quickly and with a grin. "I think the sooner we are in Ashdod the better for everyone, Mr. Howell."

I could not but agree.

Chapter 8

Lewis Prescott

August

Michael Howell should have had better luck.

The crime of piracy on the open sea occupies a special place in international law. It is the one "international" crime that has been precisely defined and that all nations have joined in condemning. Although the penalties for those convicted of it may vary from state to state, the laws on this subject have been accepted by all. Difficulties of interpretation have been rare and usually of a technical nature.

The district court in Ashdod had no difficulty in dealing with the *Amalia Howell* case. The accused were charged only with piracy, and politics were kept out of it. The chief prosecution witnesses were Captain Touzani and First Mate Patsalides. Neither of them in their evidence referred to the PAF; and the defence, whose line was that the prime offender was dead, was naturally careful not to mention it. During the course of the trial one of the defendants, Aziz Faysal, alleged that Mr. Howell had murdered Salah Ghaled, but no evidence was produced to support the allegation. The court concluded that Ghaled had been killed in a general exchange of

247

shots between the crew and the pirates when the latter attempted to take over the vessel.

Mr. Howell himself issued no formal denial of the charge. In the circumstances this was not surprising. By the time the trial took place, so many other, and wilder, charges had been hurled at his head that issuing denials had become for him a somewhat pointless exercise.

Before sailing from Latakia on board the *Amalia Howell* he had been told by Ghaled that a supply of PAF detonators had been lost in Israel. The loss had been described at the time as a "minor mishap," and, from Ghaled's point of view, perhaps that was all it was. But for Mr. Howell it was a catastrophe.

What happened in Israel was this:

On June 28 a bus from Haifa bound for Tel Aviv stopped at Nazareth to pick up passengers. These included a party of eight American tourists. Some rearrangement of the contents of the baggage compartment at the back of the bus was necessary in order to make room for the tourists' bags and cases. In the course of this rearrangement a small but heavy carton which had been put aboard the bus in Haifa, together with other packages for delivery in Tel Aviv, fell to the ground.

A series of explosions followed. They were not big explosions, but there were a lot of them, and then the carton caught fire.

Nobody was injured, and the bus was eventually allowed to proceed. No publicity was given to the incident. The police were naturally interested in finding out who in Haifa had sent the carton and who in Tel Aviv was to have been the recipient Publicity would have warned both parties. As the carton had been quite badly burned the task of deciphering the writing on the charred labels was taken over by a police laboratory. The results, if any, of the investigation have not so far been announced.

All that is known publicly is what Mr. Robert S. Rankin, of Malibu, California, heard and saw.

He was on a tour of the Holy Land with Mrs. Rankin and they

were among the passengers on the bus who joined it at Nazareth. Mr. Rankin is a motion picture executive, and when he and his wife arrived in Rome a few days later they were invited to a dinner party. One of their fellow guests was a roving American gossip columnist. During the evening Mr. Rankin told her about the exploding carton. The columnist, who was short of copy that week, used the story.

Here is Mr. Rankin's own account of the incident:

"It was the damnedest thing. The guy with the baggage dropped this carton on the ground. Not carelessly, you understand. If it had been a case of Scotch nothing would have been broken. He just gave it a hard jolt. Well, the next moment it was like the Fourth of July. Suddenly, a lot of bangs - *pah* - *pah* - *pah!* I thought it was a machine gun at first and yelled to Mrs. Rankin to get down. But no - *pah* - *pah* - *pah!* And there were these bits flying all over the place. Bits! What do you think they were? Flashlight batteries, that's what! Ordinary flashlight batteries going off like Chinese firecrackers. I picked one of the cases up and kept it. One of those that had gone off, I mean. An army man took the rest away. I kept it as a souvenir and because I thought nobody would believe me otherwise. I mean, flashlight batteries! Of course they weren't real batteries. Our guide said they had this sort of trouble once in a while. At the airport a month or so back he said they found explosive detonators in some woman's shoes, hidden in the heels. It's the Palestinians."

In Paris two days later, Mr. Rankin was asked by a reporter from a French news magazine if he could see the battery case. The magazine published a photograph of it The label had been singed, but the Green Circle trademark and the words "Made in Syria" were clearly visible.

The government of Israel tends to assign the responsibility for hostile acts committed by foreign based groups of Palestine guerrillas to each group's host country, and to determine its reprisal policies accordingly. Smuggling in detonators disguised as flashlight batteries was clearly a hostile act, no matter which guerrilla group was involved.

In Damascus, Dr. Hawa hastened to dissociate his ministry from the Green Circle trademark. In his statement he pointed out, quite truthfully, that the Green Circle dry-battery factory was a private enterprise of the Agence Howell, that no government money was involved in its financing, and that Michael Howell, a foreign entrepreneur resident in Syria, had no official standing whatsoever.

On the heels of Dr. Hawa's statement came the publication of Mr. Howell's and Miss Malandra's confessions by Colonel Shikla's department.

In Damascus they meant to defend themselves by discrediting Michael Howell, and they succeeded. The Arab press, hysterical as ever, tore into him with everything they had.

And they had plenty. Here was this Howell, a rich businessman whose family company had battened for years on poor Arab countries, revealed as an Israeli provocateur and spy. Having joined or having pretended to join the Palestinian liberation cause he had then proceeded to betray it in the vilest way. Worse, he had organized treacherous murder plots against Arabs who refused to be blackmailed by his agents. Nor was blackmail his only source of profit. In his factories he had made illegal arms and sold them to the very *fedayeen* whom he later betrayed. Among his known victims was the Palestinian patriot Salah Ghaled, lured aboard a Howell ship and murdered for Howell's Zionist masters; though perhaps Ghaled's fate was merciful when one thought of other Howell victims delivered bound to the Israeli usurper and condemned to rot in the Zionist concentration camps.

To this sort of insensate attack there can be no real defence. The victim can only wait for it to exhaust itself. Mr. Howell's initial response had been a blank and steadfast denial of all the charges. However, when the European press took up the story, he changed his tactics and began to explain. He would have done better, perhaps, to have stayed with the denials. They at least had been unequivocal. Of the explanations that could not be said.

In August I had occasion to go again to Beirut, where I talked to

Frank Edwards about Mr. Howell. He had recently been in Israel and had discussed the case with contacts there. For reasons which seemed to me very sound, the government of Israel had refused to comment publicly on either the "Green Circle Incident" or the Arab charges against Mr. Howell. Frank Edwards' contacts, however, had been more forthcoming, and he had picked up some intriguing scraps of information. The idea of someone doing a full-length feature on the subject was mooted. Frank Edwards knew Mr. Howell slightly and could set up an interview with him. As I had been the one to interview Ghaled it seemed logical that I should now interview the man who had been accused of murdering him, and write the feature.

The Villa Howell near Famagusta does not look very big from the outside, but when you get inside you know that you are in a wealthy house. It has that "old-money" look: everything is very good, nothing is very new-except, possibly, the swimming pool - and it is all slightly, pleasantly, untidy. I had been told that Mr. Howell's mother and his wife and children were all in Cannes for the summer, so I was not surprised to find Miss Malandra there with the master of the house.

They were in beach clothes by the swimming pool, where, Judging from the files scattered about them, they had been working. I was invited to take off my jacket and tie, offered swimming trunks if I would feel more comfortable, and a champagne cocktail. I refused the swimming trunks but accepted the cocktail.

Miss Malandra served it Lunch would be at one thirty, she said. There would be ample time for a second drink. Then we got down to brass tacks.

Or, rather, Michael Howell got down to brass tacks, with a denunciation that lasted for twenty minutes of the iniquities of the press. Frank Edwards had warned me to expect this, so at first I let it flow; but when he began to quote from an article written by Melanie Hammad for a Cairo paper and read long extracts from it, I had to interrupt.

"Mr. Howell, I'm afraid I don't understand Arabic."

"Ah, sorry. Well, I can tell you what she says about me in English. Hashemite lackey, running dog, murderous viper, jackal, hyena, defiler of youth. Those are some of the nicer things she has to say."

"Nicer?"

"When she comes to my crucifixion of Ghaled she is horrible. She says I wash my hands in Palestinian blood. And look at this. The name of Howell is the name of everything that is vile in our society. Only fire can cleanse us of this evil.'" He flung the paper down in disgust.

"Well, it's what you would expect, isn't it, Mr. Howell?"

"Expect?"

"Of Miss Hammad. I hear, by the way, that with Ghaled gone, she has transferred her allegiance from the PAF to the Popular Front."

"But she is still inciting people to assassinate me. I must tell you, Mr. Prescott, that this sort of thing is very bad indeed for business."

The anticlimax took me by surprise. "Only for business, Mr. Howell?"

"*Only* you say! Do you realize that Howell ships are now being boycotted in some ports? I can tell you that Touzani is very worried."

"Touzani? Is this Captain Touzani?"

"Of course. He is to be our new marine superintendent. The present one is almost due for his pension and Touzani has earned the promotion. But it comes at a bad time. He is saying that we may have to take the Howell name off our ships."

"I realize the importance of the Howell name as a business symbol, naturally," I said; "but what I would like to discuss with you is your own personal position, the position of Michael Howell."

"The two are inseparable, Mr. Prescott."

"Are they? It wasn't the Agence Howell who joined the PAF, it was Michael Howell. And it was Michael Howell who called for naval assistance against pirates off the coast of Israel."

"But sailing in a ship owned by the Agence Howell. And yes - why not say it? - those detonators which exploded in Nazareth were made and packed in the Agence Howell Green Circle factory."

I tried a fresh approach.

"On the subject of detonators, Mr. Howell, I have brought you some important information that you may not already have. Frank Edwards got hold of it in Israel. At least we think that it's important. The trouble is that we don't understand it. You may."

I handed him the photostat that Frank had given me. It was of a short news item.

In the late afternoon of July 2, two houses on the outskirts of an Arab village near the Israeli airport of Lod had been shattered by a dynamite explosion. Damage was also done to the nearby village. From the extent of the damage it was estimated that as much as two hundred kilos of explosive had been involved. Parts of six bodies had been found in the ruins, though this figure could only be estimated. Also found, scattered over a wide area by the explosion, were a number of plastic flight bags belonging to foreign airlines using Lod airport. Neither the police nor the military had issued any statement concerning the cause of the explosion.

He read it through and nodded. "I guessed it was something like that."

"Something like what, Mr. Howell?"

"As you must know, Ghaled planned to plant these bombs of his in airline flight bags and fire them with electronic triggers by radio. He had the transmitter on board the *Amalia* in that music box. Well, I gave the Israelis one of those triggers to analyse and test. Obviously they succeeded in working out the frequencies he was using."

"I'm afraid I don't follow."

"Do you know anything about making bombs, Mr. Prescott? No, I don't suppose so. I had to find out, too. The thing is this. You have the explosive, you have the detonator with a battery to fire it, and you have the electronic trigger that's going to make it all work at the right time. But these things all have to be connected up, 'armed' is the word. Am I making sense to you?"

"Yes."

"With some bombs, say a single bomb in a suitcase, you might have a little secret switch on the outside so that you could leave the final arming until the very last moment But if you are making a hundred bombs and packing them in plastic flight bags you can't have switches. Too complicated, and they would show. You have to arm the bombs beforehand, before you start planting them where they are to explode. You have to arm them where you assemble them, in other words. So you see what happened?"

"I'm afraid not."

"Well, as soon as the Israelis had worked out the radio code being used to operate the triggers they used it. Easy, really. All they had to do was order one of their military radio transmitters to send out a strong continuous signal on the trigger frequencies and keep sending twenty-four hours a day. Then, the moment the PAF started arming the bombs - boom! - up would go the lot. Even if the bombs hadn't all been in one place it would still have worked, because the triggers were all exactly the same. Then, you would have had two or three smaller explosions instead of one big one."

"You say you guessed that this would happen?"

"Much later, yes. Too late." He suddenly became indignant and started wagging his finger at me. "If the Israelis had had the common decency to let me know, things might have been easier. I consider that their behaviour to me throughout has been absolutely appalling. Not one word have those ingrates uttered. Not a single word! For them I don't exist. Silence!"

"I don't understand, Mr. Howell. If you're so worried about the Howell name in the Arab world I would have thought that the last thing you would want would be a public acknowledgment from Israel. It seems to me that they're simply being tactful."

That really incensed him.

"Tactful! Have you read those French and West German smears? 'Eichmann in the Levant?' - that was one of their captions. All right, they put a question mark after it, but how would you like that, Mr. Prescott? 'Pro-Arab businessman made bombs for terrorists.' That was another. 'Green Circle man plotted Tel Aviv massacre.' 'Howell money behind terrorists.' One of them even made out that Ghaled was *my* lieutenant, that he was only a figure-head and that *I* am the PAF! And the Israelis say nothing, *nothing!*"

"But surely if you hope to reestablish your position with the Arabs ..."

"I have no such hope. My position there is hopeless. Israeli provocateur, spy, traitor, informer, assassin - that's what they've decided. Even if they were allowed to hear the truth, none of them would believe it. I can face facts, Mr. Prescott. My family has been doing business in the Levant for three quarters of a century. Facing facts is in the blood. We're finished there now. I know that. Touzani's right We're going to have to form a new company without the Howell name showing, buy up the ships and reregister them. There's no other way. The rest of our business will go for a song. That can't be helped. It's past and done with. We've cut our losses. But what about the future? What about Europe?"

"Europe, Mr. Howell?"

He flung out his arms in amazement at my inability to grasp the obvious. "Well, naturally we're going into Europe. We must. We can't have capital lying around idle. Bonds at seven percent? Ridiculous! No, Italy's the place. We already have land in the *mezzo-giorno,* or rather Teresa has. The company is buying it Our plans are all made. Do you know about the *mezzo-giorno,* Mr. Prescott? Very farsighted the Italian government is being. Tax incentives, low-interest development loans, favourable amortization agreements - it's all there for the asking, including the labour. I already have five projects mapped out. Howell (Italia) S.A., that's what we'll be, right in the Common Market. But why should I have to go to the Italian government and negotiate the deals with all this smearing going on, with this cloud of suspicion and distrust hanging over me?"

"Mr. Howell," I said weakly, "that's why I'm sitting here. That's what I've come about. So that we can talk about the cloud."

Miss Malandra handed me another champagne cocktail. If she had decided that I needed it just then, she was absolutely right.

"What I would like from you, Mr. Howell," I went on, "is a brief, simple recital of the facts of the case as you know them. Not a reply to the charges - most of them are fantastic anyway - not an argument, not a polemic, but a dispassionate statement of the facts."

He beamed at me. "Mr. Prescott, I always try to think ahead. The statement is already prepared. Teresa has it there ready for you. I dictated it when I knew that you were coming to see me."

Miss Malandra handed it to me solemnly. Her eyes meeting mine over it were quite expressionless. She really is extraordinarily beautiful.

The statement weighed at least two pounds. It was well over a hundred pages long. I opened it at random and read an estimate of the Agence Howell's losses the previous year, item by item, on the Green Circle dry-battery operation. I shut it again.

"What I had in mind Mr. Howell, if I may repeat myself, is a brief, simple recital of the facts. On three or four pages, say."

He pursed his lips. "Bare facts are not truth, Mr. Prescott. You want the truth, I take it. There it is."

Hopeless.

"I see what you mean, Mr. Howell. I'd like to take this away, then, and read it if I may."

"That was the idea. Keep it for reference, Mr. Prescott. I have other copies. But read it and then, if you have any questions, I will gladly answer them."

"Thank you. But speaking of questions, Mr. Howell, there is one that I would very much like to ask you now, if I may."

"Certainly."

"Did you kill Salah Ghaled?"

He thought about it for a moment and then smiled. "Teresa says that sometimes I am not one man but a committee. Why don't we ask her?" He turned his smile in her direction. "Teresa, my dear, have you ever noticed among the committee members a murderer?"

She returned the smile, but I thought that there was an appraising look in her eyes. "No, Michael No, I can't say that I've ever seen a murderer."

"There is your answer, Mr. Prescott."

"Not quite, Mr. Howell. I didn't ask if you murdered him. I asked if you killed him."

"I am not a man of violence, Mr. Prescott."

No wonder he had trouble with newsmen.

"That still doesn't answer the question. Did you or did you not kill him, Mr. Howell?"

"Intentionally, you mean?"

"Yes."

He blinked. "That's a strange question to ask a man in his own house."

"The question has been asked outside."

"And answered in an Israeli court."

"I think not, Mr. Howell In Israel three men were on trial for piracy. You were not even called upon to give evidence."

"I made a deposition."

"Relative to the piracy charges, yes. You were not cross-examined on the deposition and you didn't answer any questions. No wonder there's a cloud, Mr. Howell."

"Let me explain how it was," he said.

"Thank you."

But he had taken off his glasses and was polishing them on the tail of his sports shirt. Only when he had replaced his glasses did he go on.

"When the Israelis didn't intercept us off Caesarea but gave us that new course to steer instead, I guessed that they might have found a way of dealing with the bomb threat. As it turns out they had. That piece you showed me about the explosion confirms that. But *I* did not know, at least not for certain. How could I? Nor did I know for certain the effective range of that transmitter in the music box. Well, after Ghaled had shot Captain Touzani he went straight to the box. So I went after him with Touzani's revolver in my hand. When I saw that he was setting the box up to transmit I fired at it to put it out of action. I fired at it three times."

"But two of the bullets hit Ghaled in the chest."

"Yes."

"How many bullets hit the box?"

"I can't be sure. It was smashed anyway. The Israelis took it away. They may know."

"Are you saying that the shots that killed Ghaled ricocheted off the box?"

"I haven't the slightest idea, Mr. Prescott." He leaned forward, glass in hand, his eyes wide with candour. "I know nothing about such things. You see I had never before in my life fired a revolver. Indeed, I had never fired a gun of any kind."

"The music box was a small target to begin on. Ghaled was a large one. Your feelings toward him at that moment can't have been very friendly."

"My feelings toward him were never aft any time friendly. I detested him."

"And he had just shot your captain."

"And young Aziz was shooting at the first mate, who was shooting back at him. A lot of shooting went on in a very short space of time."

"It just happened that the gun you were holding accidentally shot Ghaled?"

"It could only have been an accident, Mr. Prescott. I was aiming at the music box."

"In other words you hit the small target by design and the big one by accident."

"Mr. Prescott, it was all an entirely new experience for me, an experience that I do not intend to repeat. Does that answer your question?"

I sighed. "I guess it has to."

His smile began to return. "I do assure you, Mr. Prescott, that I am not a man of violence."

"Luncheon is served, Michael," said Miss Malandra.

She gave me a lovely smile as we went in, a smile full of sympathy and understanding.

It was some consolation, and I must say the lunch was excellent.

ERIC AMBLER

Doctor Frigo
ISBN: 978-07551-1761-1

A coup d'etat in a Caribbean state causes a political storm in the region and even the seemingly impassive and impersonal Doctor Castillo, nicknamed Doctor Frigo, cannot escape the consequences. As things heat up, Frigo finds that both his profession and life are horribly at risk.

'As subtle, clever and complex as always' - Sunday Telegraph
'The book is a triumph' - Sunday Times

Judgment on Deltchev
ISBN: 978-07551-1762-8

Foster is hired to cover the trial of Deltchev, who is accused of treason for allegedly being a member of the sinister and secretive Brotherhood and preparing a plot to assassinate the head of state whilst President of the Agrarian Socialist Party and member of the Provisional Government. It is assumed to be a show trial, but when Foster encounters Madame Deltchev the plot thickens, with his and other lives in danger ....

'The maestro is back again, with all his sinister magic intact' - The New York Times

The Maras Affair
ISBN: 978-07551-1764-2

(Ambler originally writing as Eliot Reed with Charles Rodda)

Charles Burton, journalist, cannot get work past Iron Curtain censors and knows he should leave the country. However, he is in love with his secretary, Anna Maras, and she is in danger. Then the President is assassinated and one of Burton's office workers is found dead. He decides to smuggle Anna out of the country, but her reluctance impedes him, as does being sought by secret police and counter-revolutionaries alike.

ERIC AMBLER

The Schirmer Inheritance   ISBN: 978-07551-1765-9

Former bomber pilot George Carey becomes a lawyer and his first job with a Philadelphia firm looks tedious - he is asked to read through a large quantity of files to ensure nothing has been missed in an inheritance case where there is no traceable heir. His discoveries, however, lead to unforeseen adventures and real danger in post war Greece.

'Ambler towers over most of his newer imitators' - Los Angeles Times
'Ambler may well be the best writer of suspense stories .. He is the master craftsman' - Life

Topkapi (The Light of Day)   ISBN: 978-07551-1768-0

Arthur Simpson is a petty thief who is discovered stealing from a hotel room. His victim, however, turns out to be a criminal in a league well above his own and Simpson is blackmailed into smuggling arms into Turkey for use in a major jewel robbery. The Turkish police, however, discover the arms and he is further 'blackmailed' by them into spying on the 'gang' - or must rot in a Turkish jail. However, agreeing to help brings even greater danger ....

'Ambler is incapable of writing a dull paragraph' - The Sunday Times

Eric Ambler

Siege at the Villa Lipp (Send No More Roses)

ISBN: 978-07551-1766-6

Professor Krom believes Paul Firman, alias Oberholzer, is one of those criminals who keep a low profile and are just too clever to get caught. Firman, rich and somewhat shady, agrees to be interviewed in his villa on the French Riviera. But events take an unexpected turn and perhaps there is even someone else artfully hiding in the deep background?

'One of Ambler's most ambitious and best' - The Observer
'Ambler has done it again ... deliciously plausible' - The Guardian

Tender to Danger (Tender to Moonlight)

ISBN: 978-07551-1767-3

(Ambler originally writing as Eliot Reed with Charles Rodda)
A blanket of fog grounds a flight in Brussels and Dr. Andrew Maclaren finds himself sharing a room with a fellow passenger who by morning disappears in suspicious circumstances, leaving behind an envelope hidden under the carpet. Whilst the contents are seemingly innocent, they lead the young Doctor into nightmarish adventures, culminating in the avoidance of cold-blooded killers in a deserted windmill and in the company of a beautiful redhead.

Manufactured By: RR Donnelley
                     Breinigsville, PA USA
                     December 2009